The Summer Boy

Henry Mitchell

Printed in the United Kingdom

First Printing, 2013 Alfie Dog Limited

The author can be found at: authors@alfiedog.com

Cover image: © Ronnie McCall

ISBN 978-1-909894-11-2

Published by
Alfie Dog Limited
Schilde Lodge, Tholthorpe,
North Yorkshire, YO61 1SN
Tel: 01347 827178

DEDICATION

To Mary.
It was her story first.

CONTENTS

ACKNOWLEDGMENTS

Deep and abiding thanks to Rosemary J. Kind, my editor at Alfie Dog Fiction, who thought The Summer Boy worth publishing and did not hesitate to sacrifice the author's ego to the story.

Humble gratitude to long-suffering manuscript readers, Deb Coulter, Reg Darling, Robin Rector Krupp, David Longley, Ma Fred Garrett, Amber Warren McCartney, Michelle McClendon, Michele Schusterman, Sharon Clabo, Sharon Decker and Seven Thunders who loved the story enough to cheerfully nail my hide to the door as often as they deemed necessary.

Thanks to the almost two hundred agents and editors who passed on my queries, thus compelling me to keep searching until the right publisher found me.

Undying love and unpayable debt to my main muse, Jane Ella Matthews, who listened to every scrap I scribbled, and told me to keep writing until the tale was done.

Special thanks to veteran Appalachian hiker, climber and guide, Ronnie McCall, who graciously granted permission to use his stunning photograph on the cover.

WATCHER

Oblivious to the rain, Raven perched atop a dead pine. From that vantage, he could see the Creek away down in the Gap, shining and singing among banks and drifts of fog. Across the Gap, beyond the Creek, Pinnacle and the Rim tumbled to a road dogging the creek south and west as it ascended. On Raven's side, the stream ran against Standing Stone Mountain, where his pine stood, and Lon's Anvil, a sheer escarpment of layered gneiss and schist thrusting a thousand feet above a narrow bottomland bedding the creek. A waterfall plummeted and cascaded down the face of this cliff, close enough that Raven could overhear the endless argument between Water and Stone. Stone, being harder, ever resisted. Water, being softer, would eventually have her way.

Raven had been here for several days, waiting for the car that came crawling now like a dark red bug up along the road by the creek. Raven knew without seeing him that the car was bringing the boy back to a place where he could find them all. Raven flew then to tell the others. It had begun.

ARRIVAL

At each place where the rain-swollen creek washed over the road, Ben tensed as tires slipped on loose gravel, then steadied as the wheels regained traction and the car began to gain the next hill. He pretended not to notice his father, Harry, grimace, tighten his grip on the steering wheel as the car plunged into yet another ford.

"Boy, you're not supposed to enjoy this. Ronan and Mary live rough."

Ben thought Harry sounded hopeful.

"Boy, did you hear me?"

"Yes, Sir."

"Well, answer me when I talk to you."

"Yes, Sir."

They rode the rest of their way in hostile silence. Ben concentrated on the rhythmic slap of windshield wipers and studied the writhing tracks of raindrops down the glass until the wipers swept them away. Harry strained to see the road. On the car radio, a preacher chanted between great gulps of air about how Jesus loved and trusted his father. Ben thought Jesus must have had a father very different from Harry.

Ben learned early on that the most effective way to deflect his father's goading was to appear untouched by it. He had picked up from his mother the knack of acting removed from any situation that was unpleasant for him.

He knew this tactic infuriated Harry, diminishing by a further fraction his already tenuous sense of control over his life and those souls who occupied it with him.

Harry delivered his son here to the Gap each year at the beginning of summer. So far, Ben had managed to conceal the fact that he regarded the expeditions as deliverance rather than banishment. He knew his father believed him coddled and pampered by his mother. He reckoned that since Harry thought Mary had spoiled his own childhood, he hoped she might do something like that for his son.

Having made this trip several times already, Ben knew the drill, so he tried his best to look despondent while he suppressed a secret elation at the prospect of watching the car depart back down the Gap without him.

#

Mary tore May from the Jarrard's Hardware calendar hanging beside her kitchen door as she passed, took a last look at the three puppies pictured on the page before she crumpled it and dropped it into the trash. She stepped out onto her porch as the maroon Studebaker pulled into her yard, and stood waiting while her brother and her nephew got out of the car and came through the misty morning toward the house. The boy trailed behind, grasping the handle of his bulging suitcase in both hands. The suitcase banged against his bare knees as he walked. Beyond and above them, Mary could barely make out the bulk of Pinnacle through the fog and the fine rain that had settled into the Gap overnight. She shook her head as Harry turned to look back at his son, "You're getting wet in this rain."

Mary marveled at her brother's unflagging capacity for stating the obvious. She knew Ben deliberately lagged behind, avoiding proximity so as not to be touched or herded, and she understood that Harry and his boy each felt a vague disappointment in the other, convinced they deserved something better than their lineage had granted them. She would deliver them from one another for the summer, at least.

As Mary stood with her brother, negotiating her handling of Ben for the duration of his stay, the child dragged his suitcase past them and heaved it onto a futon at the far end of the porch. This would be his bed for the season. The sun made a surprise appearance as the drizzle ceased. Ronan came out the door with his two daughters and clapped the boy on his back, "We're off to Store. You coming with us?"

A formidable old woman named Emalene ruled Store, a tiny square building barely a dozen paces across, that stood beside the creek about a half mile down the road, just past the bridge. A single gasoline pump stood in front of the store, and a tank beside the building dispensed kerosene. Store was stocked with dented canned goods and stale bread and moon pies, all overpriced and largely ignored by the souls who passed through. A small cooler-freezer just inside the front door offered soft drinks and ice cream which drew more frequent buyers. The ice cream was packaged in little cardboard cups, each with a small wooden paddle attached to the side to spoon it with. Ronan would gas his old pickup there and buy a cup of ice cream for any child he happened to have in tow.

Ice cream and the company of his cousins seemed preferable to listening while two adults debated his unworthiness, so Ben made to go with them. As the children ran down the porch, Harry reached out and grabbed his son's arm, "Where are you going in such a hurry?"

"I'm going to Store with Uncle Ronan."

"Did I say you could go?"

"May I go to Store with Uncle Ronan?"

"Did he ask you to go?"

"Yes, Sir."

"You may go."

The girls stood in the yard waiting for their cousin. As he started to go after them, his father seized his arm again.

"What do you say?"

"Thank you."

"Thank you?"

"Thank you, Sir." This was sufficient to win a release.

The children galloped across the yard toward Ronan's pickup. As Ronan stepped off the porch after them, he glanced at his wife and brother-in-law, "Try not to fight before we get back. We wouldn't want to miss the show."

The three children clambered into the bed of the truck. Harry called across the yard, "Boy, sit down!"

Ben, well sat already, shouted cheerfully, "Yes, Sir."

Ronan got into the cab and slammed the door. Before he started the engine, Ben overheard his aunt say to her brother, "Good Lord, Harry Drum, he's going to be here all summer. Do you want him to write home every time he leaves the yard?"

#

To say that Mary and her brother didn't get along was an understatement. It would not be an overstatement to say they had never gotten along. They grew up in a family of six children. The eldest, Ella, scandalized her four brothers when she went off to college and wound up marrying one of her professors. The boys were all in love with their Big Sister, and thought it unseemly that any male outside the family should know her more intimately than her own kin. Harry, the youngest brother, was expected to be the last baby in the house, and so was darling of all. Then Mary was born. Harry never forgave her for stealing away his blessing. One day, he would accuse her of stealing his son, as well. It would never occur to him that he had in effect aided and abetted her at every step.

As a child, Mary would tell anyone who asked that she wanted to be a dancer when she grew up. None in the family knew how she had come by such a notion, but the movement was in her and she danced through her childhood, amusing her mother with her antics, unsettling her father, who was a Baptist preacher, and annoying all her brothers. Ella, who could appreciate her performances, had already gone off to college and was seldom home to see.

When an eighteen year old Mary asked her father's permission to study dancing, assuming she could find a school to take her in, he responded with a story about John the Baptist and said it would be more appropriate for a minister's daughter to become a teacher or a nurse. To please her father, she became a nurse. To make him pay for his satisfaction, she joined the Army Medical Corps.

She met Ronan Darner in a hospital in France, where he was recovering from a bullet wound his doctor said should have killed him. At war's end, Mary came to the Gap with Ronan, made her home there, and found a place hidden among pines where she could dance only for herself, and for God, who she was convinced had no objections to dancing but took as much pleasure in it as she did.

\#

Ronan drove to Store just fast enough to provide his

passengers a satisfactory jostle. As they bounced along, the cousins were full of talk about bears, who had been their frequent visitors over the spring.

The older girl sounded hopeful, "I don't think they will actually come up on the porch and eat you."

"But you will be afraid," promised the younger cousin.

Ben supposed he might be, but doubted a bear would be any more intimidating than his father when angry. "I will learn bear language and talk to them," he proposed.

"Bears don't have a language. They just growl." The younger sister reinforced her observation with her most bearish growl.

"Language is more than words." Not sure exactly what he meant by that, Ben remained convinced it was so.

At Store, Emalene grabbed up the boy on sight and hugged the breath out of him. "Good to have you back in the world with us again." Ben thought her likely more frightening than any bear he might meet.

She shook an arthritic finger at his uncle, "You ought to keep this one, Ronan. He don't thrive in town." Then she said that in honor of their visitor, the ice cream was on the house, but that Ronan would still have to pay for his gas.

While they were eating their ice cream and listening to Emalene's true stories about encounters with bears, the Studebaker rumbled the bridge and passed the store. Harry, intent on his road, neither slowed nor waved. Mary and Harry had consummated their obligatory argument and he had fled the battlefield, thus sparing his son the ceremonial recitation of parting admonitions. Ben thought his summer off to a fine start and the long possibility of it stretched out ahead of him as far as he could imagine. Anything might happen.

#

Next morning, Mary went out early to weed her vegetables while the rest of the household lay abed. The sun came up over the ridge soon, and the morning warmed rapidly. She laid aside her shirt, and with her face and shoulders shaded by her big hat that had been her father's, she bent to her task. When she sensed her nephew wandering across the yard in her direction, not wanting to embarrass either the child or herself, she kept working.

Ben had to this point lived a very sheltered life managed by exceptionally proper and circumspect parents. He had not an erotic thought in his head, but when he knelt down across from his aunt to join in pulling weeds from around her radishes, he was not oblivious to the difference in their anatomies. He already had an artist's eye, and the rough splinter of gneiss, which she wore on a cord around her neck, cut his heart with the way its unyielding angularity impressed upon the firm brown breasts that cradled it. The stone made more of an impression on his innocence than the bare flesh of a ripe young woman.

Desire overcame timidity. "Do you think I could ever find a rock like that?"

"Nephew, there isn't another stone quite like this one. It was given me before you were in the world, but you can have my stone if you've a mind to share my soul."

Ben, besides having an artist's eye, also possessed a precocious caution. "What would happen if I shared your soul?" He had only the slightest notion of what a soul might be, but sharing his aunt's soul seemed to him tantamount to sharing her toothbrush, something he'd been taught was highly inappropriate.

"Among other things, it would mean you'd miss me terribly when I die."

#

From that day, the garden became his school when he wasn't out on the mountain learning wilder and deeper lessons. By the way she did things as much as by her words Mary taught him how to read the map of his life, to know not just who he was, but what was more important at his age, to know what he might become. One morning a week after Ben's arrival in the Gap, while on his way out to Mary's garden to help weed the herbs, with his nose in his book, as usual, his unguided foot came down right amidst a fine clump of wormwood.

"Mind your way, Nephew," Mary commanded sharply, then wryly, "That was mighty careless. I should turn you into a bear or a tree." She smiled as she said this.

"If it be the same to you, I'd as soon be a bear;" Ben answered brightly, "Being a tree would get awfully same-ish after a spell."

"You be a bear, then, but I will leave you a man's flesh and brain. You will go off to live in a town amongst people, and spend your days grubbing after things other people want you to have, but all your years, your soul will ache for the mountain and the woods."

A couple of hours after his aunt turned him into a bear, Ben sat to lunch on the broad porch with his two cousins, girls younger in years, but wiser in their lore of place. They were his self-appointed tutors in all things they deemed worth knowing about life in the Gap. On the wide boards of the long table Ronan fashioned while he was still building the house, Mary set a loaf of dark bread, baked that morning while the children still slept, a small bowl of goat's cheese, and a comb of rich, ruddy poplar honey from the bees they heard singing around them in the yard. Sweet ears of white corn appeared, and the tomatoes they had gathered that morning. Last, Mary brought out a pitcher of tea, sweetened with "sorghums" and minted from her herb garden.

Ben's Baptist parents would have required he recite a long and ornate blessing before he admitted to hunger, but Mary simply put the food before them and sat down. They confessed in unison, "We receive unworthily," and commenced to eat and be grateful.

"These tomatoes are better than the ones we have in town," Ben judged.

"Maters be maters," corrected the older girl.

Mary laughed, "But some be more so than others. You friended these tomatoes. You mulched and weeded and carried them water and pulled the beetles off, and now they are giving you back all that care, round and ripe and red as love. Of course these taste special; some of your own life is in each one."

#

On the hottest afternoon of the year, when the ridge-tops appeared vague and insubstantial in the blue haze of summer, Mary and her nephew worked together in her garden, picking okra.

"I hate okra," declared the boy, "It prickles so when it's hot."

Mary's smile collapsed into a laugh in spite of her valiant efforts to contain it, "You like it well enough pickled or fried. I love okra. When it is this hot, squash wilts in the shade, and peppers drop their blossoms before they set, but the heat just encourages my okra."

"Why's that?"

"Because it comes from Africa, where it is hot all the

10

time, Africans were brought amongst our folk as slaves, and gave us okra. Now what think you of that?"

Ben thought on it a moment; "I think that was mighty Christian of them."

Mary laughed again, this time without even attempting to rein it in. Her laughter would come without warning, in an instant, a soft low music, like water eddying among stones. It seemed to well up from a place deeper than herself, down among the roots of the ancient hemlocks beside her door, maybe from the stony heart of the mountain itself. Although her nephew was more often than not the object of her amusement, her laugh, dark and rich and full, warmed his soul whenever he heard it. Ben breathed at home in her laughter the way a plant is at home in good soil.

#

Ben slept on the porch all summer. He found comfort and reassurance in the mysterious lights of fireflies and foxfire, in the voicings of owls, and occasionally the rummaging and snufflings of bears among the trees beyond the yard, and more infrequently, the distant call of a big cat somewhere up on the Rim. These same sounds might have frightened him had he heard them from his bed in town. Here in the Gap, they testified to his belonging. He felt secure and at rest among the wild things.

Once, he wakened in the wee hours with the moon full in his face. His grandmother, who died the year he was born, had just paid him a visit. He must have spoken or cried aloud in his sleep, because his aunt stepped soundlessly out the door, barefoot and silvery in the moonlight, herself appearing like a ghost.

"Are you troubled?" she whispered.

"Grandmother was here," Ben whispered back.

Whispering seemed appropriate.

"She was prettier than her pictures. I wish she had stayed longer."

"What did she tell you?"

"She said, 'Find my boy.'"

"When you find the boy," Mary told him, "She will be with you to stay."

"Where do I look?"

"Somewhere close," and very quietly, Mary closed the door.

#

After lunch next day, when the children had finished drying the dishes - the cousins dried, while Ben, being taller, put things away - the girls wandered off to the spring, and he sat with his aunt on the porch while the long summer afternoon slowly gathered shadows into evening. As always, it was Ben who broke their silence. "I want to go see Owl." He inflected the phrase like a question.

Ethan Owl kept a solitary existence beside a nameless branch half-way up the side of Pinnacle, at a spot in near perpetual shade most of the year. Not far, but steep, no road, just a twisty footpath. Mary stumbled upon his place during one of her ramblings not long after she came to live in the Gap with Ronan. Ethan became her friend and confidant, introducing her to modes of healing she had not learned training as a nurse. When her brother's son began spending summers with Mary and her family, Ethan extended the umbrella of his friendship over Ben, as well.

"Well enough, Nephew," Mary approved, "But stay not if Ethan is busy, and don't hang about the place if he isn't to home. And mind you're down from there before dark."

By the time Ben finished his climb up to the old man's cabin, Ethan was off on the mountain gathering medicinals. Contrary to Mary's instructions, the child sat down to wait against the thick trunk of an old hemlock and, tired from his long day, promptly fell asleep. For the first time, Owl visited his dreams. Ben saw the old man walking up the path, a full grown bear lumbering along beside him. He laid his hand on the bear's broad back and said to the boy, "Kuma."

In the dream, Owl didn't look quite like the Ethan Ben knew in his waking life; he was strangely dressed in what appeared to be some sort of short robe, and the bear was the color of no bear Ben had ever seen. He didn't think the word spoken to him was at home in Ethan's language or his, but he was certain it meant *bear*. The word also spoke to his soul of steep mountains and deep water, and he felt the earth tremble slightly beneath him when he woke with the word on his lips, "Kuma."

Ethan had called him up to wakefulness, touching him lightly on the shoulder, "You best be off, Boy. Soon now it is dark. Our Mary will think you've been stolen. When you hear something coming fast behind you, get off the path."

Before Ben was halfway down the slope, it was dark, and he did indeed hear a furious clattering along the trail above him. He stepped quickly aside into the omnipresent laurel just in time to see a yearling bear barreling full-tilt in his direction. The bear sensed the boy's presence, slid to a stop, and poked his bristly snout through the laurel branches and snuffed at the petrified child, almost nose to nose, the bear's breath overwhelming, smelling of mud and moss and decaying vegetation, rancid, with a tangy overlay like fermenting persimmons.

"Kuma" Ben whispered to the bear, whereupon the animal wheeled and resumed his headlong plunge toward the creek below.

When he finally stepped up on Mary's porch, it was fully night. Owls held conversation, and fireflies sparked the air. Great moths flung themselves against the backlit panes. Ben expected a scolding, but Mary opened the door with a laugh, "So then Little Bear is home at last, timely for his bath."

#

The spring became a favorite haunt of the children at Mary's house on long July afternoons. Though right near the house, it hid among the laurel, sheltered by a dense piney grove, and seemed a place apart and away, full of salamanders and possibilities. Sometimes Mary came with them, as much a child as any there, enlisting the children as co-conspirators in her life-long campaign to subvert Western Civilization.

She delighted in making things for them to weave play with, about and around, as on a day the children perched silent and rapt on a smallish boulder above the spring, watching Mary add finishing touches to an elaborate miniature house, framed with twigs and thatched with needles from the white pines that shaded them. She had an audience of three, her two daughters and their summer boy, who all in the family insisted on calling Little Bear since his night-time adventure on Ethan's path. He was the eldest, though their ages varied less than three years between them all.

As Mary was done with her construction and stood, Little Bear spoke, "Is that for Elves?"

"No, Elves are as tall as you, though more slender by

far. Too wee, that, for Elves. A spirit could rest here, though, for a night or a day. Spirits are oblivious to scale." Little Bear made a mental note to find out for himself one day exactly what *oblivious* meant.

#

The summer led him on, and as Little Bear took his bearings of the ridges and hollows along the Creek, he began wandering off by himself, sometimes for a whole day, whenever Mary would allow it. She often herself felt the hills calling her out at odd times for purposes obscure even to her. She knew the psychic imperative to answer such summons, so whenever her nephew had not chores to do, she generally let him go.

Sometimes along his wanderings, Little Bear would be overtaken by a sudden shiver, not from a chill but a thrill, as if touched by an angel, and he would stop and look about him to see if a door had just opened in creation through which he might go home to stay. For the rest of his life, he felt least at odds with his world when he could wrap himself in the wild, and whenever most in need of being reminded of himself, he would traverse, alone and afoot, some country of trees and hills in expectation of these moments of revelation and liberation.

As he left the house of a morning on one of his pilgrimages, Mary handed Little Bear his lunch bundle and admonished him, "Don't wander beyond what you know," knowing as she said it that he would, that he must. And wander he did, for almost a mile upstream along the creek, regarding dragonflies and small fishes, flashing bright in the sun before darting through the shadows, themselves shadows, fluid and fleeting. Then he struck out away from the water, up the slope through laurels and hemlocks, until he found himself threading his way among boulders and rock faces near the crest of the ridge, where oaks and hickories still managed to find anchorage in the stingy soil. There Little Bear conversed with ravens and ate berries of several kinds. He was particular to partake only of those plants to whom he had been properly introduced.

Near to noon, he stood before the tallest waterfall he had ever encountered in his brief span of years, and sat down beside the rollicking stream it fed, to unwrap his lunch. As he ate, Little Bear breathed to the blessed air something like thanks for all this day had brought to him, and realized that although he didn't feel exactly lost – he felt very much at home right where he was – he had apparently mislaid those parts of the world that were familiar to him.

When he finished eating, Little Bear neatly folded the towel that had held his meal, stowed it in his sack, and began following the lively water downhill. He had not crossed a major ridge, so he counted on the stream eventually bringing him close to home. Along his way, he came upon a sizable pool among boulders where two does and a fawn drank from the cold water. They lifted their heads as he stopped and spoke respectfully, then resumed drinking as he moved off down the branch. Eventually he came upon a larger stream he did not recognize, but instinct, or perhaps some energy of the water, told him that he had come to an upper reach of the creek he often played in near home. Not far beyond he surprised a slate hued heron at her lunch. She lifted and glided away swift and soundless over the descending waters.

As Little Bear followed Creek down into the Gap, she gathered breadth and voice, and he began to see here and there an old tree whose shape he thought he remembered, and eventually boulders he knew by name. Then, among the shadows of an encroaching laurel thicket, he saw the bear. He was certain it was the same bear he had encountered on his night ramble back down the mountain from Ethan's cabin.

The bear, unmoving as a stone, looked at him. The boy looked back at the bear. As he looked, he saw it wasn't a bear at all, but Ethan, who smiled then, broadly, as if he had been waiting for him. "Well, sure then you took the long way round to come visit me."

On their way up the laurelled steep toward Ethan's cabin, where the old man would nourish the wanderer with cornbread and honeycomb before sending him back to Mary, Little Bear made a confession. "Owl, down there next to Creek, I thought you were the bear."

Ethan's great booming laugh echoed against the gneiss cliffs on the far side of the cove, "And so am I Bear, Little Brother, and so are you. And Bear is us and the water in Creek and the stones that are Mountain's bone, and every soul, scaled or furred or feathered that moves in air or woods or water. We are each and all one in our Mother's body. The breath of Earth fills every lung. Her one heart pumps her blood inside us all. If you learn anything from this old man, know that you need not be ever striving to make a place for yourself in this world. Just watch and listen, and your place will find you."

"What place is that, Owl?"

Ethan reached out and laid his hand atop Little Bear's head, as if in blessing, "The place that waited for you before ever you were birthed."

#

Mary kept rituals she had not learned growing up in church. Some of them had been taught to her by Ethan.

Most were of her own devising, fruit of her own personal revelations. Whenever Spirit called, at odd times of the day or night, she slipped away on the mountain to some place where her heart kept lodgings, and there, with sky and earth and creatures for witness, she enacted the exchanges emblematic of her kinship and communion with the other souls through whom Maker is manifest in the world. A few times, at Ethan's urging, she took her nephew with her, more as observer than participant of her sacraments. Once on an August night, at the close of an invocation, she gave to the fire her handful of corn flour. It blossomed and flared in the flame as it was intended to do, a reminder of the unfailing power and presence of Spirit who held them. Little Bear, wide-eyed and awed, whispered, "Magic!"

Mary turned on him, as if he had uttered blasphemy, fixed him with a gaze so stern and commanding, it frightened him. She spoke quietly then, but her voice carried an edge. "There is no magic in this world, only Spirit; everything not of Spirit is an illusion or a lie."

#

His uncle Ronan was never much about the place. When questioned concerning their father's absence, the cousins said, "Daddy works away, don't you know?" On the infrequent occasions when Ronan kept at home for more than a day, he and Mary invariably fell into argument. Their tension did not unsettle their summer visitor. Such was the default relationship of his own parents, but Mary and Ronan both seemed pained by their differences, and went to lengths to avoid them. Even when at odds, they remained tending and helpful toward one another. Obviously, they were more of one heart than of one mind, but they nurtured a mutual tenderness, even in their shouting.

The last day of Little Bear's sojourn with the Darners, Ronan stayed home all day. It had been raining for most of the week, leaving the woods muddy and slippery and dangerous for loggers to work in and he had given his crew the day off. He had no major disagreements with his wife, and while they all sat out on the wide porch after their supper, still at table, listening to the rising voices of the coming night, without prompting or cue, Ronan reached for his guitar leaning against the wall behind him, brought it to tune and began to sing as he played some old melody that seemed to Little Bear to come from dark hills across wide waters.

Flow gently, Old River, beside our green hill,
Flow constant, Old River, and never be still,
My Mary is sleeping beside your bright stream,
Flow quietly, Old River, and sing in her dream.

Tired and filled after his long day, Little Bear closed his eyes, tilted his chair back from the table and fell into the song. The chair tilted a bit farther than he intended, and before he could catch himself, toppled onto the floor with a resounding crash. Only his feelings were much hurt. He opened his eyes into a vast and sudden silence and saw familiar and concerned faces peering down at him. They sounded like a Greek chorus, "Are you hurt?"

Little Bear sat up, rubbed his slightly tender noggin, and laughed at them. Everybody laughed then. He was happy. The long night stretched ahead of him as far as he could imagine. Anything could happen.

RIVER

Little Bear woke with a start before first light, whether from a dream or into one, he couldn't tell, The summer of his becoming had come down to its end. The Studebaker would arrive in a few hours to carry him back to town. There, he would be Ben again, and sent away to a school where Harry hoped the faculty could perform a task so far he had been unable to accomplish on his own - turn his son into a reasonable facsimile of himself.

From his bed on Mary's porch, Little Bear thought he saw Owl's bearish face peering through the screening. Then he realized it wasn't Ethan at all, just a bear, who, when the boy sat up, snorted, turned and shambled across the moon washed yard toward the dark line of trees beyond. Little Bear knew what to do then. He dressed and slipped out the door, taking no provisions, not even water. As he went out, he borrowed Mary's staff to ease his way; it seemed important to him that it should be hers, familiar to her hand, tested by her weight, and that it be with him. He walked in the cricket-riddled darkness down to the Creek. Disregarding his usual instinct to follow the stream upward toward the ridgetops, this time he headed downstream. He belonged to Creek, knew her well by now, and expected she would take him toward settlement and responsibility and return. Instead, he was surprised to find the terrain grew wilder and more difficult as he descended. Often he had to wade in the swift water among the boulders there in order to pass the laurel that thicketed the shore. Several times, the current swept him off his feet, but Creek carried him on his way and always deposited him more or less intact on some gravel bed or half-submerged log.

Deep within himself he knew what he was looking for. Although he couldn't have said it, he was looking for the place where two streams merged, where his Story became his life.

All morning Little Bear followed Creek on her bouldered course down the valley, sometimes scrambling through mazes of rhododendron and laurel, sometimes floundering among stones over his knees in icy water. Occasionally, there would be a relatively clear stretch of shoreline where he could stroll along in the deep shade of hemlocks older than any human alive. It puzzled, though not alarmed him, that he did not recognize any of the landscape around him, nor see any sign of the road he knew ran along the side of the ridge above the stream. He thought he might cross to the opposite bank if he found a decent place to ford, and try to find the road. Being lost had always been a temporary experience for Little Bear, however, and had never been particularly unpleasant. He was as much at home in the woods as anywhere.

But by mid-day he was tiring, and hungry and thirsty as well, and finding comfort in the thought that at least he could follow the boisterous stream back up the hill to home. If he turned around now, he'd be at Mary's table again by dark. Then he saw a little hemlock sapling bent over in the downstream direction, it's tip weighted by a stone, as Ethan would sometimes do to mark a path he wanted Little Bear to follow after him. Hung across the arc of the bent trunk was a burlap bag, which Little Bear folded and tucked into his belt. Then he lifted the stone, watched the treelet spring sunward, and continued on his downward way. Before he had gone far, he came upon an abandoned apple orchard, overgrown and untended for a long time. Nevertheless, it offered some surprisingly mellow and juicy fruit which satisfied his hunger and eased his thirst. He ate a couple of the apples, rested, gathered a few into his bag, and walked on into the afternoon.

The first Rule of his journey was already formulating in his mind- to accept each gift of the Way as it presented, trusting that although it might not always be what he wanted at the moment, it would prove needful, therefore should be received thankfully and honored for what it was.

#

For a time that seemed a long time to Little Bear, he continued making his way carefully along his Creek. Toward mid-afternoon, he came to a clearing that once had been some human's cornfield. He saw a coppered fluttering among the tall weeds and saplings there, and discovered a young hawk, who had attempted to take a groundhog. Her prey had managed to scrabble into his burrow, with the hawk still hanging on, and died there, wedged into his hole. The hawk, her legs fully extended into the burrow, could not release her grip, and left to nature, was doomed to starve with her meal in her grasp. Using the wire-bound end of Mary's staff, Little Bear was able to remove enough of the soft soil between the stones and gravel to dislodge the corpse, and the hawk, who had been assailing and pecking at the offending staff during the whole operation, could finally relax her talons. Freed at last from the body of her death, she staggered around a bit, flailing at the air before she lifted up with a flurry of wingbeats about Little Bear's startled face, circled once above, and vanished over the treetops. His heart pounding, his senses shaken by the drama of resurrection, Little Bear lay for a while on his back smelling the sunbaked grasses around him, savoring one of the apples from his bag, and marveling at how little equipment one required to bring life out of death when granted the opportunity to be a miracle.

#

A little further along Creek, past the overgrown clearing where he had given Hawk back her life, Little Bear began to discern slight traces of a path. Whether worn by two leggeds or four, or both, he couldn't tell. In places the path had been more traveled and it broadened, became more distinct, then for stretches it tapered to no more than a hint of passing there. From time to time side trails led up from the water's edge, and away through the trees and boulders on the slopes above. The ridgetops, when they could be glimpsed through the heavy growth, seemed higher than before. Little Bear could not judge whether the mountains were taller here, or if he were just deeper down among them. As he followed his path, black clouds billowed up over a ridge beyond the far side of the narrow valley. Thunder echoed back and forth between the hills, and suddenly, as if by a word spoken, it commenced to rain.

A flood fell upon him. There was no wind, just sheets of water streaming down until the whole world was awash. Even the thunder was drowned out by the roar of the swollen Creek. It was impossible for Little Bear to lift his gaze against the downpour for more than a moment.

The path became a miniature manifestation of the torrent beside him. There would be no crossing it now. Though soaked to the skin, his insides felt like he was in a desert. He paused from time to time, cupped his hands beneath the edges of broad rhododendron leaves, and caught a few sips of water. Thus, head down, clutching his staff, his sodden bag with its few treasures slung over his shoulder, Little Bear walked on deeper into the storm.

#

He had no feeling for how long he had been walking under the unrelenting rain. It might have been an hour, a day, a season. To Little Bear, it seemed as if it had always been raining. Then, as suddenly as it had begun, the rain ceased. The skies gleamed blue between the sunlit crests of the ridges either side of Creek's valley, while Little Bear slogged on in the deep shadows of the cove below. A half-mile farther on, the ground trod dry and firm underfoot and there was no sign of a recent rain. The afternoon was nearly spent. In his soggy clothes, Little Bear trembled from the chill. As he walked, his path widened into a double track where wheels had passed, though not with great frequency, as grass grew between the stones in the twin traces.

When only the highest summits of the surrounding mountains remained ablaze with the dying day, he saw a wider valley opening before him, and Creek bounded off into a broad river flowing away westward. At the confluence of Creek and river, the road turned sharply away from the water and wound off upslope to disappear among trees. Here in the narrow floodplain, Little Bear discovered a well-tended vegetable garden. Along one side of the garden, farthest from the water, ran a wire strung atop posts cut from black locust where grapevines had been trained. And just where the road angled left to begin its climb into the forest above, pinned on a rope stretched between two sycamores, hung a boy's shirt and trousers. They looked remarkably similar to the clothes he wore. On closer inspection, he found them considerably more worn than his own. They had been mended and darned repeatedly, used hard, and well kept. They were sturdy yet, and clean, and most importantly, dry. Little Bear stripped off his soaked garments, and pulled the clothes from the line and tried them on. They were still warm from the afternoon sun. They had appeared to be large for him, but to his mild astonishment, they fit him perfectly.

Leaving his shoes and wet clothes in a heap with his bag at the foot of one of the sycamores, he leaned his staff against the tree, and in the fading light made a barefoot tour of the garden. He passed down long rows of tomato vines and green beans tied to stakes. He pulled one of the tomatoes and ate it as he walked. It was of darker hue than any he had seen before, deep crimson, tending almost to purple. The taste was sweet and tangy and the pulp springy and crisp. The juice soothed his parched throat. He thought it even better than one of Mary's. He found potatoes, and several kinds of squash, melons and chard and all sorts of greens and herbs. Then he encountered a couple of rows of sweet corn and a whole row with stalks of okra, taller than a man, laden with pods and furled blossoms. When he rounded the far side of the garden he noticed some of the grapes were fully ripe. Having made his circuit, he went back to the sycamore, hung his wet clothing on the rope stretched there, and began to wonder where he might shelter for the night.

He noticed, shadowed in the tall grasses along the

water's edge, a flat-bottomed skiff pulled up on the shore. He retrieved his staff, picked up his bag and wet shoes and walked over for a closer look. The little craft was old, made of wide boards, calked with what appeared to be wax and rope. A long time past, someone had painted it green. A few flakes of paint still clung to the wood. The skiff was clean inside, obviously used regularly. A paddle lay along the bottom, and on the single seat, a squarish bundle in a bright yellow wrapper, tied with a stout piece of hemp cord. Beside it sat a clay bottle, stoppered, with a cradle of string netting woven about it. Little Bear dropped his shoes, bag and staff into the skiff, picked up the bottle, loosed the stopper and sniffed at the contents, then sipped warily. It was water, light and cool, as if fresh drawn from a well or spring. He drank deeply and gratefully, and when he closed the bottle, he was no longer thirsty.

Having trespassed to this extent, Little Bear saw no harm in opening the bundle. He sat down on the seat, placed the package in his lap, and loosed the cord. The wrapper turned out to be a water-proof poncho. Inside it, he found a light blanket, an old cloth hat, floppy brimmed with a chin strap, and a small metal canister with a screw cap. He removed the cap to find nine wooden matches and a small square of sandpaper that had apparently been used for a striker.

Little Bear closed the canister. He was spent. It was almost dark. Fireflies strobed the night around him. He gathered the gear and his two remaining apples to the bow of the skiff, flipped aside the seat, which hinged at one end, wrapped the blanket around his shoulders and lay down to rest, pulling the poncho over him to shield against the dew. Almost before his head dented the pillow he fashioned from his rolled-up bag, he fell sound asleep.

#

His dreams came vivid and wild. He saw darknesses and lights, tempests and earthquakes, bloody moons and black suns. He walked through stony deserts and deep forests. He traversed swamps and mountains. He met strange animals and stranger humans, and beings who might have been either or both. Owl walked beside him for a way, not the Ethan he knew awake, but the not-quite-Ethan of his dreaming. Before Owl disappeared, he turned to face Little Bear and said simply, "Trust the River."

Little Bear woke to night and dark. He heard thunder far away. He became aware of the slight rocking of the skiff, like a cradle. Rains up on the mountains had lifted the level of the river during the night, and the little boat was half in the water. He sat up, suddenly wide awake. At first, the whole world was black. Even the fireflies had doused their torches. As his eyes accustomed to darkness, he made out the faint glow of the fog rolling in off the water, and ahead of him, among the unseen trees above the garden, a lighted window, no doubt the house where the gardeners lived.

Little Bear knew what to do then. He planted the end of Mary's staff into the muck and pushed the skiff out into the water. He sat swaying gently to the rippling pulse of the river beneath, watching as gathering fog devoured the window light. Darkness folded round him. Sometime during the long night, he felt the current taking the skiff. It was impossible to see where he was going, but it did not trouble him at all that now he belonged to the River.

Little Bear lay on his back in the dark, waiting for something to happen, as the skiff rocked along its way, revolving slowly in the grasp of the flow. Eventually, he drifted back into sleep. This time, his dreams were quieter, moving him through vast spaces beneath star-strewn skies. In some of his dreams, his body seemed strange to him, furred or scaled, cradled by water, close to the earth, or away up in trees. The shapes of himself kept changing, and oddly, he felt at home in them all. In one of his dreams he looked down on the river as if from a great height. His shoulders burned with the delicious stress of living flight. He rejoiced in the air feathering through his wings. The moon had risen full above the black hills behind him and he saw his skiff, a tiny shadow on the water directly below. The fog had begun to dissipate, and persisted in banks against the flanking mountains. Ahead of the skiff and the sleeping boy, the moon laid a silver road straight down the River until it was hid between the hills.

#

Little Bear woke with the sun in his face. The river had become wider and shallow here. Rounded boulders of varying sizes protruded above the water all around, like a pod of whales swimming upstream, each of them trailing in their shadow a rippled wake. One of these rocks, barely submerged, had scraped the bottom of the skiff, waking him. The sun was not yet high, but reflecting off the river around him, made him feel need of some shade. He picked up the hat he'd found the night before. He could make out the letters the previous wearer had inked on the inner band, *B. A. R. D.* He pulled the hat down over his head, found it snug enough to stay with him in a stiff breeze, but not overly tight, and the chin-strap would hold it to him in a gale. He told himself it fit well enough for free, and ate one of his two remaining apples.

When he finished it, he was still hungry, but thought

he'd best save his last apple for some leaner hour. He wished he had gathered some of the grapes from the garden before he embarked, and as if in response to his thought, the river began a wide southerly turn. The current carried the skiff in an ark near the longer bank, and as he passed under some overhanging maples, Little Bear saw they were festooned with fox grapes. He grabbed as many grapes as came within reach, piled them at his feet, and savored them over the rest of the morning.

As the river straightened into another reach, a gaggle of small brown ducks passed him, paddling purposefully downriver, chatting softly among themselves. As they overtook the drifting skiff, a couple of them looked inquiringly at Little Bear. When he spoke to them, they answered in the way ducks do. Now and then one or the other plunged her head beneath the water, and feet in the air, snatched some morsel from the depths. Little Bear tossed the tough skins of a few of his grapes overboard, and the ducks took them, with more curiosity than enthusiasm.

Soon the ducks moved on, intent on whatever duck business was calling them. The mountains drew in closer to the shore. The river narrowed a bit, became deeper as the current gathered speed. Little Bear saw ominous black clouds banking over the peaks ahead, and heard thunder rumbling beyond the nearest ridges. He thought he might not want to be out on the water in a storm.

Suddenly, a searing spear of light leapt toward the clouds from a huge dead white pine on the farther shore, and the whole top of the tree exploded in flames. Immediately, a wave of blue sound clapped Little Bear's ears like a giant's hands, then echoed between the surrounding mountains as he sat there stunned and blinded by the bolt, hardly realizing what had just happened. In the silence that followed, he heard no sounds but the crackling of flames in the stricken pine.

Little Bear recalled the older of Mary's girls once saying to him quite seriously, with certain conviction, "Lightning never strikes in the same place twice." He knelt in the skiff, gripped the paddle, and clumsy with haste and inexperience, pulled furiously toward the burning tree.

#

The current proved swifter than he thought, his paddling less efficient than he wished. He pulled his skiff up on the riverbank at the mouth of a meandering brook about fifty yards downstream from the pine, which still blazed like a torch. Beyond the tall reeds and grasses along the shore, he saw ahead of him a dirt track that appeared to have been graveled sparingly none too recently. The road forded the brook, and ran roughly parallel to the river. A path from the road followed the brook toward a tree-shrouded slope rising steeply and abruptly from the bottomland. Little Bear glimpsed among the shadows there a dark opening that might have been a cave.

He pulled the poncho over his head, quickly tied his blanket into a roll with the piece of corded hemp, stuffed everything loose into his bag, dropped staff, bag and blanket roll aside while he flipped the skiff bottom up to keep the interior dry during the coming storm. The skiff was heavier than he had reckoned, but he managed, as mist-laden gusts began tossing the tall grass around him.

Little Bear laid the paddle atop the overturned skiff, glanced behind him to see the surface of the river splintered white with hail and rain as the squall front bore down. He picked up his staff and bag, slung the blanket roll over his shoulder, and as the first grape-sized chunks of ice pitted the dust at his feet, crossed the road at as close to a run as he could manage under his burden, and took the path along the brook toward what he prayed was shelter.

He ran among the trees before the full force of the storm fell around him. The rattle in the leaves of the oaks and poplars above him suddenly magnified into a roar. Bits and shreds of greenery torn loose by hail came floating down around him amid fluttering birds seeking refuge deeper within the canopy. Occasionally, a hard bit of ice found its way through to smack the ground beside him. Once or twice, a hailstone met his head, made him glad to have even the cloth of his hat between ice and scalp. But the grove mostly sheltered him from the hostile elements until he reached the opening he had seen, a squarish door framed in rough timber. Not a cave at all. It had been somebody's spring house.

The brook disappeared through a low opening in the stone wall laid up around the door. Someone had found the spring here where it emerged from a fault in a large rockface, walled it in with stone, and covered it over with a sod and timber roof. At one corner, a small boulder had loosed from the slope above and come crashing through the roof, leaving a bushel-basket sized opening through which hailstones rattled now in the dim light from above. The natural stone of the place formed the rear wall of the little enclosure, and most of the floor. The brook had been channeled into a rough trough chiseled out of the stone, large enough for jugs of milk and pots of butter to be kept cool and fresh. Shards of some of these containers still littered about.

Entire human lives had been lived around this spring.

A family Little Bear would never know, who were likely gone from this world before he ever came into it, had come this far into the mountains, and decided that was far enough. He wondered how long might it have been since a boy like him last sheltered in this place.

#

While the storm vented fury outside, Little Bear dozed beneath his hill. He woke to sun shining down through the hole in his roof. The angle of the light said the afternoon was well gone. As he watched, the pool of light at his feet dimmed and vanished as the sun dropped behind the ridge above the spring. He went over to the door and peered out. Small limbs and branches and leaves littered the ground. To his right, the brook wandered down through the wood and across the road to the river. To left groved a stand of young poplars that may have once been a cleared field, or a yard. Little Bear walked out among them, gathering a handful of the broad leaves as he went, intent on appeasing an urge that had been building for some time. He hunkered down beside a pile of stones, apparently the remains of a chimney, the only surviving trace of the house it had once hearthed.

As he re-entered the spring house, in the shadows just inside the door his foot caught on a fair clutch of firewood. Obviously he was not the first pilgrim to spend a night here. There was still enough light to make out the blackened area on the stone floor below the hole in the roof. Little Bear gathered enough leaves and sticks from the corners for kindling, and laid out wood for burning. He took one of the matches from the little metal canister in his bag, struck it on the sandpaper and lit his fire. The flames took and he still had eight matches.

He unrolled his blanket then, set his can of matches in

the center. They would more likely stay dry rolled in his blanket, he reasoned, than in his wet bag. He pulled out the water bottle, which fortunately survived his flight stoppered and whole, and after a long swallow, brimmed it at the spring, although, strangely, it seemed about as full as it had the night before.

The night wasn't cold; Little Bear built his fire mainly for light and company. He felt, as he often had during his short life, lonely. He also felt hungry. He sat for a time watching the dancing shadows on the walls around, trying to read the voices in the flames, wondering if the time had come to eat his last apple. He thought he heard someone speak his name. A young voice, a girl? And then he woke, and it was morning.

#

Little Bear had no memory of falling asleep. If he had dreams during the night, the clear light of morning rinsed them all away. He stepped out of the springhouse amid a great clamoring of crows in the poplars west of the path. Whatever they were disputing had nothing to do with him. Their debate continued unabated as he walked through their throng to the brook.

Where the water pooled above a stony ledge, Little Bear took off his clothes and settled into the chill. He scrubbed himself with coarse sand from the stream bottom until his pink skin tingled. He wondered if he might be growing up, for at that moment, a hot bath with real soap seemed to his mind a fine thing. Then he lay on a mossy rock while the early sun dried him. He was starving, he thought. Time now to eat that last apple. As he stood in the dappled morning, buttoning his shirt, he heard from behind him the voice that had called him to sleep the previous evening, "Mama said you would be needing these."

Little Bear whirled around, startled and unnerved that another human had been able to get so close and he unawares. How long had the girl been there? Where had she come from? She looked like one of the sepia-toned photographs in his grandfather's old album. Barefoot, in a long dress, long sleeves, with yoked front, green, with tiny red and yellow flowers printed on it. Long dark hair hung straight down her back to below her shoulders. Her expression looked profoundly solemn until she suddenly smiled the most guileless and welcoming smile Little Bear had ever seen, and held out to him her basket.

Whatever was in the basket smelled like thanksgiving. Wrapped in brown paper, oily from its contents, Little Bear found a sweet potato, yet warm from the baking, several cakes of fried gritty bread, a wedge of goat's cheese, mouldy, but tastier for it, a boiled egg and a ripe peach.

While Little Bear attacked his meal, the girl offered commentary. "Mama told me, 'That boy will be hungry down there by now.'"

Little Bear grinned at her around the egg he was swallowing more or less intact, "Tell your mama this boy is not as hungry as he was a while ago, but he will be thankful for a good while to come. How did you know I was here, anyway?"

"We used to live down here by the spring. That was a long time ago, but Mama still watches the place."

Little Bear wondered about that. He judged the girl about his age, maybe a year older, but girls looked older than boys. She was nowhere near as old as that chimney he had seen. Maybe her family had lived here for some time before she was born. "Where do your folks live now?"

"Gannies we live all over this old mountain," she said ever so serious, then instantly all alaugh, "Well, I've fed you and now I'm off," and the girl jumped across the brook like a bird in flight, and swept herself away up the slope.

"Wait! What's your name?" Little Bear tried to shout after her, his mouth still full of her mama's goodness.

"Elizabeth," she laughed over her shoulder, but she was already just a glimmer among the trees. He could hardly see her, and then he couldn't see her at all.

"You forgot your basket," He said to the trees, and realized he had lost it himself. He looked all around, and finally spied the handle emerging from a riotous shock of sourgrass. When he reached for it, the handle separated from the body of the basket and the whole structure collapsed into a scattering of mildewed fragments. This basket had not held a hot lunch for a boy or anyone else in a very long time.

If Elizabeth were a ghost, as Little Bear strongly suspected, the food she had brought him was solid and real. He felt filled and anchored now, present and part of the place he was in. He neatly folded his piece of oil-slicked craft paper, the only evidence of his visitor left to him, stuffed it into the pocket of his shirt. When he got back to the spring house, he rolled the square of paper along with his match canister into his blanket, tied it at both ends with his cord, leaving a span in the middle to sling over his shoulder. He took a long drink from his bottle, stoppered it, and looped its string webbing through his belt. He pulled on his hat, picked up his bag, which now only held his single apple, hoisted that with the blanket roll over his left shoulder, and with his staff resting against his right, stepped out into the day.

As he walked along the brook toward the river, he heard a commotion approaching from somewhere beyond the trees. Just as he stepped up to the road, an ancient truck, reddened from old paint or recent rust, came rattling and banging along the road, following the river downstream. Rickety wooden sideboards swayed and shuddered around the bed, and within stood a doleful looking cow with swollen udder. Her calf stood beside her, too traumatized by his ordeal to suckle. The cow bawled mournfully at Little Bear as they passed. He stood gazing after them until the truck disappeared around a bend. He stayed where he was, listening, until the hills muffled the truck's cacophony.

Then he walked up the road to inspect the lightning-struck tree. What was left of it, blackened and shattered, stood between the road and the river to his left. As he approached, he found bits and shards of charred and blasted wood scattered in a wide circle around the tree. Fires had kindled at several places in the tall grass there to be doused by the rain. Coals still smoldered in the heart of the dead pine. A thin trace of smoke spiraled listlessly heavenward like a hopeless prayer.

For the better part of an hour, Little Bear rummaged around the dead tree, poking with his staff among the fragments and debris strewn about the place. Apart from a few broken bottles, probably left behind by fishermen, he turned up nothing of recognizable human origin, except for a small porcelain bowl, which, once he shook out the clumped mud, revealed a pattern of twined ivy painted inside. It was cracked, but of a piece. He put it in his bag. His mostly fruitless search bothered him, as he had attributed to the tree some considerable significance.

This tree, after all, had called up the lightning, which compelled him to this shore, where he found shelter and sustenance and companionship in an unlikely place and out of time. He concluded that even dead and done, one might have important work to do in the world.

Finally, he returned to the road, looked up and down it, feeling no particular call in either direction, and heard far above him, Hawk's wild cry. He glanced up and saw her, sun-gilt and high, out over the river, flying westward. Little Bear walked back along the road to the brook, and followed it down to the riverbank, where he had left the skiff. He bent among the tall grasses swaying about him in the late morning sun, picked up the paddle, and stared at it wonderingly. Then he straightened and took a long slow look all around. There was no sign at all of the skiff.

ROAD

Little Bear pondered his options until he realized he had no notion of what his options might be. Finally he decided to continue following the river downstream. The truck had taken that direction. He'd seen Hawk flying that way. Maybe something waited there for him. He had no more idea on land where he might be headed than he had on the water, but walking under his own power, choosing the path of his unknowing, made his journey feel more purposeful than just drifting with the current. Because he was working at it, he felt as if now he was going somewhere. Where that might turn out to be, he still hadn't the slightest inkling.

Trucks and cattle traversed this road. Somewhere along it, he would find companionship if not purpose. The road had brought him the only human presence he had encountered since he left Mary's porch, although he reminded himself Elizabeth might well be anything but human.

This was the third day since Little Bear left home with nothing but Mary's staff to shore and comfort him on his way. It could as well have been three years. It seemed to him as if he had always been on this road. The river had taken him to a different world, a different life. Along the way, he had become a boy of some substance. He had a poncho that shed rain, a hat with somebody else's name on it, a bottle of water that stayed cool even in the noonday sun, a blanket, eight matches, a scrap of greasy paper, and a burlap bag holding an apple and a bowl with a crack in it. And his day was just getting started.

Little Bear watched as he walked. He hoped from here on there might be signs and warnings before he met with anything drastic for good or ill. Whatever came to meet him on the Road, he meant to be ready for it. As he walked out of morning into afternoon, he encountered wild raspberries growing along the ditches, some black, some red, all tart and juicy. He picked as many as he could carry in his hands and ate them as he walked. By the time he thought he might like some more, he came come upon another patch of them. As long as he didn't get tired of berries, he figured he wouldn't be hungry.

Once, he thought he heard far up ahead the old truck that had passed him that morning, but the sound faded and he walked on, his lengthening shadow trailing him like a faithful puppy, as the sun shone more and more in his eyes until he had to lift his hat brim to see as far as the next turn in the road. Dust swirled around his feet with every step. It occurred to him that Harry would not like to drive his shiny new Studebaker here.

The road continued to follow the river to his right. As he walked, the River kept trying to sing him something. There were definitely words in the music, but he couldn't quite make them out. Occasionally, crows would offer translation, but he couldn't understand them. There was no music in their speech at all.

Neither rain nor hail nor lightning assailed Little Bear that day. The afternoon waned; heavy clouds gathered over the ridges farthest west, and thunder mumbled faintly away and beyond, but the storms moved off in

another direction, and none came close to him. Apart from
the road, and the occasional artifact he kicked up along
the shoulder as he walked, no sign appeared of human
passage or habitation in this country. The road ran close to
the riverbank on his right, the trees grew close to the road
on his left, and although after a few miles the mountains
ahead did not appear quite as tall as those behind him,
their forested slopes were steep, often with massive
outcroppings of boulders protruding above the canopy.
The hills themselves crowded close upon the road. Every
mile or so, he saw thinning among the trees that could
indicate the land had been cleared at some point, but
never in all that long afternoon did he pass anything that
might have been a trace of house or barn or fence or any
structure put up by human purpose. No faces or voices
came to him here, except the memories he carried within
him. There was the boy and there was the road, trailing
through vast heaving silences that filled the whole world.

The longer Little Bear walked, the more full those
silences became. His habitual loneliness began to fade.
The river sang, the wind whispered, squirrels chattered,
birds called and cried and piped and shrieked in whatever
manner they were disposed to do. Within him sprang a
sense of all these voices speaking together the earth's own
language, the One Tongue. Eventually, he might begin to
learn that language, but for now his part in the
conversation was simply to listen. It would be a long time
before his brain could attempt to formulate these realities
that were being imprinted on his psyche. Even had he
conscious understanding of them presently, he could not
have framed words to express the truths he was receiving,
but he was beginning to feel them in his bones, in his tired
muscles and sunburned arms and aching feet. The germ of

a belief began to take hold in him, that all of these small lives, his own among them, were each and all merely steps and measures in the Great Dance. The One Mother breathed in them all, and they were all Her.

#

As the sun began sinking behind the farther mountains, shadows of the tallest oaks and hickories crowning the nearest ridge crept across the road. A few steps in light alternated with brief immersions in deep shadow. Hawk sounded again her shrill, piercing call. Little Bear never heard a hawk cry but he felt the almost invisible hairs on his arms stiffen, and breathed to the air a prayer for wings. The prayer, of course, had never elicited a response, but this time, the river who had been sighing and murmuring to him all day, suddenly spoke quietly, and quite clearly, *Patience - soon.*

Little Bear took off his hat and squinted into the setting sun, made out the descending raptor against the light and followed her with his eyes as she dropped down below the ridgeline, becoming a pale shadow against a darker one, and settled into the top of an old sycamore whose base was concealed somewhere just beyond the low ridge nearest him. Hawk called to him once again from her perch as he walked on down the road, rounded about a little hillock and was slightly shocked to see people.

A two-storey stone house stood at the foot of Hawk's sycamore. An exceedingly lean old man sat on an up-ended keg by the door playing a banjo. The tune carried clear and far in the still air. Two grown men in overalls pranced a tight circle around one another in time to the music. Across the dirt yard to the right, Little Bear saw a timbered landing at the riverbank. A heavy frame above it anchored a single cable that stretched across the river, sagging in the middle to the water, then rising again to a similar structure on the opposite bank. Alongside the farther landing floated what he took to be a ferry. Parked before the near landing, the truck that had passed him on the road that morning waited to cross.

As Little Bear approached the truck, the cow lifted her head over the rails and bawled in recognition. The banjo fell silent, the two men broke off their dance, and one of them began walking toward the truck, as the other called after, "Robberlee, don't you stray away now. Give us a chance tonight to take the rest of your money."

#

As Robberlee strode over to the truck, a large golden cat and her two half-grown kittens followed him out from the house, the cat deftly twining between his feet as he paced. "I believe I saw you this morning," he said to Little Bear, who had been standing in silent communion with the cow. "You are a fast walker." Robberlee reached through the rails into the truck bed and felt the cow's inflamed udder. Then he clambered over the sideboards, stroked the cow's side, and when she settled, squatted down beside her and began to pull her reddened teats. "This calf has turned sickly on me and won't take his milk. Old Nancy's going to bust herself here if we don't help her out," Milk streamed onto the truckbed and dripped between the boards into the dirt below. The cat sniffed at it and the kittens mewed piteously. Robberlee squinted at Little Bear through the sideboards. "A shame to waste this good milk. You wouldn't have a bucket on you somewhere, would you, boy?"

"I have a bowl in my bag. It isn't very big."

"It will hold more than my fingers do, Might it please you to let me see it?" Little Bear fetched out his bowl and handed it through the rails to Robberlee, who wiped out the remaining dirt with the edge of his cupped hand, and after a few draws had brimmed it full. Carefully, he passed it back through the sideboards to Little Bear. "Mind you to set this down there for me, so Lucy and her young'uns can get their supper?"

The cats fell to furiously lapping up the milk, and emptied the bowl in moments. This sequence of events repeated several times as Robberlee continued milking, the cow giving more milk to the earth than to the cats. Meanwhile, across the river an engine fired and sputtered to life, the cable swayed and trembled, then tightened to the creaking frame of timbers that anchored it, and in the gathering dusk Little Bear could see the ferry slowly moving out from the far bank in their direction.

"We'll have to wait until morning to cross," Robberlee predicted. "Charon will not be wanting to haul us over in the dark."

His milking done, Robberlee climbed down from the truck bed and stood beside Little Bear watching the approaching ferry pulling with fits and starts along its cable, which vibrated and flinched and set its anchor frame at the landing to groaning with the stress. The river narrowed and deepened in this place, thus flowed faster here and tugged the ferry downstream so that midway across the river it hung twenty feet or more out of plumb with the landings at either end. It made for slow going.

Little Bear knew better than to ask such things of adults, but as they waited and talked, his curiosity bettered him, "Why did that man call you Robberlee? You don't seem like a robber to me."

Robberlee seemed to think this was the funniest thing he'd ever heard. He slapped his thigh and laughed so hard that he had to sit down on the running board of his old truck to recover. Finally, with tears of mirth brimming his eyes, he looked at Little Bear to answer, "They call me Robberlee because they're just too lazy to say all the names I've accumulated before Lee, and also as a sign they appreciate my well-known ability to close a handy deal."

"You're a storekeeper?"

"Not a merchant, boy, I'm a Trader by heart. I will turn goods for coin if I meet someone who would benefit by being separated from theirs, but my main game is to swap and trade from here to there. It is my greatest delight to give some soul something they need and take in exchange something they don't. Trading is a strange business, though. People will get the best bargain in the world and be upset over it. Some folks might say I'm tight in a deal, or even that I would cheat them if they give me the chance, but nary soul ever traded with me who didn't walk on less burdened than he was before we met."

As they watched, the ferry panted and moaned its way along the cable, gradually closing on the near shore. It was an ungainly flat-bottomed craft with a drop gate at either end. The only occupant was the ferryman. Just before the ferry jarred against the landing, he pulled a lever on an overhead rig, which disengaged a metal-faced wooden shoe from between two drive wheels. A chain looped to a sprocket powered the wheels. The sprocket shafted to a decrepit gasoline engine bolted to blocks attached to the deck. It was a contraption, but it worked. Once the engine started and the wheels were turning, the operator could ratchet down the lever, and the shoe, grooved to guide the cable, would press the cable to the wheels and gain enough friction to set the whole mess in motion.

The ferryman was a beefy man, with massive shoulders and arms, and broad hands, who looked as if he might be able to pull his ferry across the river by his own strength, a feat he claimed to have accomplished once or twice. As the ferryman went about securing his craft for the night, Robberlee said to Little Bear, "This here's Charlie Charon. His daddy kept this ferry before him, and his grandpappy before that. Charons have been hauling folks across this old River for as long as there has been a Road."

"Longer than that," Charon informed Little Bear, as he wiped the grime from his hands, then he said to the Trader, "Robberlee, whose cow do you have in that truck?"

"I took her in a trade yesterday over to Poplar Spring, and as a mercy, took that sickly calf with her."

"How much did you pay for them, Robberlee, if I might be pokey enough to nose?"

"It was a good trade, Charlie; they were a steal."

Charon lifted a brow. "I don't have a doubt they were. Otherwise they wouldn't be in your truck." Then he looked at Little Bear, "I've seen everybody who's come along this road since I was no bigger than you, but I don't believe I know you, son. What's your name?"

Suddenly, Little Bear was painfully shy about telling anyone his name. He remembered, of course, the names he had gathered along his way to this place, but every one of them seemed to him belonging to some alien country far away in a time long past or not yet come. Not one felt like his name anymore. He couldn't bring himself to say any of them aloud. Charon waited for his answer.

The speechless boy stared at the hat in his hand, finally found his voice, "Bard."

Charlie glanced keenly at Robberlee as he spoke, "Well now, Bard, you're in some unreliable company here. We'll go over when the sun comes back. Right now, I'm off to see what Callie has been cooking. Any who are hungry can follow me." And with that, he strode off toward the house, the cats schooling around his feet.

Bard looked his silent question at Robberlee, who said, "His Callie cooks for travelers, and they let rooms to people on the way. Do you have any coin, Bard?" Bard shook his head.

"That won't stop you from being hungry now, will it?" Maybe you can trade to old Robberlee for your supper. That's a mighty fine walking stick you have there."

"I can't. It's borrowed."

Robberlee bent down and picked up the empty bowl the cats had licked clean, "This bowl has a crack already, but it might still feed a boy on the road."

"I found it."

"Done deal, then." pronounced Robberlee. He opened the door to the cab of his truck and slid the bowl under the seat. "Put your gear in the truck here, and let's go catch up with Charon before he eats everything in sight."

#

As night fell down around them, the two walked after Charlie toward his house. Light shone from the windows on the lower floor, and streamed out across the yard from the open door. They found Charon with his big arms submerged up to his elbows in a large basin of water, one of several upon a long table set against the back of the house. Towels hung on pegs along the front of the table. Several bars of dark soap lay among the basins. Bard laid aside his hat, bent and lifted water to his face. It felt cool to his hands, and falling through his fingers, sounded like a little brook. Despite his hat, his face had a mild burn from the sun and wind on the road, and he expected the water to sting. Instead, it was instantly soothing, oddly restoring, almost like sleep. He wished he could take a bath in this stuff. He rolled up his sleeves and plunged in his arms as deeply as he could. Robberlee noticed his enjoyment and informed, "Callie's herbs."

As they dried themselves, Bard noticed a large detached kitchen, connected to the main house by a dogtrot, through which people rushed presently with armloads of crockery. Past the kitchen he glimpsed a long low shed, open-walled, but partitioned with hung canvas. The splashing and laughter in its vicinity evidenced it might be a wash house. Beyond that, he could see what appeared to be a large privy set among trees close against the rising ridge behind. A bold creek tumbled down from the ridge and away through a sycamore grove beyond, then off toward the river. Just opposite the house, a squarish wood frame building straddled the creek. Light shone through the window, and Bard could hear a steady throbbing of machinery within. A column about six feet square made of heavily chinked cedar logs, somewhat taller than the roof, adjoined the upstream side of the building; it looked like a chimney, except for a trestled raceway that brought water from further up on the ridge to empty into the open top of the column. This was a tub mill. Water pressure would build in the log stand, and be released through a small pipe at the bottom with great force to turn a relatively small wheel on a vertical shaft. Properly geared and pullied, it could power a gristmill or even a small sawmill. A large amount of energy was thus attained from a relatively small natural flow of water. In a dry season water could be stored in the stand and the mill could still be powered for a few hours each day. From the light and the sounds coming from the mill, Bard judged the miller was working late. In the failing light, he could make out stacks of lumber in the mill-yard. Bard wondered if all this enterprise belonged to Charlie Charon.

Coming round the house, they went in through the wide front door to a large room walled with square-hewn walnut logs, spanned overhead by stout beams of yellow locust. Atop these beams, ran wide heavy boards, serving as floor for the storey above. A huge stone fireplace dominated one end of the room. A fire burned briskly on the hearth, and about a dozen people stood chatting around it or sat on assorted kegs, chairs and boxes. Bard noticed a couple of women among the men there. Two long tables occupied the center of the room; each of which could seat a dozen or more. Plates of varying design were arranged on the tables, and glasses or mugs, utensils; the places more or less set.

As the three entered, a huge woman with skin the hue of the walnut logs that sheltered her domain set her eyes on Charon and let out a whoop. She was formidable in her glee, not fat so much as just large, a mountain of a woman and a woman of the mountain. Charlie was no slight human himself, but Callie grabbed him up in her stout arms before he could evade her and pressed him to her ample bosom, nearly pulling him off his feet, to the enormous amusement of the company gathered around the fire. Her great voice filled the room, making the walls seem to tremble, as if the very earth were shouting her delight, "Charlie, you've left me here apining all the long day, and now you've come to cheer me so late and last."

She held him at arm's length, smiled on him like the

sun, pulled his face close and kissed him like a lover. Charlie just stood there, grinned and suffered it all, clearly as pleased in sharing her company as she was to have him there. Callie turned him toward the nearest table, "Sit ye down here, my Charlie," she ordered, "and let me feed you from the fat of the land. I don't want you fading on me again like you did last night." As Charon ambled like an obedient bear toward his place at the table, she swatted him smartly on his wide rump. All this brought much laughter and applause and stamping of feet from the group around the fireplace, and was apparently the signal to begin the meal, for the whole assembly began to converge on the tables.

No chairs flanked the tables, only low benches on which people arranged themselves according to their previous conversations. The tables were stoutly horsed with some dark wood and topped with wide poplar boards, that polished with time and use and countless spills and wipings, shone in the light of the lamps along the center of each table. Both tables were roughly the same size. Two or three could sit comfortably at each end and five or six along a side. As the meal progressed, one or another soul would wander in from the road, warm at the fire, and as if by invitation, come over to a table where those already seated lifted their plates and slid along their bench to make room for the newcomers. More plates and drinks appeared, food passed around, and the feast continued. Now and then, one or two folk would finish eating, rise and leave, or go stand by the fire. There seemed always room at the tables for several more.

Callie and her helpers would come from the dogtrot, unload heaping platters of all manner of goodness at the head of one or other of the tables, and the platters would get handed down the table, arriving at the other end nearly empty, whereupon someone carried them off again to the kitchen until they reappeared filled with more of the same or with some other sustenance. Whole platters of fried and baked trout emerged from the dogtrot, along with chicken and goose and steaks or cutlets of beef or pork or venison or bear, fried, baked, broiled or roasted. Bard noticed that some at table did not share the meat, but no one had less of anything than they wanted. Bowls as big as washbasins arrived, full of beans green or black or red, and all sorts of leafy greens, cooked with peppers and onions and flavored with roots and herbs, supplemented by balls of cheese soft and hard, wedges of melon crimson and gold, squashes baked and fried, some of them stuffed with beans and spices. Bard tried to sample as many things as were passed in front of him, for most of them he had never seen the likes of. He found several he liked more, but could not say he liked one thing on his plate any less than the rest.

Along with the food, pitchers and urns came by him offering all sorts of drink, hot and cold, a few sweet and spicy and headily aromatic. Wisely, he mostly drank the water, which didn't add to his sleepiness, and as Mary would have put it, "made his taster work better."

Several of those who were first to eat their fill got up from table and went back over by the fireplace, and began to stir up music. The thin old man who had played for the dancers in the yard picked up his banjo, and one of the women the boy had noticed earlier brought a cello from the corner. A pink, plump, fifty-ish man who wore a funny little round hat with a narrow brim sat at an old piano over against one wall and began to tinker on it. A younger man, maybe twenty, in orange coveralls brought up a tin whistle. An older man who resembled him, could have been his father, put a fiddle to his chin. The other fiddler was a young girl several years older than Bard, not really a girl any longer, but a young woman. She wore a long green skirt and her blouse was printed with thin red and yellow stripes. Her dark hair hung straight and long down her back to just above her waist, and was secured with a comb of polished cherry wood that gleamed and flashed fiery in the light. The girl lifted her fiddle, stroked a few notes that soon resolved into a lively melody, drawing all the random tootling, plinking, plunking, strumming, and picking of the other musicians after her into a reel, and they were off.

People came and went and ate and drank, and the musicians played and played on. People listened and talked and laughed and dozed by the fire while the music carried them all deeper into the night. Time to time, a few would rise from the table and dance, in couples, or alone. The music spun out in reels and waltzes and steps and jigs, in wild tunes and slow tunes, some that sang to love and some that spoke of war. Hours or days or weeks into the evening, when the tables were finally being cleared, most of the people who had found their way to Callie's door that evening still remained, gathered in the spell. Then the musicians stilled, the room fell into a vast and sudden hush. Bard, by now teetering on the brink of sleep, with his head resting against Robberlee's arm, jerked upright wide awake, as the girl tucked her fiddle beneath her arm, and dangling her bow vertically by its tip before her, lifted her face and closed her eyes as if in prayer, and began in a clear fine voice to sing:

Nobody played for money
And no one sang for pay,

We only loved the music
And gave our love away;
All who were with us that night
Got caught up in our sound,
Dancing in the golden light
And passing love around.

She sang on, verse after verse, each evoking at the same time warm healing for old hurts and gentle sadness for old losses. When she had sung her story and ceased, everyone in the room believed they lived in her song.

As the music died, Robberlee nodded toward the three men across the table from them, said to the sleepy boy, "I've some business to discuss tonight with these gentlemen. There's a wash house out back. Count that as part of our supper trade. You'll sleep better if you're clean." Tired though he was, a real bath sounded mighty compelling to Bard. He spoke his thanks sincerely and headed for the door. He hoped he wouldn't fall asleep and drown himself before he finished his bath.

Bard walked out the back door into the dogtrot, saw off to his left the lanterns hanging in the wash house, moved to step off in that direction, when he heard from behind a voice he had heard before, "Mama said you would be needing these."

He turned to see the fiddler girl standing in the lighted doorway, holding out to him a big towel, folded, with a thick piece of black soap on top that looked as if it had been cut out with a hatchet, as it likely had been.

"Who?" he asked, flustered and astonished as if he had been visited by an angel.

"Callie, my mother; Robberlee told her you meant to have a bath." Confusion upon confusion. Bard could scarcely believe this willowy young woman was the daughter of Charon and his wife. She seemed the very opposite of them both in appearance and manner. They weren't even all the same color.

Still waiting for him to take his towel and soap, the fiddler read the puzzlement in his face and blessed him with a broad smile, "I was a baby left on the road. They took me in." Then, instantly all seriousness, "You look worn out."

He was. As she handed him the towel and soap, he grinned and confessed, "I'm dead."

She burst into a laugh that warmed him instantly, like sunshine through morning leaves, "We're all dead, don't you know? We are only real when we are in the Music."

Bard thanked her for his soap and towel. She pointed toward the bath house, "There's a vacant tub at the far end. Leave your things in the box by the door when you're done," and disappeared back into the house.

He went off then along a graveled path under a black and starless sky. The windows in the house and the lanterns in the open structure ahead gave him barely enough light to make out his way between rows of some tall large-leafed flowering plants, their blossoms curled tight against the dark. He stepped up into the wash house, just a large shed, open on three sides, elevated a couple of feet off the ground on locust posts. Wide-spaced stringers overhead revealed the underside of split cedar shakes that were the roof.

The shed divided into cubicles with canvas sheeting hung over saplings fastened horizontally just over a man's height to the posts supporting the flooring and roof. A row of these enclosures stretched along each of the long sides of the shed with a clear walkway through the middle. Suspended from the rafters overhead, above the canvas, hung a grid of pipes, some metal, some fashioned from hollowed cedar poles. A vertical pipe descended from the overhead plumbing into each cubicle. As Bard walked the length of the shed, he found the center of the roof open to the sky above a broad, roughly circular raised hearth, paved with large flat stones, the smallest of which he might have been able to move with some help. A deep bed of burning coals glowed and flared upon this hearth, over which, on a stout iron cradle, perched a huge metal vat, which would have displaced the roof had it been enclosed. An elevated raceway, similar to the one at the tub mill, delivered a small but steady stream of water into the vat. On a short ladder beside the vat, the thin banjo player was emptying a large basin full of some sort of pungent greenery into the brew. He waved from his perch and pointed farther along the shed, "Down to the end, son."

Most of the cubicles appeared vacant now, but here and there, aromatic steam drifted over the canvas walls. Bard could hear splashing and scrubbing and contented sighs behind them. The banjo man climbed down from his ladder and followed. When they reached the end of the shed, he pulled back a corner of a canvas sheet to reveal Bard's tub, steaming and redolent with restoration. The tub was constructed like a giant cedar bucket, banded top and bottom with metal, with the bottom boards grooved into the sides. The bottom had been fitted dry, so that when filled with water, the wood swelled and expanded, and rendered the joints quite watertight. Sturdy and well-made; if cared for, it could be expected to outlast the humans who bathed in it. The old man stepped aside to let Bard enter, and left him to his bath.

Bard sat on a stool alongside the tub and took off his

shoes, undressed, piled his clothes on the stool, and laid the towel on top. Folded inside the towel he found a rough cloth to scrub himself with. Soap in hand, he tested the water with one sore foot, then gingerly eased himself down into the water to his chin. The effect was instant and sustained. It soothed like the water he had washed in before supper, except this was hot. He wished he had a bucket of creek water to cool it with, but after a moment, his tender skin reconciled to the heat, which seemed only to magnify the lively properties of the herbs. The bath nurtured like sleeping, lifting away from him not only the dust and bruises from the road, but his weariness and wariness as well. For a while he could not bring himself to move. He watched the steam rising around him like mist from a river after a summer rain. He listened to the sputter of the old man's fire, and the dripping from leaks in the make-shift plumbing. It made a soothing, percussive sort of music. Bard thought that if he listened for a while he might be able to make out the melody. He closed his eyes, and breathed in deeply the essences of the infused herbs. Unnoticed, the Banjo Man reached beneath the canvas and deftly removed the clothes from the stool.

Either Bard roused himself occasionally to scrub his hide with the fierce black soap, or he dreamed he did. Later he was pretty sure that at one point during his bath he had plunged his head beneath the water and opened his eyes there, expecting it to burn, but overridden by a curiosity to know if the water from Charon's creek felt different from the water in his own Creek back in the Gap, a point of experience that would attract only a boy's inquisitiveness, but he had felt only coolness, more like a light than liquid, and when he sat up and looked around him, he thought everything appeared more sharp and real, colors more vivid and intense. The moths darting at the lamp lighting his cubicle had the presence and power of eagles. Even the night sounds in the dark beyond seemed closer, more potent, as if echoing from some place deep inside his own small self. Crickets and frogs, owls and larger animals off among the trees wove a music older than any song, that enveloped and infused his body and lifted his mind away into dreams and worlds wondrous and exalted that would terrify any sane adult.

Bard may have dreamed thus for years or centuries, but he returned a little later that same night, when sound asleep, he slid down into his tub and strangled on Callie's potion. He came up abruptly, coughing and sputtering, whacking his noggin on the brass faucet just behind his head in the process, as Banjo man looked in, said, "I see ye be done, then." and left Bard's clothes, folded and clean, and as he discovered when he put them on, mended in a couple of places.

By the time he had dried and dressed, he was convinced that however astute at trading, Robberlee had shorted himself in the deal this time. He was also beginning to entertain a growing suspicion that time might not work here in exactly the same way it did in the world he left behind in the Gap.

#

Only a few lamps burned here and there as Bard walked back through the wash shed. The fire beneath the vat was banked. The banjo player had disappeared. Fewer lights in the house, too, though a dim light shone out the back door and from a couple of lighted windows on the upper floor. The kitchen was dark. He figured his best course might be to go back to the truck and get some sleep. The thought occurred that sleep might seldom be a priority with Robberlee. Bard left his soap and towel in the box Liza had told him about, and crunched back along the gravel path. He saw no soul abroad but him. As he stepped through the dogtrot, the doorway suddenly darkened, and he looked up to see it filled with Callie. With the faint light behind her, he couldn't see her features. She really did look like a mountain.

"Take this, Bard, and see if you can get some of it down Robberlee's calf. It should help him." Callie handed him a large bottle filled with a liquid he couldn't identify in the near dark. A cloth rolled into a sop was stuffed into the mouth of the bottle. He thanked Callie and walked on past the tables where he had washed his hands for supper, and nearly dropped the bottle when, with low deep-throated growls, a huge three-headed dog bounded out of the darker dark along the creek. He was too frightened to yell or do anything but watch as the apparition hurtled toward him. As they separated, he saw it was not one dog but three, running close together. They didn't attack, but took stations around him several yards away and silently walked with him to the truck. He didn't know if he were being warded or herded.

When he reached the truck, the dogs lay some distance off, and appeared to be watching not Bard, but the darkness beyond. He saw that someone had brought hay and a bucket of water for the cow, who lay placidly ruminating in the bed of the truck. Her calf off in a corner looked gaunt and miserable. Bard climbed into the truck bed, patted the cow on her head. She seemed to consider him a minor event in her long evening. He squatted before the calf, who gazed at him listlessly. Bard inverted the bottle until the sop began to drip, and sniffed at the sop. It smelled a lot like the soap, only stronger. Consciously imitating his father's voice, he said to the calf, "Boy, you're not supposed to enjoy this."

As he expected, the calf refused it, but he had promised Callie that he would try, so he wet his fingers with the concoction and pushed them into the side of the calf's mouth, and when the calf began to suck at his fingers, he slipped in the sop beside them. The calf took the potion greedily, and in less than two minutes, Bard held an empty bottle. The calf bleated, stood shakily, and begin to nose his mother's belly, looking for his favorite parts.

Bard climbed over the side-boards and jumped to the ground. One of the dogs barked softly and glanced in his direction when his feet hit the earth. He opened the door to the cab, found everything present and accounted for just as he'd left it. He picked up his bottle, unstoppered it and took a deep swallow, wishing he'd remembered to take it to the house and refill it. But the bottle seemed about as full as it had that morning. The water in it tasted just like the water at the house.

Bard looked off toward the house then and was surprised to find he could barely see it. A heavy fog had rolled up from the river, completely hiding the opposite shore. Although there were no stars or moon visible, the fog itself seemed to be alight, emitting a faint, but steady glow that illuminated all it did not conceal. He put all his gear in the floor of the cab, curled himself on the seat like a puppy, and consigned himself to sleep, which took him immediately.

CROSSING

Morning did not bring sunrise. Darkness gradually paled eastward until the light in sky overhead grew brighter than the glow of fog below. Robberlee slapped on the door of the truck cab with the flat of his hand, startling Bard to life.

"Rouse and rise, Bard; you dreamed your breakfast away. Fortunately for you, I took more than I could eat and was ashamed to turn it back." Robberlee tossed through the open window a small package wrapped in what looked like old newsprint. Bard untangled the crinkly paper, found inside it, still mostly intact, two oversized biscuits, each enfolding a fried duck's egg. He crawled out of the cab and stood eating while the Trader emptied two large jugs of clear liquid into the gas tank of his truck. "This was brewed for drinking," Robberlee informed, "But has some miles in it for this old truck."

Bard didn't see the dogs. The little bull calf stood hungrily attached to his mother, bestowing her an occasional sharp butt of his bony head by way of encouragement to let down more milk for her baby.

Robberlee took note, "Ye done fair good there, Bard," picked up the calf's bottle from the night before, hefted it against the light, then reached through the window of the truck cab and dropped it behind the seat, as he said to the calf, "Somebody yonder is already needing that more than you do." He gathered the bucket and the two empty jugs and handed them to Bard, "Son, would you mind greatly running these back to the house for me and leave them by the dogtrot?" Robberlee tended to disguise the slightest instruction or directive as a request.

Bard put one of the jugs in the bucket, picked them up with one hand, and with a jug in the other, started for the house. In the heavy fog, he could not make out any sign of the buildings, but saw Charon emerging toward him from the gray, carrying two full jugs of his own, so headed in that direction. As they passed, Charon said, "Stay straight on, Bard, and you'll come round right."

When Bard returned, Charon already had his engine running, and the ferry gate open to the landing. Robberlee was bent over under the hood of his truck, up to his elbows in its greasy innards. Once he flinched and jumped back as if burned or bitten by something hidden there. As Bard approached, he said, "Son, this will go faster if you help me. Ever drive a truck?"

Bard shook his head.

"Nothing to it. All you have to do is sit up there, I've got everything set. Do you see that little knob just right of the steering wheel, little round black thing?"

Bard nodded.

"Now pull that all the way out, and when she starts, let it back in slowly until I tell you."

Bard got up behind the wheel and pulled out the choke. Robberlee unclipped a crank from its place just forward of the cab door and walked around in front of the truck, and inserted the flanged end of the crank into an opening in the grill. Bracing himself against his knee with one hand, and taking hold of the crank with the other, he carefully folded back his thumb to avoid the kickback, and gave the crank a mighty heave. The crank made a half circle, then hitched, barely missing Robberlee's knee on the backswing, and the engine coughed and exploded into an insane clatter.

"Ease her back, Bard," yelled Robberlee, and when the thrashing of the engine had more rumble than clatter to it, he shouted, "Slide over," jumped into the cab, throttled down, put the truck in gear, and eased them onto the ferry. Then he killed the engine, clapped Bard on the shoulder, said to him with a big grin, "You'll be a driver yet," set the brake, and hopped out onto the deck.

Charon had been watching the whole operation with silent amusement. When he judged the show was over he stepped forward, "Well, boys, we can start the instant I have my fare."

Robberlee hauled out a long leather pouch from his jacket pocket, loosed the drawstring and shook out a bundle of wadded papers and some coins. He sorted out two large bronze coins and dropped them into Charon's outstretched palm, complaining good naturedly as he did so, "I ganny you'll want one for the cow, too."

"You knew I would ask," replied Charon placidly, as he received a third coin. Then he looked at Bard. "Are you traveling with this person, Son?"

"No sir, We both just happened here."

"Then, you'll have to pay your fare like any other man on the road."

"I don't have any money," Bard admitted.

"What's in your bag?"

"I have an apple."

Charon winked at Robberlee."I'll take you over for an apple." Bard brought out his apple from the bag, handed it over to the ferryman, who wiped it on his sleeve and took a big bite. "That's a good one, Bard" Charon appraised, "This will take you far."

Bard stuffed the poncho into the end of his blanket roll, folded his now empty bag and tucked it into his belt alongside his bottle. He slung the rolled blanket across his shoulder, and clutching his staff, stood by watching as Robberlee and Charon lifted the gate and locked it down, then cast off the two lines securing the ferry to the landing. Charon adjusted the throttle on his ancient engine, which looked like it might once have belonged in a truck like Robberlee's. Then he pulled down on his lever. It clicked and clacked into place. The wheels overhead screeched against the cable. The cow bawled one last goodbye as the calf did a sudden jig between his mother's legs, and the ferry with its tiny contingent of souls, lurched out into the fog.

The whole world gradually dissolved into that fog. Holding his staff with both hands before him, his hat pulled down to his ears, Bard stood on deck as the fog consumed the shore. Through a momentary rift in the gray he caught a brief glimpse of the shoreline. He tried to find Charon's house. For a second or two, he discerned a grove of tall sycamores, the ruin of a stone chimney and what may have been the tumbled corner of a wall. Then the fog closed and was whole again, and the trembling cable stretched into the unfathomable gray void. It was as if everything Bard had experienced the night before had never been, or had existed only as a spell woven from the lives that had come together there out of their needing one for another. *We are only alive,* the fiddler girl had said, *When we are in the music.*

The only music now was the striving of Charon's engine, the creaking and shrieking of the drive wheels upon the tortured cable, and the barely audible lapping of the water against the side of the ferry. Charlie and Robberlee maintained earnest conversation about something, as Charlie kept a watchful eye on the cable, but their voices didn't carry over the sound of the engine.

Bard heard a familiar cry, and looking ahead along the cable, saw a shadow materialize out of the fog. The shadow solidified into Hawk. She passed a little upstream of the ferry, flying low and fast, as if following the cable. She called once again as she faded into the mists behind.

The fog gathered itself, becoming more dense. It enveloped the ferry like a falcon enfolding her prey beneath her wings, so thick now as to conceal the water. The ferry floated in a cloud. The cable behind stretched out to vanishing, and it was the same before. Bard had a strange sense that the ferry wasn't moving at all, was a still-point, like a spider in her web, relentlessly drawing the future to them. Suddenly, a wave of vertigo seized him, as if horizontal had become vertical, and the ferry was pulling him up to heaven – or down into hell.

The river might have been a thousand feet wide or a thousand miles. It seemed to Bard as if he had been on the fog-bound ferry forever. Without any reference on land or water, the rhythmic laboring of the engine, the shrill protest of the overhead drive wheels as they crawled along the cable, and the pulse of the river beneath provided the only measure of their progress. It was as if the fog had obliterated time itself. Now, in the fourth day of his sojourn, Bard felt as if his whole life had been lived on the road and the river. Callie, the Fiddler girl, Elizabeth, the landing, the springhouse, the lightning, the skiff, the river itself, resided real and vivid in his memories. Everything leading up to those experiences might have been imagination, or half-recalled dreams. But here he was, set down out of time with Robberlee and Charon, a cow and her calf in an old truck on a decrepit ferry whose greatest mystery was how she stayed afloat. The ferry now carried the sum of his life. This was all the world he could know until the fog lifted, or until Charon brought him to the other shore.

As if he had read the boy's thoughts, Robberlee left off his conversation with Charon and walked over to stand beside the truck. "Bard, it's clear you be not from around here. Charlie there says Bard is not even your real name. So you're here with us now, with none of your own to look after you. Do you even know where you are going?"

"Across the river and over the mountain, I reckon." Bard spoke as close to the truth as he knew of his situation.

"Aren't we all?" Robberlee, managed to subdue another onset of relentless mirth, "But being on your own now, the time's upon you to order your own life and make it fit you, or to fit yourself to it without complaint. As I see it from here, you have three choices. You can go back across the river with Charon and be part of all that is there. You would live a fine and worthy life and be well loved by people who value whatever is in you to give for them.

You could come with me down to Beaverdam, which is where I'm headed, and become a Trader. You have the heart and the head for it. I've noticed you take nothing lightly, but value every common thing you come across, knowing it just might be able to save your life one day. You also regard things not just for what they bring you, but for what they might do for another's need. But a Trader's life turns around people and towns. Somehow, you don't strike me as being cut out for living in places where all the roads are marked. Your third choice is that you can leave this road and strike your own trail up the mountain, or at least turn along some path walked by only a few who are somewhat like yourself. Finding your own way is the hardest way to travel, but for some souls the road is the only home they ever come to. Before today is done, you will have to decide your way for yourself. Me and Charlie either one would be glad to take you in and teach you our way, but we can't tell you what to do, and we can't go with you to watch after you. Stay with one of us, and you will be as safe and prosperous and befriended as it is possible to be in this strange country. Take up the road again, and you're on your own, but you might be happier that way. You're the only one who knows."

"If I don't go with you, Robberlee, or with Charlie, but go off some other way, can I ever come back?"

"Bard, the next time you come this way, every heart will welcome you and every eye will be glad to see you home."

As they talked, the timbre of the engine altered, began to labor. Now and again the wheels slipped on the cable and Charon would have to pull his lever down another notch until they took hold. Aft, the ferry swung downstream a bit. Waves piled up noticeably to starboard as if the ferry were bucking the current slightly.

Bard asked an earnest question, "Is Beaverdam where you live?"

"At present," answered Roberlee amiably, "I'm living on the river with you and Charon and two bovines."

"I mean, is Beaverdam your home?"

"Well, Bard," Roberlee suddenly seemed more serious than the conversation merited, "Beaverdam is the one place in all the Laurel where I'm allowed to show my true face. Ganny that makes it home."

"Here we come," yelled Charon cheerfully, as the fog began to lift and vague shapes of trees coalesced ahead. Suddenly, the anchor frame loomed up in front of them, Charon released the lever, and the ferry glided up against the landing with an unsettling thud. Charon jumped onto the landing; Robberlee tossed over the lines, which Charon secured, and they let down the drop gate.

The fog still hung thick overhead, veiling the sun, but had receded from the ground as far as the tops of the nearest trees. The filtered sun cast an eerie brassy light over everything in sight. No grand establishment here such as Charon maintained on the opposite side of the river; just the landing, and a small closed shed, which appeared to be barred and shuttered. In front of the shed, stood the strangest family Bard had ever seen, a man and woman of indeterminate age, and two others, a male and a female, the size of children, about his own height. They looked as old as their taller companions. They all appeared gray in the strange light, completely devoid of any coloring. Even their clothes were ashen beyond life.

Charon noticed Bard's stare, "They've come up from Beaverdam."

Robberlee chuckled, "I'm the only fool in the Laurel who ever wants to go the other way."

Gaunt, hollow-eyed, and deathly silent, the four figures waiting at the landing watched immobile as the passengers disembarked. As soon as the truck had moved off the ferry, the gray man stepped up without a word, dumped some coins from a pouch into Charon's palm, then the little clan filed onto the ferry, and stood in a huddle on the deck while Robberlee helped Charon close the gate, and cast off the lines.

Charon looked across at Bard, "Whatever advice Robberlee gave you would be well-heeded, but remember; the widest road always takes you most directly to your undoing. Choose another whenever you can." He turned abruptly without further word, took hold of his lever, and the ferry sought the river one more time.

Robberlee sat in the idling truck, resting his elbow in the open window and grinned at Bard, "Are you riding down to Beaverdam with me, then?"

"I reckon I'll just walk awhile."

"I reckoned you would." Roberlee put his truck in gear and it lurched forward only to slide to a stop a dozen feet away. "One more thing, Bard,"

Bard walked up to the window.

Robberlee reached under the seat and pulled out the ivy bowl, blew the dust out of it, cupped it in his hands and turned it about, looking at it intently. Then he reached out and handed it to Bard, "This is yours, Son."

"But it was a proper deal, Robberlee; I'm content."

"This is for taking care of my calf last night. Look at this now; it has your name written all over it. Take it, Bard. It will serve you better than it ever would me," and before Bard could respond, the truck catapulted down the road, spraying him with dust and gravel. The cow bawled once more in delight or despair, and they clattered around a turn and out of sight.

As he stood in the road, listening to the receding chaos, Bard studied the bowl in his hand. What he had thought a painted design of woven ivy now appeared to be incised into the surface, the grooves inlaid with a pigment that looked like blue summer sky, and instead of ivy, wound an impossibly complicated labyrinth of swirls and figures that twisted around one another, lacing and intertwining among their elements so as to weary and confound any eye that tried to trace them. He turned the bowl over and around. He could find no sign of the crack.

#

For a while, then, Bard stood in the middle of the road, leaning on his staff, watching the fog rise up the slopes until ribbons of blue sky began to show overhead. Without calling his attention, the morning light had shifted from brass to silver. He stowed his transformed bowl in his bag, and lashed it to his blanket roll. He unstoppered his bottle and took a long swallow, which was cool and sweet and something else he couldn't name, but it thrilled his senses. The bottle seemed as heavy when he stoppered it again as it had before he drank.

He realized he was lonesome. He had always been lonely, apart from other souls, never quite free to engage other lives, an observer, even in his own. His parents and the people in their world had greeted him into their realm with their concepts of who he ought to be and to become already fixed before his arrival. They never saw him; only their expectations of him, which were theirs, not his, and they could never understand why he failed to live up to them. As a result, parents as well as child grew older believing that those souls bound closest to them were essentially strangers, who either by will or weakness might betray their trust and hope on any given day.

Mary, Ronan, the cousins and Ethan had been different in that they simply shared their days with him and allowed him to be within that space whatever he found was in him to be. They opened for him doors and windows into a world that was not real in any sense his parents would understand or accept, but was true in every way their world was false.

Seeing the door wide open, he'd had no better sense than to walk through it. And now here he stood, all by himself on some nameless road to a town that he knew only by name, beside a river that flowed from and to no places he had ever seen. He thought about the lives that had touched him on this road. Bound by no ties of blood; no obligations of class or clan, yet they had all been kind and generous to one another, welcoming each to each in whatever way was opened to them. Bard realized he loved them all, strange and unsettling as they were. For they had all been true to one another in the only way that anyone can, by each and every one of them refusing to be false to their own given natures.

Now, on his separate way, he could not reach out to any of them and touch a hand or face. He could not hear a laugh or see a smile. He could not sit at table before a great feast and look around and see his own pleasure and gratitude reflected in faces he knew as well as he knew his own. And so he was lonesome. He missed those souls who had so lately, so briefly, been his life.

Lonesome indeed, but not lonely. Not alone. He stood listening to the river singing along her way, the breeze sighing lazily up the mountain's face, crows quarreling among the poplars along the ridge above. He heard cicadas; he heard Hawk, and as he listened on, more voices than he could count or identify, all sounding out their parts in the Great Song. All souls lived in this music, whenever and wherever they might sing, and they were all present with him to this moment, for the Song had never begun, and would never end, and in the Music, they were forever real.

Of course, Bard did not think about his condition in

quite these terms. He hadn't yet the language for it, but he felt in his bones and muscles, in his tissues and in his blood, his shared connection with all other souls. He felt bound to those he could not touch, near to those he could not see. Alone and apart, he was neither. He walked away down the road in the company of angels. The sun rose higher above the ridgetops. The fog melted into clouds and the clouds into deep and deeper blue. For no reason Bard could name, a quiet and ruthless joy possessed him there.

As he walked, the road edged up alongside the riverbank, and the mountain crept right up to the road. He began to wish he had saved one of his biscuits, along with the egg that was in it, when up ahead he heard, then saw a bold creek, laughing and splashing across the road on its way to the river. As he came closer, he found the water too deep and wide to cross without removing his shoes. He wondered what might be down that road to make it worth the trouble. The rest of his life might be easier, he considered, if he went back to the Ferry and waited for Charon.

Hawk's high-pitched call came to him from his left, out over the river. Bard turned and saw her flying straight at him. Something small and dark dangled from one of her taloned fists. She seemed about to crash into him. He dropped his staff and threw both hands above his head. Hawk passed directly above, close enough that he felt and heard the air sliding beneath her wings. Bard wheeled and followed her with his eyes as Hawk glided low over the road along the creek, released her burden, which narrowly missed falling into the water, raised her great wings once and brought them down, lifted and then disappeared among the treetops.

Bard picked up his staff. Heart still pumping adrenalin, he walked across the road to see what Hawk had left behind, picked up a small pouch on a plaited leather thong long enough to slip over his head. He thought at first the bag was made of leather, but on closer inspection, it evidenced to be closely woven of some very fine fiber, either naturally a russet hue, or perhaps stained so with some kind of berry juice or bark. A design had been worked into the fabric with dyed quills or needles. He couldn't discern what the image represented, but it looked to him contents into his upturned palm. A single tiny black pebble, about the size of a grape or a cherry, fell into his hand. He lifted it to his nose and inhaled. It smelled of pine sap and beeswax and one or two other pungencies he couldn't name. Rolled and polished into a tiny sphere, it was a piece of the same sort of soap with which he had bathed on the other side of the river.

There was something else in the bag. He pulled out a folded scrap of paper which bore a message written in pencil, *Mama said you would be needing this. -L.* He stared at it with more wonder than comprehension. The music the mountain was making suddenly seemed very loud around him.

Bard returned his talisman to the medicine bag, hung the bag around his neck. He folded the note and tucked it behind the band of his hat. He peered up through the trees along the creek where Hawk had vanished. From the road, following the creek uphill on the nearer side, he made out an old wagon trace, nearly lost in leaves and new-growth laurel; but here and there a track grooved into the soft earth bore witness to at least occasional traffic. Charon had said to steer away from the wide road.

Bard decided to do just that.

Although overgrown with brush and weeds, often impinged upon by laurel and rhododendron thickets, the wagon track was easier walking than the surrounding tangle. The trees grew tall and densely groved. Even though it was not yet midday, the dim and filtered light made it seem like late afternoon. Now and again an opening in the canopy left him half blinded until his eyes adjusted to the glare. The road never climbed steeply, but wound around and steadily upward. Once it veered away from the creek for a distance and skirted a massive rockface, and Bard stopped to appraise view. He was astonished at how far and above the river he had come. Hot and tired, he drank frequently from his bottle.

As he climbed, the creek diminished, forking from time to time into lesser branches, the wagon track always turning along the stronger one. Several times he forded the stream, now hardly more than a brook. Eventually a spring presented itself beside the road. Previous travelers had taken time and forethought to lay up stones around it. Salamanders, some little ones the color of moss, some larger ones bright as clowns, lazed among the stones. Bard knelt then, pushed aside a few floating leaves, and drank from his cupped hands. Flushed as he was from the exertions of his steady climb, the water felt icy cold. Restored considerably, he filled his bottle. It was only half empty.

After he left the spring behind him, the road leveled somewhat, although it still tended in the main moderately uphill. The ground began to fall away east of the track. Here the little road traversed the flank of a ridge, although the heavy forest permitted no long view to judge the shape of the landscape beyond. Near the middle of the day, Bard found himself walking through a heavy stand of mature hardwoods, mostly poplar and maple, where the limited sunlight sifting through the canopy allowed sparse undergrowth. It looked almost like a park in that other world where his parents lived. Everything had a kept look about it, almost manicured, like some rich man's yard. Nature had done this, though, and nature had maintained it just so for centuries, perhaps millennia. In spite of his weariness and his hunger, the calm beauty of the place touched him, though he could not summon words to name his feeling.

Bard rounded a turn and there the road appeared to end. Before him opened a brighter circular space ringed by trillium and anemone and carpeted with leaves and mosses. In the center grew a single tree, taller than the surrounding woods, with a wide spreading crown, and broad serrated leaves, which gentled the sunlight coming through them without blocking it entirely. Spiny pods burdened the tree, and littered the forest floor around it with large nuts, some of them still half-encased in their prickly husks. Bard found a fist-sized stone and cracked one of the nuts and tasted it, sweet and meaty and moist. He cracked a few more. He sat back on his heels and laughed for pure joy and gratitude at the entirely impersonal largess of the mountain. Because he had no ghost girl here to say the words to him, he said aloud for himself, "Mama said you would be needing these."

Then he ate his fill of the nuts, accompanied by generous gulps from his bottle. His stomach protested his intemperance later, but the last nut he ate tasted just as good as the first. When he could not eat even one more, he gathered a pound or so of them into his bag. Occasionally while he engaged in this harvest, a nut falling fresh from the tree cracked him smartly on his crown. He kept his hat on.

CIRCLE

The venerable chestnut in its shaded, cloistered space gave Bard a sense of standing in a great church. He knew about churches. His grandfather had been a preacher, usually wound up warring with any congregation who dared invite him among them. Too addicted to telling the undisguised truth to really be successful as a clergyman, he stayed with it because he loved quiet places that make worldly folk restive. He nurtured a rich interior life and taught his like-natured grandson to do the same. At a family dinner, when the boy's mother complained, as she often did, that she needed a larger house, the old man would lean over to his grandson, who invariably sat beside him, and whisper, "There's never room enough for a crowded soul." The boy had no clear idea of what that meant, but he liked the conspiratorial tone of the whisper; it told him that he had an ally, somebody who might be counted upon to leave the door open for him if he ever needed to escape.

Done with his nutting, Bard roused to his feet, beginning to realize he had consumed far more than was good for him, and took a couple of circuits around the tree. For a space as broad as the spread of the chestnut's crown, the ground was clear of any tall growth. Among the fallen nuts and leaves sprouted little patches of short grass, green almost to black, lawned by the habitual grazing of deer, and an assortment of wildflowers, some of them spectacular, some delicate and half-concealed by their neighbors. The flowers endured by being less tasty than the grass. Moss and ferns and gill grew rife among them. A few parson's berries had begun to flame, along with scarlet orbs of Solomon's seal. The circle was as well appointed as the altar of any church.

Bard's road entered on the south side of the circle, and opposite, on the north, a more traveled stretch took up again and wound off farther along the crest of the ridge beyond. This ridge rose up from the west and south, then continued climbing north and eastward past the circle, and fell away sharply on the right into a deep valley. A single track, showing sign of human passage, as well as horses or mules, ran up the spine of the ridge, entering the circle from the west, exiting eastward to wind down into the valley. More or less midway betwixt each of these junctures, less defined, but clearly evidenced paths converged, ways of pilgrimages and forays by any number of forest creatures, their nature and form difficult to guess from the sparse sign they left behind. The circle was thus divided by common passage of many souls in all manner of shape and race into eight parts, aligned with the compass. Eight ways led into and from the circle, and allowing for the chestnut tree, with her crown away above the earth and her roots deep within it, her massive trunk marking a vertical axis between darkness and light, a ninth way. Around the edge of the clearing, among the trillium and crested iris, centered between each path and track, resided eight flat stones, large enough to seat a human, or perhaps an animal. Bard had wandered into a Council Circle.

He spent a good part of his afternoon inspecting the

Circle. He saw it was obviously a place of meeting and gathering, but could find no traces of its specific use beyond the convergence of trails. He thought perhaps four-leggeds and two-leggeds alike came here only to gather sustenance and change their direction.

At length, Bard noticed the breeze had become cooler, the light grayer. Above him, the lowering sun barely fired the toppermost leaves in the big chestnut. The air was yet relatively warm, but the slight breeze drawing night up the slopes felt cold on his skin. Suddenly, he shivered uncontrollably. Bard had dallied about moving on, in part, because he didn't feel well. Now, he was becoming downright sick. He felt feverish, and his belly hurt as though he had swallowed a rock.

He cried out aloud in agony and surprise when, with no warning at all, a pain like being speared in the gut with a rusty spoon brought him to his knees. As he sat there on the ground with his legs stretched out before him, his eyes full of tears, one of the stones opposite him in the circle suddenly darkened, folded in on itself, and then with a sound like an old gate swinging on a rusty hinge, expanded and unfurled, blossoming like a flower, looking for an instant very like the design woven into his medicine bag. Involuntarily, he lifted his hand to seize the bag around his neck as the stone became a stone again, upon which stood an imposing bird whose darkness was so deep and unrelieved as to devour any light that fell on it. He thought at first it was a large crow, but it was too sizable and hefty, too thick of beak to be a crow. Up among the rocks above Ethan's retreat, he had encountered such a creature. Yes, he recognized him now. On a stone not more than twenty feet away, still and mute as the rock beneath him, perched a silence in a shadow.

Raven.

#

Raven, head turned, stared unblinking at Bard out of his right eye, a baleful glare as if he had seen into the child's very soul, and found it wanting. The boy had received such looks from his father, and was only mildly impressed. He stared back, silent as Raven, imagining some portentous utterance about to come forth from the majestic corvid.

What came was a rending groan from Bard's innards and a wave of nausea that filled his throat and sent him stumbling and crawling past the chestnut and away beyond the opposite side of the circle. Shadowed in the laurel that bounded the clearing, where he hoped Raven's relentless watching would be frustrated, for a time he squatted and knelt, strained and heaved, retched and gasped, and when everything unwholesome and hurtful within him had been given to the earth, he cleaned himself up as best he could, wished for a tub of Callie's water, opened his medicine bag a little, breathed in the scent of pinesap and beeswax, and for the first time since he had taken Mary's staff from beside her door, he cried. He wept as any sick boy would who is on his own in a strange country, longing for a home he has never seen. And when he was empty even of tears, he pulled himself upright, tottered back to the tree, gathered up his gear beside him, and being careful to keep the broad trunk of the chestnut between him and Raven, Bard lay down on his back upon the dewy sod, spread his arms wide. And fell into stars.

#

Sometime during the darkest dark of that long night, a chestnut hanging in the upper reaches of the tree slipped from its husk and meeting neither leaf nor twig to deflect its descent, plummeted straight to land squarely in the middle of the sleeping boy's chest. The impact was more startling than painful. Bard felt the slight blow before he was awake. He breathed deeply, looked all around, was relieved not to see Raven standing on his chest, waiting to peck out his eyes when he opened them. He had been dreaming something similar. The chestnut's collision reverberated through his small corpus, faded into the ground beneath his shoulders. He took another breath. Then the wave returned like an echo, welling from deep in the mountain, far beneath the roots of the tree towering over him. He gasped for breath, as he felt the impulse rising up through stone and soil, through his own thin skin and frail structure, and up through the tree above, rattling the leaves and loosening more nuts, which drummed the turf all around him. At that, his skull resounded with a concussion like a vast drum. The soil under him dissolved into a swarm of vibrations and attenuations in indescribable flux and variation. The stars in the sky above him wavered before his gaze.

Bard took another slow deep breath, trying in vain to slow his racing heart, all his senses acute to the threshold of pain. He waited for the crashings and thunderings and rumblings within and without to settle and cease. He hoped the stars might steady themselves.

They did not. They were not stars. They were fireflies, swirling and schooling out of the top of the chestnut, innumerable tiny points of vivid light, blue and bright as a morning sky, each one showing itself sharp and instant like sparks from a fire. Every moment more of them circled the tree from east to south to west to north and back again, ever descending in their circuit, weaving a cloak of living light about its trunk.

Bard could not quite fix in his mind what he had just been seeing. He waited for another nut to fall, and when that didn't happen, he took a deep breath, raised his right hand above him, and still with his back to the ground, brought his fist down upon his chest. It did sound like a drum, he thought, a sound bigger than himself, and as he heard it, the dancing lights filling the air around him pulsed brighter, and the whole mountain throbbed, a deep and low percussion, immeasurable as a soul and as close as a beating heart. Bard lay unmoving because that was all he could do. He lay as silence was swallowed up into silence until even the crickets and frogs were beyond voice. He lay as the spiral of light above and around him slowed in its revolving about the tree and the glimmering gyre seemed to hang motionless above him. He lay there wondering what obvious thing he was missing, until he felt it through his spine. The lights had not stopped at all. The tree and the circle on which he lay, and for all he knew, the whole mountain, were turning with the Light.

In the deep silence that followed, Bard's breathing sounded to him like a gale. He held his breath and was held in turn by the slow drumming of his heart. He no longer needed by act of will to call up the Drum's music. The music was in him. He was in the drum. For a time, he simply lay and listened. It was not time that could be kept by a clock. If measurable at all, it would be in eons and millennia. To Bard, it was not a long time. He lay still, beyond any will to move, and then deeper still, beyond any thought at all, carried into night in harmony with the tree who sheltered him, with the lights above and the earth beneath, with all the great dark mountain around him and all the souls fleet and slow, large and wee, hale and broken, that lived upon it. He felt himself loosening, expanding outward. He felt the glimmer lights of the fireflies flickering among his atoms, felt roots and leaves and stones and waters shifting and reaching and flowing through the widening spaces within his matrix. He felt all the myriad of lives from the surrounding forest finding their form and way through the maze of his being, until he knew he wasn't a boy any more. And then he knew nothing at all, and he knew them all. He was the mountain.

The mountain that had been a boy looked down for a thousand years or so upon the tiny circle of lights held in its lap, slowly revolving beneath the stars. It saw the lights dancing unceasingly, saw Raven on his stone, endlessly watching, saw the chestnut tree keeping the Circle, and saw the sleeping boy beneath. Consciousness tightened then, descended, souls slipped aside, become unique to themselves again, and the boy who had been a mountain awoke looking and feeling just like a boy, spent, exhausted and human.

#

When Bard opened his eyes, the lights had ceased their swirling, but the circle was carpeted in an emerald light like foxfire. The Chestnut thrust up above him until it wrapped itself in night. He held his breath. If he could, he would have willed his heart to still, He wanted to hear what he knew was in the silence. Then Raven spoke. Raven yet sat immobile as a stone upon a stone. Raven didn't open his beak, didn't utter a sound, but the words lay in Bard's mind as clear and shaped as if they had been spoken aloud. It was not a voice he had heard before, but was a voice he would know if he heard it again.

I am Raven, spoke the bird, mind to mind, from his

stone. The tree took up the thought among her manifold branches, re-framed them into familiar speech and sent them on to the boy, for the chestnut had stood in the Circle over generations of blooded lives, and had heard much of all languages spoken by those who passed there.

Careful not to let a sound pass his lips, for it seemed important not to break the silence, Bard laid the words out in his mind, *I hear you, Raven*.

For a moment, there was only quiet. Bard wondered if he must speak aloud to be heard, then Raven spoke again, *We have heard your drumming; we are coming to your Council*.

But I am not the drummer, Bard protested. He sat up then, surprised at the effort it required. His head swam, and he stared at the stone opposite him on the circle's rim to steady himself. He sensed movement in the shadows beyond the stone. A shadow separated from the wider dark and brightened and took form and color and he saw Hawk, perched on her stone across the circle from Raven.

You are not the Drummer, said Hawk to the boy; *You are only the Drum. But your voice has called us.*

I'm not a drum, either, I'm just a boy.

And I am just Bear, spoke a voice from his left, a voice Bard had heard before in his dreams. From the night emerged an indistinct shape, shifting and changing as it approached. First, he seemed to be Ethan, then a bear, then the not-quite-Ethan of dreams, who, as he sat on his stone beside the south road, settled into Bear again.

Bard was so taken aback that he cried aloud, and at the sound of his voice the whole scene rippled before him. He held his breath until it stayed.

Kuma he said in his mind, wonderingly, genuinely glad to see the old bruin. Elusive and mysterious though he was, Bear remained a connection with a world left behind.

Yes, said Bear, *I heard the Drum, and I am here.*

From down the south road then, the sound of some large animal traveling fast. Bard could hear the beast's labored breathing as it lunged up the slope. Then, the three-headed dog that had surprised him at Charon's house erupted into the circle, shook itself into three, and took their seats, one on either side of Raven and the other between Bear and Hawk. When they spoke, it was with one voice. "We are Three, warders of the Drum, and we have come."

Bard felt too tired to breathe. He did not think he had strength to stand. For a moment, the ground seemed to be rising around him, but it was only the lights of fireflies lifting from the leaves and ferns and grass that carpeted the circle until the air was full of their sharp strobing. As they began once more spiraling about the Circle, Callie stepped out of the tree. At first, Bard thought the tree itself was transforming, for Callie's own coloring and her clothes mimed the chestnut's bark. She emerged from it like one stepping through a waterfall. It looked as if the tree had decided to become Callie. As she stood beaming down at Bard, the lights drew in close to the tree in a fast rotating column about the trunk. Those at the bottom began moving swiftly upward inside the column, and as they rose, the chestnut wavered and dimmed and went with them, until the circle stood open with a seething dome of living sparks above it.

Callie looked around the Circle and said aloud with her big voice, "I see you all are come before me. I am the last to get word of anything that happens around here."

She reached down and took Bard by the hand, "Well, they've saved us a place. Come sit by your dog," and she towed him away toward the two vacant stones by the road to the north, his feet barely touching the ground, as if he were a weightless balloon being pulled through the air on a string.

As Callie closed her large hand about his, Bard felt a surge of life from her. Heat and light and love and will, soul and sustenance all came flowing into him, so that by the time she set him upon his stone, he felt gathered and centered again, his mind clear, the fire in his belly no longer just a smolder, but bright and vital. He was a boy, alive, weighing upon his stone, blooded and embodied, and filling his place in creation.

Bard looked at the dog to his left, then at the other two who were Three. None of them faced toward the center of the Circle as all the other souls in Council, but, ears erect, eyes ever watchful, were staring out into the surrounding dark.

Callie asked him then, "Bard, do you know why you are here?"

"Because this is as far as I was able to come," It was an obvious truth, but it was as much of the truth as he knew.

"And it was far enough for now." said Callie, not at all put off by his honest answer, as adults often are when children tell the simple truth, "But there is more to your being here than any of us can know tonight. Let us explain to you as much as we do know." She nodded to Hawk at her right.

Hawk looked at Bard, and when he returned her gaze, she began, *In the Beforetime, when the world had not yet been broken, there were no languages as there are now. All creatures and souls talked to one another in the One Speech as we do now in Council. All souls rested in our Mother, the Maker, and her heart beat in us all. Not only blooded things, but stone and trees and waters, even the air had voice. Her knowing was in us all and every one, so that all who knew were known.*

Hawk fell silent at this point, seemed to decide she had said her part, and nodded to the one of Three seated to her right. The Three all barked softly in unison, "Ho!" which apparently was sign of their agreement, as well as of their desire to listen, for Bear then took up the conversation,

Two-leggeds, your kind, Bard, came late and last. From the first they were striven. Their hearts turned inward, so they forgot the One Speech. They assailed the same earth they were shaped from. In time they made many languages, for their mind was sundered even among their own kind. They no longer remembered Maker. They did not love her world and the creatures upon it. They lost all respect, even for themselves, and preyed and warred upon one another unceasingly.

Bear looked at the one of Three to his right, The Warders assented, "Ho!" and speech passed to Raven,

Unchecked, their need to subdue and diminish all about them would have wrecked the whole world. So they were set apart into Shadow until such time as there may be a Mending. But for the Separation Maker has wrought, we who live in the Laurel would be vanished from the earth and there would be none here to sit in Council.

All of us are still in the world, but the Shadowfolk cannot see us and we can cannot touch them. To their minds we are not real, and to us, they are unfettered death. But in spite of the Separation, there are seasons when their violence intrudes upon us. From the great anguish and aloneness Shadowfolk inflict upon their fellows, and upon such of the world as they are able to know, now and again the Separation is rent. Through these openings some small healing may spill through to them, or some measure of their dark may seep through to us. If these breaches are left untended, the whole of the Laurel might become blighted and barren and gray.

Raven fell silent and looked to the one of Three at his right. The Three spoke then, sometimes singly, one or another, or two or all three in chorus, *Among the remnant of two leggeds who remain this side of the Separation are those we name Traders. Their calling is to watch and maintain the Separation. If there is a breach, they will seek to make whatever exchanges are required to restore balance, and may send out Riders to secure order and stability. Sometimes the Riders must capture and return predatory Shadowfolk to their own realm, although some gray souls desperate for escape from Shadow may be given sufferance and resettled in the Laurel. It takes a long time, but once here among the souls of Laurel, a gray soul can often be nurtured again to the One Life.*

The Three ceased their speech and looked at the boy. He looked to Callie, and she spoke, "So, Bard, you, in your unknowing, called the Council to consider the problem that faces us now, even though your presence here is at the heart of our dilemma."

Silence then around the circle, and when no one spoke, Bard said, "I don't want to make a problem for anyone. I just needed to find a place to be before I was sent away."

Callie laughed her great laugh, then said quietly, "We understand your heart, Bard, but here is our problem. We have not been aware of any new rift in the Separation, yet here you are. You have either made or found a way into the Laurel that was not opened by force, else we would have known of it. We need to understand how you came here, and why, although we think now you may not be aware of your own purpose. We were afraid of you at first, but now we believe that somehow, you may be as one of us, even though you came out of Shadow. We began to sense that you were not gray hearted when you saved Hawk's life."

Bard raised his hand as if he were in school.

"You have a question?" asked Callie.

Bard looked at Hawk. "Was it really you I dug out of the groundhog's hole?"

Your mercy to any one of my kind is a mercy to me, Bard, for we are none of us only one, and any one of us is in all. Hawk continued, *Do you see that if you, who are one of us, has come out of Shadow, then there may be others of us there. If so, Shadow may be lifting and the Mending may be at hand, or it may be the Separation is failing and the whole of Laurel is about to fade into Shadow.* She looked at the one of Three seated next to her, and they spoke as was their fashion,

We are the Warders. It is our task to ward the Laurel against you, Bard, if you by will or weakness would bring harm among us, or to ward you against encumbrance until you achieve the purpose for which Maker brought you here. We were still uncertain of your intent until we found you on your way to help Robberlee's calf. Since, we have watched you. You live close to the ground, walk lightly on the earth, and tread on no innocence if you can spare it. Whatever your given purpose, your heart and intention are pure.

After the Three, Bear spoke again, *The Traders are bound to know you are here, Bard. One of them has seen you, though he may not have guessed your origin at the time. They must all know of you soon, certainly, for they will have word of the Council. They will send out a Rider to find you, and to determine how you got here. Their main concern will be to close your way from Shadow. That may or may not be Maker's intent. There may be a time in Maker's mind when even the continuance of the Laurel serves no further end. We must decide now whether to give you to the Rider or to help you on your way.*

The one of Three to the right of Bear came to the center

of the circle where the other two of Three joined him. They spoke in chorus, *We will prevent the Rider if we must. We will ward the boy until his purpose is clear. If that purpose is desolation to the Laurel, we will prevent him, in turn.*

All in the circle, except Bard responded, "Ho."

Raven said, *I will watch the Rider,*

Then Hawk, *I will watch the river to see if any follow the boy.*

Bear spoke in turn, *Do not worry about how the boy came here. I know where his passage is, having traveled it from time to time myself. Any who find it would likely be welcome among us, but I will guard the passage.*

Callie lifted an eyebrow at Bear, "Bear, you are as full of secrets as an old owl. We will talk more about this later. But are we agreed then?"

From around the circle, even Bard, "Ho!"

"Let it become," shouted Callie, raising her big hands high over her head and clapping them together with a sound like thunder.

#

Bard woke to the grumbling of a distant storm. Above him, the stout limbs of the chestnut reached up until they were swallowed into the fine mist that swirled across the ridge. The fog prevented him seeing much beyond the edge of the clearing in which he lay. He had slept on the ground, beside the great tree. His chilled muscles ached. His clothes were damp from the fog and the dewy earth. He thought about unrolling his blanket and going back to sleep. Then he remembered what the Council had said. The Rider would be coming for him. Bard thought that a meeting he preferred to put off as long as possible.

He no longer felt sick, at least. He was hungry. He gathered a few nuts from the wet grass, cracked and ate some of them, not many, just enough to feel a presence in his empty belly. His legs felt steady when he stood. He slung his blanket and sack across his shoulder, took a long drink from his bottle, stoppered it and looped its cording into his belt, and hefted his staff. He laid his hand on his medicine bag in an unconscious gesture of supplication and turned about the Circle hoping for some sign or trace that would tell him his further way, for he felt in his bones that he had to go from this place.

Bard had thought he was alone, but as he turned, he saw Raven sitting on the same stone the dark bird had occupied the evening before, still glaring unblinking at him, offering neither solace nor judgment, just seeing deep and all. All through the Council, Raven had always watched him with that same right eye, never turning. Bard wondered if they could still talk to one another. He laid out the words in his mind, *Well, Raven, Where do I go now?*

Raven did not reply, but turned his head toward the opening beside him, where the wagon road left the Circle to continue down the east face of the ridge. Down the left side of Raven's head, running through where his eye should have been, down into his body to the base of his wing, wound a jagged white scar, like a lightning bolt. Bard thought the question to Raven, *Can you see well enough to fly among the trees?* Being still a child, after all, he had no fear of delicate questions.

Raven answered promptly, *Where there is no vision, there is sight in pain*, and flew away.

Bard pulled his poncho from the end of his blanket roll, slipped it over his head, pulled his hat down to his ears, and pushing away with his staff, headed down the east road. Charon had said to avoid the wider road whenever possible, but the mists had coalesced into a fine rain. Bard wanted shelter. He wanted to sit at table with human faces and be warm and dry and listen to a fiddler girl sing him into a dream. He wanted people.

DISMAL

The Rider was angry. Though he spoke to a man who had been a surrogate father to him, his question came out almost a shout, "Robberlee, you had him with you; why, for the sake of Laurel, did you not bring him back here?"

Robberlee smiled ruefully and spread his hands wide, "I bear your blame, Rider; but understand there was no gray about the boy at all. He had more of the One Life in him than either of us. His intention was pure, if untaught. He had a fairybowl in his possession and had no idea of what it was or how he might use it. It seemed best to let things play out in their own order until we learned enough to act with some purpose. Besides, you know that away from Beaverdam, I could not have compelled him to do anything."

The Rider was not above sarcasm, "So now, according to Owl, there has been a Council drummed up by some mere child who is not of the Laurel. Things seem to be playing out very finely indeed."

"You have made your point," Robberlee spoke quietly, offering no further defense of his judgment. "We have a soul among us who is from some place we know not, by some way we know not. That means there is a rift in the Separation that we have not been aware of. Would you have a mind to go find the boy and determine where he slipped through, and what must be done to close the way before others follow?"

The Rider counted it a point of honor to follow no directive not his own. "I have a sense about this boy of yours, Whether sent or not, I would go after him. I must make some preparation, but I will leave before night."

#

Bard made good progress on his down-hill way, although to what destination, he had no way to tell. To his right, the slope fell sharply away. Through the trees below he could glimpse a bold stream, tossing among boulders as it plunged and cascaded down the shadowed valley. To south, beyond the valley loomed a long range of dark mountains taller than the one he had climbed the day before. To his left the ridge rising from the Circle crested north and east, gradually pulling away and above the road. He guessed the other well-traveled track he had seen at the Circle ran along this ridge.

As the road descended, the drizzle of the morning became a steady rain, not heavy, but constant and soaking. Bard saw nothing resembling human presence, other than an occasional overgrown clearing beside the track. The land seemed not so much unsettled as long abandoned.

A fine white dust covered the road, which the rain did nothing to suppress. It boiled up from the ground with every step until his shoes and his lower legs and the end of his staff were ashen with it. Bard kept his hat pulled low, but water was beginning to trickle down his neck, and finding its way through the arm-slits in his poncho. He was getting wet. He needed someplace with a roof where if he couldn't warm, he could at least dry out. He was also noticeably hungry.

The road made a sharp turn, skirting the base of a high

bank of red clay. Pumpkin and squash vines, yellowed and unfruited, straggled over the top of the bank above the road. Some excuse for a garden apparently subsisted somewhere beyond the brink. Someone had dug notches into the face of the bank, and short lengths of plank were secured in them with wooden stakes, to serve as a stair. Bard clambered up, once slipping and nearly falling, but managing to save his balance with his staff. Atop the bank, a bedraggled garden, more needy than weedy, sprawled to his right. Before him, crowded upon a wee sloping yard, as if leaning toward one another for mutual support, a tiny house, unpainted, with a sagging porch across the front and what appeared to be a corncrib attached to the side, and right of the house, a smaller building that may have been a spring house or a smokehouse, and a sad little barn huddled together under the bleak sky with scarcely enough room between for a man to walk.

Bard surveyed the dismal homestead, then stepped up on the porch and knocked on the door, intending to ask someone's permission to wait out the rain on their porch. The door rattled on its hinges, but excited no sound from within. Bard stood for a few moments, listening to the drumming of rain on the shakes above his head, watching the line of drops cascading from the eaves over the steps. He thought this might not be a place where trespassing counted as a minor offense, so he stepped back down into the rain and the mud.

As he made to cross the yard toward the road, "Mama said you would be needing this."

Bard turned to see the open door. From the shadows inside the house, a tall, too-thin woman peered out at him. He couldn't discern her features. On the porch, at the top of the steps, stood a girl about his age, maybe a year younger, who looked as if she might have been a friend of one of his cousins. Over a red shirt with a chain of large yellow circles printed across the front, she wore bright green overalls, too long for her, that covered her bare feet to her toes. Her hair hung behind her in pigtails, not dark, nor red, nor blond, but gray as the dust that covered the boy's shoes. She held a bowl full of some steamy contents, and a wooden spoon. When he approached the steps, she did not hold the bowl out to him, but set it down on the floor in front of him, as if he were a puppy.

Then she spoke again, obviously trying to imitate her mother's tone, "Mama wants to know what's your name, boy."

"Bard, I reckon" The name still did not rest easy on his tongue. "What's yours?"

"Pappy calls me Lizbet, but the brothers call me Lizard Breath," and she stuck out her tongue at him. Some trick of the light made it appear that she really did have a forked tongue like a lizard's.

Bard looked into the bowl at his feet. It was full of a colorless oily liquid in which floated bits of matter that might have been either plant or animal in origin, although he thought he could see tufts of fur or feathers submerged in its depths. It was hot, whatever it was, but the smell of it promised neither nurture nor nourishment. Bard thought it safer to risk an apology than his stomach, "I thank you for your kindness, but the rain seems to be slacking and I reckon I'd better be walking on now."

He turned away and started back across the yard, as the girl was reaching into the pocket of her overalls. He wasn't aware she had thrown the rock until it met the back of his head, and then he was aware of nothing at all as he sprawled face down in the bloody dirt.

#

The Rider stepped out of his door, finally ready. The tops of the buildings ahead still flared in the setting sun, but the street itself, in deep shadow, appeared almost deserted. His longbow and quiver hung snugly across his back. A pair of leather satchels draped over his shoulder. He removed the glove from his right hand. A dark, elongated mark like a bruise traversed the back of it, had been there a long time. He made a fist, raised it above him in the air and said softly, like a lover, "Millicent."

She emerged from whenever she had been waiting, lifting him upon her as she conformed herself to his present. He twisted as he rose, laying the satchels across the broad darkness behind him, knowing that his Flyer would meld herself to them and keep them secure. The Rider always felt more than himself when they joined, as indeed they both were. Of wholly different orders of being, yet souls so attuned each to each that often they thought and moved as one mind and will. Millicent would carry the Rider through whatever places and times his seeking might lead them. They would not be parted until one of them released the other, or until one of them no longer lived.

They moved away then through the town, a darkness upon a darkness, Millicent, a glint of hoof, a flash of mane, an elusive presence, at once there and not there, ever arriving, ever departing, and the Rider above her, a stillness borne upon her movement, a calm and implacable terror. As they went, the grayer folk along the street stopped to turn their old, expressionless faces toward them. Whenever a Rider left Beaverdam, there was trouble somewhere in Laurel. The Rider knew in his bones that some of the grayest half-wished that Shadow might reach out even yet to reclaim them, carry them back to a place where they bore no responsibility for their own suffering, where there was no possibility or imperative for them ever to be more than they already were.

As they turned up the road east along the river, the Rider ordered his thoughts. Robberlee, like all Traders, interpreted every new thing that happened solely in light of what had been before. Even in the Laurel, where time became more fluid than in Shadow, many remained addicted to chronology, and Traders more so than most. Riders did not keep clocks and maps, however. The Rider was used to seeing things from both their beginnings and their endings. He thought that Robberlee had missed the obvious. They were not aware of any place where the Separation had been torn because there was no such place. The rending occurred not in a landscape but in the mind of the boy. By will or by unknowing, he had attuned himself to two worlds and made of himself a door. As long as the boy possessed an awareness of the Laurel, the entire Separation remained in danger of unraveling. The Rider had no wish to be part of a world where Riders were useful only as spies and assassins, and where Traders measured misery and murder in terms of the money it gained them. He would find the boy, and do whatever necessary to render him unaware.

Once well clear of the town, they left the road and moved upward among the trees. The Rider settled himself deeper into her presence, and Millicent began to flow, transforming into a rushing shining under the moon, a stream flowing by will rather than gravity. They gathered speed. They lifted above the trees. They would be at the Circle by morning.

#

Three men, one a generation older than the others, stood in the fading day, looking at the fallen boy lying face down at their feet. Rain still fell lightly and intermittently. Ash streaked their arms and faces. They looked as if they had been painted with the dust of the road and the rain had washed some of it away.

The older man pulled on a worn and shredded pair of work gloves and gingerly picked up Mary's staff. Keeping as much distance as he could between himself and the boy, as if handling a venomous serpent who given the chance might strike, the man managed to work the end of the staff under and through the unconscious child's belt.

He gestured to one of the younger men, "Grab the other end of this thing, and help me drag him to the crib." His son took hold of the free end of the staff and immediately released it, jumping back as if he had been burned.

"Not with your bare hands, you fool. This boy's hot. Everything he's touched reeks of Light."

The other brother snickered, pulled off his shirt, wrapped it around his hands, took hold of the staff, and together, the two men lifted the boy enough to drag him across the yard and deposit him in a heap in the corncrib attached to the house. In the process, his bottle came loose from his belt, lay unnoticed in the dirt. They came back and very gingerly gathered up his blanket roll, bag and hat, carrying them at arms' length to throw them into the crib. In the deepening twilight they failed to see the earthen bottle.

#

Bard came back into the world with the parting words of Raven in his head, *Where there is no vision, there is sight in pain.* In pitch blackness now, he was in pain. His head, neck and shoulders throbbed. He lay face down in musty husks and bits of corn stalks. A few stray mouldy kernels bit into his cheek. As his eyes adjusted to the darkness, he could see faint light filtering in from the night through the wide spaced boards in the walls. On the wall the crib shared with the cabin, horizontal threads of light gleamed where the chinking had crumbled away. He could hear voices on the other side.

When he tried to turn over, Bard discovered his poncho was wrapped up around his arms and his belt behind looped over his staff. He tried to move quietly and it was several minutes before he could loose himself from all his encumbrances and crawl over to peer through one of the cracks in the chinking of the log wall. He saw the emaciated woman and a man he guessed was the girl's father. He heard the girl singing a strange keyless dirge to herself somewhere off in a corner beyond his view. There was no sign of her brothers.

"What are we going to do with him, Jude?" The thin woman whined on, "The last thing we need here is a dead boy on our hands."

Her husband was trying to placate her. "He be not dead, Min. He's a thick-headed young'un for sure then. We shut him in the crib. With a boy like that abroad, a Rider is bound to come looking for him. We'll trade him back for a thing or two."

"I don't know what we're going to do with that girl of yours, Jude. She might have killed him."

"Well, Min, sure we got lucky this time. That old man who came through last summer, when she tied him to a tree and poured live coals down his pants, I was afraid we might have to give her back to the Rider after that."

"A live boy is worse than a dead one, Jude; I'm afraid to have him on the place."

"It won't be for long at all." Riders don't dally. He'll show up here in a day or so, and we'll give him the boy, and gain something for our trouble."

Accustomed to hearing adults in the next room discussing his future, Bard in this case didn't intend to be a participant. He crawled over to the door. The vertical boards of the door were spaced apart an inch or more, and as he peered through the openings, he could see the stout wooden bar that secured the door from outside. He pushed the door slightly. It gave somewhat and he saw the bar move. Good. It wasn't tight.

Finding his blanket roll, Bard removed the cord, reached into his medicine bag, which still hung about his neck, and took out the little ball of black soap, softened now from the heat of his body. He pulled one end of the cord through the soap and pressed the ball firmly around it. Going back to the door, he managed, after numerous attempts, to swing the soap on its string through the crack and out far enough to drop down on the outside of the bar. Then, by jiggling it and blowing on it and with much prayer and one or two childish curses, he finally brought the soap swinging back to the door close enough to snare it with his fingers. He pulled the cord through to him, removed the soap, returned it to his medicine bag, then lifted the loop of cord above him. At first the bar resisted. He nudged the door, trying to maintain quiet. The bar lifted out of its cleat and fell to the ground, one end knocking against the door as it fell. The conversation inside the house continued. No one had heard.

Bard found his bedroll, unrolled it, took out the canister of matches. He gathered some of the husks and rubbish from the corners and piled them in the middle of the crib. They flaked and powdered in his hands as he arranged them in a wee pyre. He thought that people would not be chasing him if they were trying to keep their house from burning down. He struck a match and touched it to the tender pile. He held the match until it burned his fingers, then dropped it on the pile. It flared and went dark. It seemed that nothing he had laid hands on could inspire light or heat. He had seven matches left.

Bard gave up then on fire. Partly because he was reluctant to risk another match, and mainly because Callie came unbidden to his mind at that moment and he couldn't imagine her burning down someone's home, even if they were an enemy. As quickly as he could, he gathered his gear and secured his blanket roll. He found his hat, but couldn't locate his bottle. He had no time to look for it now. His staff and bag in one hand, and his blanket roll under his arm, he pushed open the door to the crib and looked straight into the faces of the brothers.

They both stood twice his height. He hadn't time even to be afraid. Bard thought very calmly, "I am going to die now." He dropped his bag and brought up his staff in front of him in a final hopeless gesture at self-preservation. In the tawny light spilling from the cabin's single window, the staff appeared to flare with some weird luminance of its own. The brothers stared open-mouthed at Bard, as surprised at the confrontation as he was.

One whispered to the other, "Lor', Brother, it's loose!"

The other brother whispered back, "It wants to kill us all!" And they ran. Skittering across the yard, whimpering like scalded pups, they tumbled down the bank and were gone. Bard could hear them splashing through the puddles along the road as they fled.

He picked up his bag and went, not to the road, but through the trees, straight up the slope behind the house, at first along a path, which he could barely follow in the dark. It led to a privy, but he did not stop there. He left the sickly sweet smell behind, and as best he could in the dark, worked his way up through laurel and along a creekbed. It was slow going, and rendered him wet and bruised and scraped and scratched, and his clothes ripped and torn. The thickets kept trying to separate him from his blanket and bag. He lost his hat a couple of times, but managed to retrieve it. Finally, whipped and winded, he stopped to rest. He had no idea of his bearings, but as he looked behind him down the mountainside he could see no light from the house. No shouts of alarm carried on the night air. As yet, at least, there was apparently no pursuit. He prayed they didn't have dogs.

#

Raven sat at the top of the chestnut as the fog of morning submitted to the ascending sun. He watched the Rider and his Flyer come slowly up the slope from the west, the Rider studying the ground before them as they went. When they reached the Circle, Millicent stayed while the Rider walked to the tree, knelt, examined the ground around it, then walked deliberately around the Circle, scrutinizing each stone he passed. When he came to Raven's stone, he reached down and picked up one long feather, black as night. He raised it above him and looking up into the tree, said to Raven, "I know you are watching. Keep crossing my path, old Friend, and I may have occasion yet to rid you of your other eye." Then he removed his hat, stuck the quill into the band, and resettled it on his head.

Satisfied that he had seen what was there to be seen, The Rider meld again to Millicent, and they moved off without haste down the road to east, into the deep and narrow valley the folk of Laurel called the Dismal.

#

Bard woke to see a dim light filtering down all around him. Dawn had overtaken him while he slept. If he had been adept at cursing, he would have. For all he knew, the gray man and his sons were already coming up the mountain after him, or their little sister might be. He was more afraid of that wee girl than all the burly men together.

He had meant only to catch his breath and get his bearings, but sleep had claimed him before he thought against it, and propped against a hard and dripping stone he had dreamed dreams strange and wild, most of which fled from him when he opened his eyes, but he held to one when the not-quite-Ethan, the dream Owl had appeared, standing with his brother bear, and looking more and more like Bear, until the boy could not with certainty recall who was which. Then Owl had said simply, "The Weaver waits above."

If there was more to the dream, Bard had no leisure to recall it now. He gathered to himself all that was his, and with the liberal aid of his staff, began toiling upward again among the boulders that bounded the stream.

#

The man was not entirely gray, but such color as he evidenced only accentuated the essential poverty of his being. He stood before his door in the mid-morning sun, in earnest discussion with the Rider. The Rider, still on his Flyer, glared down at the gray man. The Rider's broad-brimmed hat was as black as the feather in its band, and with the sun behind him, shaded his face, rendering his features invisible, like looking beneath a shadow to find only a deeper darkness still. Everything about the Rider was dark, his hat, his duster, the creature he sat upon, his trousers and boots. Looking at him, one found it difficult to discern if he were visible at all, or if one were looking into a total absence of light and seeing only the pale dust gathered on its surface from the road.

Millicent, at the moment, looked like the blackest, largest horse any human ever saw, except there was a glimmer about her that hinted of some essential insubstantiality. Focus eye on an edge or an outline and she seemed to be shifting and reforming as a horse continually, ever on the verge of dissolving and resolving into some other shape closer to her true form.

The Rider, as he often did, sounded angry. "Nobody seems to be able to hold on to this boy. He's just a child, Jude. I can't believe you couldn't keep him locked up. Did your sons let him out, or did your daughter want to have another go at stoning him? I'd hoped she'd outgrown that murderous streak of hers by now."

"The boys have run off," Jude confessed, "They'll be back when they are hungry enough. We kept Lizbet in the house with us all night. I'm pretty certain, Rider, he got loose all on his own. But he did leave something behind." Jude pointed out toward the center of the yard.

The Rider disengaged from Millicent and walked in that direction. As he paced, he unfastened his longcoat revealing beneath it a shirt of undyed linen, open at the throat. The fabric shone bright like pewter against the dark above it. The vest buttoned over the shirt was spectacular, crimson and glowing, like satin, embroidered with an elaborate labyrinth of thorns and ivy woven in deep greens and gold, a sumptuous feast for eye and spirit, though seldom visible to the world the Rider frequented.

When he reached the spot Jude had indicated, the Rider bent and looked closely at the earthen bottle, half buried, almost the same color as the ground. He removed a glove and passed his hand over it slowly twice, without touching it. Then he pulled his rivener from the scabbard concealed under his coat. It was a strange weapon, with a straight unguarded handle about a foot long, and a slightly curved blade, almost an arm-length, that held its width right to the end. He brought the stout handle down upon the bottle and shattered it asunder. The water inside seeped into the half-dried mud, turning it red as blood until the earth absorbed it all.

The Rider stood wordless as the shards dried in the sun. Then he raised his hand. Millicent came to him, and he reached into one of his satchels, drew out a small metal box, removed the lid, and deliberately, one by one, picked up the pieces and dropped them into the box, then closed it and returned it to his bag. Meld again; Millicent carried him over to Jude, who stood mute, his hand held out like a beggar. The rider brought several bronze coins out of a pocket in his vest, and dropped them into the man's outstretched palm.

"This place isn't healthy for you, Jude. Get your people across the river, where there's some good water."

Jude winced as if in pain, but held onto his coins.

From his perch in a hollow and decaying, half-dead persimmon tree, Raven watched as Millicent and her Rider turned back along the way they had come. The Rider twisted about, met Raven's gaze, and tugged the brim of his hat, then turned and rode on. He saw no need to make a frantic search for the boy at this juncture. He had caught no fresh scent of him on the road, so the boy had not been on it since the rain the night before. He had obviously gone to the woods, could be anywhere on the face of the mountain above by now. But the Rider felt no hurry. He had the means to track him now. He would take care of the boy in good time.

DAVEY'S WOOD

Bard's traverse up the face of the mountain on his sixth day in the Laurel proved more of a climb than a walk. Without a path, he followed the creek as closely as he could, clambering over boulders, often on hands and knees, slithering under close-grown rhododendron and laurel. Every torturous step up the unremitting slope carried him higher up and deeper into the mountain. As he climbed, the creek gradually dwindled to a brook, swirling and pooling among mossy stones, singing and warbling on its way like some bright and elusive bird.

Above the Dismal, he ascended into old growth forest, massive trunks of beech and hickory and poplar and holly and oak and maple, standing close in a crowd on the tilted land. The unbroken canopy of their foliage allowed no view at all of the valley below. Even the rhododendron and laurel thinned in the dense shade, although a throng of wildflowers flourished there. Now and again, a slant of sunlight found an opening in the green barrier above, told him that along his way morning had been swallowed up into afternoon, and now the day was well toward evening. The trees ahead and above presented their smooth or craggy trunks like the shields of a guardian army. As he passed them, and looked back down the way behind, they resembled a shaggy congregation of old men, all garbed in green and gray moss and lichens. Among the trees, great outcroppings of stone, with boulders as large as houses, projected from the humus. Occasionally, a large fragment, freed by the thaw and freeze of ten thousand turnings about the sun, had tumbled down hill to rest against some tree stout enough to withstand the assault, or to topple some tree that wasn't. In other places an indomitable seedling had sprouted in the detritus atop a boulder, and as time carried the mountain toward the valley, the growing sapling had extended its roots to the remaining earth, until the tree, perhaps an old beech, stood towering above its stone cradle, gripping it with roots curled around like the fingers of a giant's hand.

Spent and bruised, hungry and above all, thirsty, Bard grieved the loss of his bottle. When he finally concluded that the mountain extended right up into Heaven, and that he had been and would be climbing forever, he came to a steep incline of moss-covered gneiss, several times his height. Cracks and crevices laced across the rocky face, upon which the brook, or what remained of it, coursed down like tears. The way around seemed more formidable than the barrier ahead of him, so slipping and grappling, nearly losing his bag several times and once almost pulled over backward by the weight of his blanket roll, Bard managed with judicial use of his staff to work his way to the lip of the ledge above and pull himself over the brink.

Exhausted, scraped and abraded, he lay on his back for a while, as two squirrels discussed the implications of his intrusion into their personal space. He looked around and saw he was lying on a broad, nearly level stone shelf over which the brook wandered from a small pool in a hollowed depression at the far side, at the base of a fractured vertical wall of stone, taller than a tree. The brook emerged from a crevice in this stone, and dropped through air into the natural basin below. It made a sound like small pebbles falling in a cave.

Bard took off his shoes, limped sore-footed into the shallow pool. He cupped his hands underneath the tiny waterfall, and when he had rinsed the dirt and dust away, drank from them. Then he sat down in the pool and wept for sheer relief and gratitude.

#

Millicent brought her Rider into Beaverdam just as they had left, in the light of the setting sun. People still on the street as they went through town turned to stare and wonder. A Rider seldom returned from a hunt without his quarry. Millicent halted before the potter's shop. The Rider took the small metal box from his satchel and went in.

"Amos, I need you to make something for me."

The potter, a man never gray, but with a gray and grizzled beard, looked up from his wheel, smiled amiably at the Rider, and came over to meet him at a table near the front of the shop, "Whatever I can".

"I want you to make a fairybowl for me; can you do that?"

Amos looked surprised, "You know I can, or you wouldn't be here. But when did Riders start taking short-cuts?"

"I'm tired of riding, Amos. I want this trip over sooner than later." The Rider opened his metal box and dumped the broken pottery onto the table, "I need these ground into the clay."

"That isn't a problem. When do you want it?"

"I'll be leaving again in three days, I need it by then."

"Thorns or Ivy?"

"There are thorns enough in Laurel. Make it ivy."

"You will have it then," Amos promised.

The Rider pulled back his coat, drew out his rivener, laid his left hand with the fingers spread wide upon the table, and with one expert blow, severed the small finger. There was little blood. Whatever pain it caused him, he swallowed without flinch or grimace. "Use the bone from this as well," he told the potter, sheathed his blade and walked out the door.

#

Perhaps Bard dozed. Perhaps he was just lost in the wilderness of his fatigue. But when he stood up, dripping with water from the spring, no sun shone through the leaves above him, and in the deepest shadows frogs carried on debate with crickets, while off among the trees, owls declared themselves to the oncoming night. He was hungry. He went to his bag, opened it, took out a handful of nuts, found a stone at hand to crack them with, and took his bowl back over to the spring to fill it. Setting the bowl beside his little stash of nuts, he took off his wet clothes, hung them on a scraggly laurel branch, hoping they would dry, unrolled his blanket, wrapped himself in it, and sat down to his supper.

His thirst still raged. Bard lifted his bowl to drink, thought he caught his reflection in the water it held, just as a stray breeze rippled the surface. He held the bowl steady until the water smoothed again, and was startled to see reflected there a face not his own. Within his bowl, he saw, as if seen from high and away as Raven would see it, a man standing, holding his wide hat in one hand and with the other lifting above him a long black feather and looking up directly at him. The man's hair was as dark as the feather. There was a long mark, the hue of plowed loam, on his brow above his left eye. His eyes, a luminous gray, shown like molten silver in the light. Their hue was not an absence of color so much as if all the colors they had ever beheld blended in them. But it was the features of the face that caught Bard's breath away. The man gazing out of the bowl looked enough like Bard's own father to be a brother to him.

The vision faded. When nothing remained to be seen through the water but the inside of his bowl, Bard drank. He paused after a couple of swallows to seek his own reflection, but in the dim light, he could find no semblance of anything except the intricate design inscribed there that wound over and under and around itself until it was lost in its own intertwining. He opened a few of the chestnuts. As he ate them, he drank from his bowl until it was empty. He thought about using one of his matches to light a fire to warm by, but he was tired and it would be a hard job gathering fuel in the dark.

He lay down upon the stone, which still held slight warmth from the departed day, and pulled his blanket tight around him. Lights flickered among the leaves of the oaks surrounding the spring. Bard could not decide if he looked upon fireflies or stars. While he was trying to make up his mind about them, he slept.

#

He woke as the first light of dawn began to infiltrate the forest. A mockingbird perched somewhere nearby, singing his heart out. As the bird worked his way through his repertoire, to Bard's surprise he could not identify any of the patterns. Either most of the birds in the Laurel were unknown to him or this mockingbird was an original soul who felt himself above borrowing music from his neighbors.

As Bard gathered again to his waking self, his senses

inventoried his world. Apart from the singing bird, who sounded quite near, but had kept so far unseen, he heard a distant quarreling of crows. A couple of squirrels, perhaps the pair who had scolded him the evening before, barked their good mornings, and apparently having judged this wandering vagabond harmless to squirreldom, commenced going about their business for the day. The little spring measured out the metrics of her music, echoing slightly within the stone ramparts from which she sprung. Wonderful aromas filtered down on the still air, which explained why Bard had awakened from a dream about the feast at Charon's house, for the smells coming to him now were like the smells from Callie's kitchen, declaring to the world baking bread.

Now wide awake, lying very still, he traced with his eyes upward along the stony height above the pool until, at the very top, almost hidden by overhanging oaks, he saw a light, and as the sky brightened behind it, discerned the shape of a wee house, perched on the edge of the precipice, like a swallow about to take flight.

Quickly Bard was up and into his clothes, still damp, but he reckoned they could dry on him as he went along. He wished for time to wash himself, but the spring with its little pool seemed now too pristine for such a purpose, become in his mind a sacred fountain. The smell of cooking, and the house above him conveyed his close proximity to human society. He thought he'd best ready himself to join it. Hastily he gathered his bowl and his bag, folded the bag close around the remaining chestnuts, and rolled them with his canister of matches and his poncho into his blanket. He bound them all up with his cord, put on his hat, took up his staff, and questioned the trees, "Which way do I go now?"

Scanning the rocks about him, on his second turn Bard discerned to the easterly side of his ledge a narrow stairway of stone rising away along the top edge of the craggy steep behind the spring. Some of the steps seemed natural stones, and these had been augmented by carefully shaped and placed slabs of the same sort of stone as birthed the spring. The steps lay mostly clear of leaves and debris. Obviously someone traveled them every day. Bard figured they led to the house he had seen above. This spring was probably the occupant's water source. Grateful he did not desecrate the little pool more than he had already, he breathed a thanks to the spring for her kind mercies to him, and prayed to the air he might find as generous a welcome at the other end of the stairs.

Conflicted between anxiety and anticipation, Bard began mounting the stairs. The predominance of one emotion or the other alternated with each step. He measured his ascent with a firm thump of his staff on each stone he passed. The blows echoed low and heavy, like a muffled drum in a funeral march. But with every step upward, the sound grew higher in pitch, perceptibly lighter and brighter than the one below. Bard imagined himself a cat walking on the keyboard of a piano.

Flowers crowded the path, and hung over the edge of the precipice to his left. He encountered a host of native forest plants, a few of which he recognized, although most were entirely new to him. They jostled against cultivars, lantana, and cone flowers, and several kinds of flowering sedum. All these thrust upward toward the light from a veritable sea of ferns and wild iris.

The trees above the spring were wider spaced than on the slopes below, and the forest much brighter. Among the large trees, slightly smaller holly proclaimed themselves with scarlet berries. A few maples towered here and there, their upper leaves already tipped with gold and crimson. That, with all the flowers, made the forest seem like a festival ground. Among the trees browsed deer, feeding on the heavy mast crunching underfoot. They paid Bard no notice, except for one old buck, weighed with a massive rack of antlers, who raised his head momentarily and looked at the boy, then went back to grazing.

Bard would not have been surprised to meet Owl and his Bear in such a place. He remembered the dream that came as he fled from the gray man and his tribe. Owl had told him, "Find the Weaver." Since then, the stream had led him straight to this place, then disappeared into the mountain. He wondered if Owl's Weaver dwelt in the house at the top of the steps. As the stair took him in a steady ark along the rocky brink above the spring, he could still now and then catch the steady strumming of the little waterfall at the pool. Then, he was at the topmost step; the path veered just ahead between huge boulders whose shape reminded him of Charon's dogs. When he passed among them, he found the house in its clearing there before him.

Bard could not recall seeing a stranger or more wee dwelling anywhere. It stood off the ground high enough for a human to walk upright beneath, resting at either end on sections of a rounded and mossed boulder bigger than the house itself. Some cataclysmic event away ago when the mountain was young had split the great rock down the middle. The boulder seemed poised to roll and drop to the spring below at the slightest provocation. The house was twice its width in height, which only made it appear more precarious on its perch than it was. Actually, it was constructed solidly enough, and anchored to a rock that had not been moved in at least ten millennia. Probably no human ever dwelt in a structure more stable and secure. A narrow deck ran the length of the house and broadened to turn around one end farthest from the escarpment. A configuration of thick chestnut timbers, barely a stair and almost a ladder, lead up to the deck.

Bard stopped and stood for a minute in the open yard before, so that he could be seen and inspected by anyone inside the house. Based on his brief experience in this country, that seemed to be the etiquette of the Laurel. When nobody came out to inquire of him, He climbed up to the deck, intending to knock and ask his way, and hopefully to be offered hospitality. Good manners in the Laurel apparently also required that no householder allow a wayfarer to pass without opportunity for shelter and sustenance. Even the gray family had offered him what they considered food.

As Bard approached the door, the aromas that had awakened him below assaulted him in force, watering his mouth and making him swallow. He paused at an open window, and peered inside. The little house was just a single room on the lower floor, with another room directly above. The far end of the room, which overlooked the spring's hollow, was windowed to the beamed ceiling. A ladder ascended through an opening in the ceiling to the room above. If this was the Weaver's house, he or she apparently worked upstairs, for Bard saw no sign of a loom.

But on the windowsill right in front of him, set on a long cedar tray to cool from the oven, presided three fat round loaves of golden and crusted bread, crowned with melted butter. He had an intense desire to make them a part of himself. Then he heard a voice from behind and below, "Help yourself there, Pilgrim. You look like you could use some."

Bard jumped as if he had been stoned all over again, feeling as guilty for his covetousness as if he actually hid the loaves in his bag and was about to slip away with them. He turned sheepishly and saw none anywhere to own the voice until, at the steep little stair, a head bobbed into view. First appeared a round, bald noggin, brown as a nut, ringed with a corona of white hair, which gleamed in the morning like a silvered cloud. Underneath bushy eyebrows, two eyes, blue as summer sky, sparkled at him from behind a pair of battered spectacles. A face that had obviously been lived in under the weather much more than under a roof, folded about the eyes with much crease and wrinkle. The spectacles perched precariously across the bridge of a short round nose, like a ripe persimmon, over a full pink mouth, not wide, around which an audacious white beard seemed intent on filling as much space as possible in all directions. The face wasn't the most handsome Bard had ever seen, but he couldn't recall ever seeing a happier one. The jolly little head was attached to a limber but compacted body scarcely taller than his own. He wondered if he were being visited by an elf or a leprechaun. Having nothing at all in his head to say to this merry apparition, he asked,

"Are you the Weaver?"

"Oh, Mercy no, Pilgrim. The Weaver is miles and promises from here. I'm the Keeper, although most who come by here just call me Mad Davey."

"What do you keep?" That seemed a safer question than asking point blank why someone was called crazy.

"Pilgrim, I keep the Woods, I do, and on my own time

I try to look after all who wander here."

"Lost people like me?" Bard was warming to the little gnome, who exuded trust and welcome.

"None of us is ever lost, Pilgrim, though many who happen by seem unaware of their destination. I offer them a space to rest and nourish, and if they can't get to where they're going from here, I try to give them directions to a place they can start from. Pilgrim, do you have a name?"

"People mostly just call me Bard."

Davey projected a probing gaze; his smile dissolving barely for a moment into thoughtful seriousness, before returning undiminished. "That is a name not entirely inappropriate to you, but ganny you got it from somebody who doesn't know you. If it doesn't ruffle you at all, I'll just call you Pilgrim for now." Bard decided that as long as he resided in Davey's company, he would answer to Pilgrim. His smile then, a little crooked, a little crazy, and altogether joyous, presented a fair approximation of Mad Davey's own.

Davey clapped his hands and rubbed them together. He fairly danced a little jig as he observed, with cackling good cheer, "You look like you fell off a mountain. Eat some of this bread while I fix our breakfast, so you won't gobble up everything on the table before you taste it. Then we have to get you cleaned up."

He pulled Bard through the door, propelled him into a chair at a small table covered with a red-checkered oil cloth. Davey brought a loaf from the window, pulled a big knife from a drawer, and wielding it like a cleaver, cut off a thick slice of bread amounting to nearly a quarter of the loaf. He slathered the bread with butter and honey, and inserted a corner of it into the astonished boy's open mouth. Bard managed to get his hand up in time to prevent his appetizer from falling onto the table.

"Now be that tasty or not?" queried Mad Davey, beaming at him beatifically, as he held a plate under Bard's chin until he could take hold of it and lower it, with his serving of bread, to the table. Still warm from the oven, the bread was tasty. Indeed, it was delicious. Bard had never eaten such bread. Davey pretended to take no notice when Bard finished it, reached for the knife, and cut himself a second slice almost as large.

From an earthen jar on one of the many shelves that lined the room on practically every available wall surface, Davey poured some coarse-ground corn, which he brought to a boil in a small pot of salted water, then added butter and milk and several other things chopped and diced, and set it to simmer atop the diminutive and ornate iron cook stove that stood in one corner of the room. As he worked, he paused now and then to stuff bits of wood into the firebox below. From a large basket hanging from the ceiling, Davey fetched half a dozen eggs the size of chicken's eggs, but of all colors, green and blue and brown and pink. He broke them into a bowl, chopped up a handful of green onions and threw them in, then added a liberal splash of some sort of red power to that, beat all together with a fork before pouring the bowl's contents out into a frying pan atop his little stove. He stirred the mix continually for several minutes until it was no longer liquid, and divided it between the boy's plate and another. Then Davey spooned out the grits, after stirring in a dash of what appeared to be coffee from a large enameled pot on the back corner of the stove. He filled two cups with the liquid and set them along with his plate on the table, brought a couple of large wooden spoons out of a drawer, tossed them at Bard who caught them in the air and laid them beside the plates. From a nook or cranny Bard hadn't noticed, Davey produced a small golden melon not much larger than a grapefruit, which he halved with the same gusto and abandon he had exercised toward the bread. He sat down across from Bard at the little table, laying half the melon on the boy's plate.

Davey raised his eyes toward the ceiling, intoned with all apparent sincerity, "We give as we receive," then spooned up a heaping mound of the corn grits which miraculously vanished all at once into his little mouth. He savored this for an instant, swallowed, then beamed at Bard once more, "Be this all tasty or not?"

The rustic fare was all Davey said of it and more. It nourished a hungry soul as much as it did starved flesh. They ate it all, and finished the loaf of bread before they left the table. The cups held not coffee, Bard discovered, but some mixture of tea, milk and spices, laced with honey. While he ate under Davey's approving smile, he forgot about being sore and aching and scratched and dirty. He even forgot about the gray man and the Rider.

While Bard finished eating, Davey set several pots and kettles full of water atop his little stove, and fed it liberally until steam began to cloud the air. Then he went outside, took down a large metal tub hanging on the wall beside the window, and brought it with a clash and a bang to the center of the deck. He came in just as Bard downed the last of his melon, handed him a thick towel and said, "Help me get these out, will you?" They carried the water onto the deck and poured it into the tub. Davey plunged in his hand and judged it not too hot, brought out a bar of some strong green-colored soap from an unpainted wood cabinet set against the house, handed it to Bard and said, "Let's see what color you really are."

"Out here in the open?" Bard found himself suddenly shy in company in a way he had not been alone in the woods.

"Don't worry, Pilgrim; these trees have looked down on my old carcass for more years than I like to count, and they never laughed once." And with that, Mad Davey bobbed down the stair and was gone.

Bard took off his tattered and filthy clothes and very carefully deposited himself into the tub. The heat eased his aches, but the water fired a hundred scrapes and cuts he had scarcely been aware of acquiring during his flight the day before. He wished for Callie's herbs, but as he gingerly began to scrub his bruised and worn flesh, the soap, which smelled something like grass, proved soothing as much as cleansing.

The back of his head, though, hurt at the slightest touch. When he explored the wound tentatively with his fingers, they came back tinged with red, and he did not protest when Davey clambered up the ladder, walked over to the tub, squatted behind him, took the cloth, and with the gentleness of a mother, began cleaning his broken scalp.

"When you're dry, Pilgrim, We'll put some ointment on that." Then Davey grabbed Bard's face between his hands, peered at him intently for a moment, and whistled softly to himself, "Be there a big knocker afront then, too. It will be with you for a while. He tapped the boy's forehead above his left brow and made him wince. "Sorry, Pilgrim; I have a hand too heavy,"

Apology offered, Davey scurried off into the house, taking Bard's clothes and shoes with him, leaving just the hat behind. A moment later a tiny square window in the gable swung open with a creak and a thud, and clothes began flying out to land on the deck near Bard's tub. Davey's cheery voice floated down through the opening, "These may be a little loose for you, Pilgrim, but they will serve. I'm thicker than you, but not a hand taller. You'll have something clean at least to cover with."

It was impossible to hear the little man speak about anything and not be touched by his irrepressible glee at being alive. Bard thought Mad Davey would make people laugh at a funeral. As he finished his bath, he could hear the old man bustling around in his little house, making enough racket for a whole crowd of Daveys.

Bard washed as clean as he could reasonably expect to render himself, stood and dried, and wrapping the towel round his waist, walked over to inspect his acquired costume. He picked up a pair of gray woolen drawers, a garment strange to him, with legs almost to the knees and a multitude of buttons. With a little trial and error, he got them on his person and buttoned to him in order and to his surprise found them quite comfortable. Amid the pile lay a pair of canvas trousers dyed a deep umber, perhaps with walnut shells or the tannin-laden bark of oaks. A set of leather suspenders buttoned to the waistband. He found a flannel shirt, without collar, the color of a robin's egg, which he put on, then pulled up the trousers and looped the suspenders over his shoulders. The fabrics, which had appeared rather rough to his eye, felt as soft to his battered and abused body as the breeze that set the trees whispering around the house. He found no socks, but a pair of sandals that fit him well enough. The sandals were the color of the dark gneiss above the spring. He could not tell if they were made from leather or from some heavily-oiled and closely-woven fiber. Last came to hand a light jacket, the same material as the trousers, the color of dark moss or sage, with three buttons on the front. Feeling cool in the morning breeze after his time in the steaming tub, Bard pulled on the jacket.

As Davey had predicted, his borrowed garments felt loose upon him, but as he walked toward the door, they settled around his frame, as comforting as they were comfortable. Bard thought they felt just right.

He nearly collided with Davey coming out the door at full speed with a bucket of steaming hot water in which floated a stout brush.

Davey motioned him to take one of the handles on the side of the tub, "Give me a hand with this, Pilgrim, if you would be so kind." The full tub made heavy lifting for Bard, but together they hoisted it atop the rail, with most of the bath water still inside, and dumped the soapy liquid over the side into a rampant bed of sorrel, cone flowers and wild garlic. If this was their steady diet, they appeared to be thriving on it. Then Davey poured the bucket of near-boiling water into the tub, scrubbed the inside severely with the brush, and emptied it over the edge onto the boulder that ran under the deck. "Hang 'er up on the house yonder, Pilgrim, and we'll go down to clean the spring, and maybe we'll stay to watch it clear"

Bard hoisted the tub up until the handle slipped over the rusty nail driven into one of the lapped boards siding the house, and turned to see Davey already across the yard and about to start down the stone steps to the spring, a long-handled rake with wooden tines over his shoulder. Bard grabbed his hat and clapped it on his head, grimacing as it bore on his hurts there, climbed down the stair to find a large basket woven of white oak splits waiting at the foot. He assumed Davey had left it for him, picked it up, and followed after the old man, who by now was half-way to the spring, hopping and bounding down the steps as if he were a boy himself.

By the time Bard reached the ledge below the spring, He found the stone almost covered with large acorns from the broad-leaved oaks on the slopes around and above. Davey had already raked the leaves away from the little pool, and scattered them among the ferns and trillium growing about the verge of the stone. With his rake, he was dredging out a few branches and some of the acorns that had settled in the water. He said to Bard over his shoulder, "Pilgrim, while I finish here, gather up as many of these acorns as you can, should you please, and put them in your basket."

"Are you going to feed these to your pigs?"

"I keep no stock, Pilgrim. There be hogs about these woods, but none a boy would necessarily want to meet. They are well put to find their own mast." He turned, lay down his rake, picked up an acorn, peeled it with his fingers, and popped it into his mouth. As he chewed, he grinned at Bard, "Be these right tasty or not?"

Bard picked up one for himself, broke away the hull, and ate it slowly, expecting to taste the bitterness of tannin. Instead he found it nutty and sweet.

Davey hopped from one foot to the other and clapped his hands joyously, "Pilgrim, we can grind these to flour finer than any wheat we could swap from a Trader. This is bread to fill the belly and warm the spirit over the long winter. The only pigs to savor these will go about on two legs." Then he burst into a string of vocalizations that came out somewhere between a laugh and a song.

Bard gathered as many of the acorns as he could in his hands and hat as Davey went about clearing the spring and the steps. When they both finished, he had nearly filled his basket.

On their way back up to the house, Bard climbed before, as he was not quite as tall, and Davey followed, each holding their side of the basket. They stopped often to gather what edibles grew among the flowers beside the steps, including wild leeks, pungent and pervasive. As Bard sniffed his hands after handling them, Davey said to him, as if it were the biggest joke in the world, "Eat a few of these, Pilgrim, and no enemy will get close enough to do you any damage."

Peculiar squashes, long and green, trailed among the trillium, and parsley, and toward the top of the stair, where more light reached the forest floor, basil, and eggplant, with violet colored, trumpet-shaped blossoms and long, thin purple fruit. All of these things, and more, they added to the basket as they climbed, and by the time they reached the boulders guarding the top of the steps, they had the makings of a feast.

As they hauled the basket through the door of the wee house, and Bard very tentatively removed his hat, Mad Davey's unflagging smile faltered for once. He looked stricken as he exclaimed, "The Holy Mother would not love the way I've neglected you Pilgrim. Sit down!" Bard sat in a chair at the table, while Davey poured water into a basin and washed his hands.

"Stay," he commanded, and vanished up the ladder into the room above. There came sounds of things falling and sliding about, then Davey appeared again, sliding down the ladder like a fireman down his pole, He came over to Bard, opened the small jar he held, and with the barest touch, parted the hair on the back of Bard's head, and spread something very soft and very cool on the hurt there. To Bard, it smelled like the cough drops he had been given when he was sick the previous winter. When he had finished his ministrations, Davey kissed his Pilgrim on the crown of his head just the way Bard's own grandfather might have.

While Bard absorbed the blissful healing of Davey's balm, the old man pulled out from a long low cabinet next to the stove, several large cedar buckets bound with brass bands.

"If we want to eat tonight and be clean tomorrow, we need some water, Pilgrim. Would you be good enough to fill these for me while I go tend to lives in the woods?" Without a word, Bard hauled himself up from his state of grace, and while he calculated how long it would take him to make even one trip to the spring and back with one or two of these buckets filled, he seized two of the buckets and started for the door.

Davey fairly exploded into a fit of jollity that sent him rolling under the table, knocking against the chairs, kicking the floor in mirthful ecstasy. When he could breathe again, he rose to his knees and tried to speak, "Mercy, Pilgrim, who taught you to live your life the hard way?" Then he pulled open one of the windows in the wall overlooking the spring, and pointed to a small windlass mounted to the exterior wall beside the window, with the crank handle extending before the casement. "Use this, Pilgrim," he said, submitting to another, less extended fit of laughter, "I have things to do." He patted Bard on the shoulder as he passed, giggled to himself as he went through the door, and was off to whatever chores awaited him.

Bard found it easy to attach the handle of a bucket to the hook at the end of the line on the windless, and it lowered without hindrance straight into the little pool before the spring. Hauling it back up full of water required some work, but not hard work. In as much time as it would have taken to make one traverse of the stairs, he had all eight buckets filled and stowed in their cabinet. Bard picked up his blanket roll, bag and staff from the floor where he had left them by the table earlier when Davey had first ushered him into the house, and set them in the corner amongst Davey's walking sticks and brooms, and walked out to the deck to get his bearings.

Several small buildings occupied the far side of the clearing, a privy walled with wide boards set vertically, and two square log sheds, one of them not much larger than the privy. The smaller, built into a slope behind, Bard surmised to be perhaps a root cellar. The purpose of the other, which had a wide door and windowless walls, he could not guess. He saw several hens scratching about among the trees at the edge of the yard. From farther off in the woods, he caught the sound of someone chopping or splitting wood with an axe. He guessed he heard Davey at work.

Bard wondered if he should go find the old man and offer to help, when he heard another sound, the steady rumble of galloping horses, drumming deeper and louder as they neared, a rhythmic pounding on the earth, with the occasional flinty discord of hoof on stone. North and east past the yard, he could make out beyond the nearer trees the pale snaking of a road. As he watched, two horsemen came into view, their mounts lathered and tested. In their peaked caps and green tunics, the riders looked like soldiers. They bent low over their horses' backs and seemed as weary as their animals, but on they went, never slacking. In moments, they passed out of sight to his left, wrapped again in the forest, and the sound of their passage faded in their wake until Bard heard only the wind in ceaseless communion with the trees, the chattering of squirrels, and the raucous complaints of crows.

He went out to find Davey then, which turned into a more protracted search than he anticipated. Sounds carried far in the clear air of the mountain, and Davey was much farther away than Bard had reckoned. He walked for a time among the ancient trees, standing wide apart here, as if in a park. He passed little stacks and piles of sticks and brush the old man had cleared and gathered, and along the way met portions of Davey's garden. In one place or another where there was suitable light and moisture, a few squash vines trailed up a dead laurel, or tomatoes ripened red in a mound of rich humus built up among stones. In a little clearing, he came upon a small potato patch. A handful of purple potatoes heaped at the end of one of the rows. Davey had apparently dug them that morning, planning to fetch them home when he came back by. Bard collected them in his hat. Oddly, none of Davey's plantings seem much molested by deer or bear. The wood was rife with mast and roots and berries of its own to sate the hunger of all the souls who lived there.

Eventually, Mad Davey, on his way home, found Bard. They walked together through the wood, enjoying the mild day, glorying in the golden light, as Davey lovingly identified and named to Bard every tree and plant and creature they passed. Some time beyond noon, ahead of them appeared Davey's little house atop its boulder at the limits of the land, like the aerie of some cliff-dwelling hawk.

While Bard washed the potatoes and set them to dry on the window sill, Davey prepared their simple lunch of bread, with soft cheese, some sliced melon, and a small piece of honeycomb. After they ate and cleared the dishes, they sorted through the things they had gathered in the morning. The acorns went into a wire mesh basket hanging by the door. Davey planned to grind them as soon as they dried. The other succulents and vegetables, they cleaned and set aside with the potatoes for supper. The rest of the afternoon they spent in the woods, at whatever tasks presented. For Davey, one task or another was ever presenting. Whatever rest and repose his spirit was capable of he found in doing and making, in keeping and tending. He kept in perpetual motion during all his waking hours, yet, behind his antics and laughter and the banter and flashing blue eyes, he seemed to carry within himself a profound stillness and unshakable calm.

#

Late in the day, as they started toward home, the lowering sun still burned above the mountain's rim, casting long shadows across the forest floor, lighting the underside of leaves overhead, bathing the land, which had been shaded for the most part through the long day, in an autumnal glow that made Bard think of the light in Callie's house the night the fiddler girl had sung them all into her song.

At length, the Keeper and his young pilgrim reached the house, and tumbled through the door, laden with new treasures from the woods. Davey filled a basin with water, and set it just outside the door where they washed hands and arms and faces, then he cleaned and anointed Bard's battered head once more, commenting that it would be well-healed in another day or so, as if that made him the happiest old man in the Laurel.

As he commenced preparing their meal, he directed Bard to gather his gear and haul it up the ladder to the room above. "You'll have to sleep up there, Pilgrim. I want to rest close to the ground tonight."

The last rays of the setting sun washed the upper room in a light as warm as love. Davey had furnished it with a small bed, covered with a quilt and bedding over a tick mattress. Beside the bed stood a tall, narrow chest of three drawers with a drop-leaf which perhaps served as a desk of sorts. When Bard lay on the bed to try it, the smell reminded him of the grasses he had rested in the day he freed Hawk. It seemed a long time ago. As in the lower room, windows opened all along the wall above the spring. Above the windows, the steep roof peaked into shadow, making the boy feel as if he were in a little church.

Whatever of Davey's possessions could not be fit into the chest, hung in bags and baskets from the beams above. Shelves of books lined all the walls floor to ceiling. Bard had never seen so many books. They all looked old and much handled.

In one corner, on the floor, weighted by several books that apparently had found no place on the shelves, three stacks of large paper sheets the dimensions of an unfolded newspaper invited perusal. When he looked closer, Bard saw they were covered with drawings populated with crows and owls and bears and rabbits and falcons, as well as flowers and trees and long, humped mountains. Among all these images, a few human faces gazed out of the pages. Obviously, whatever time Mad Davey could spare from keeping his woods and tending the stray strangers who wandered there, he spent drawing everything he loved, which Bard thought included just about everything.

He replaced the books, made a mental note to ask

Davey if he might look through all the drawings later. A small mirror, cracked and tarnished, sat atop the chest. Before he went back down the ladder, Bard stood on his toes and looked into the mirror to assess his damage. He tried to angle his head to inspect what impression the stone had made upon him, but found the wound too far back and behind for him to see. On the left side of his forehead, though, was an angry hematoma the color of a ripe plum. From the shape of it, he guessed he had hit his head across the end of his staff when he fell in the gray man's yard. The bruise soon healed. The mark stayed with him.

He heard from below clatter of skillets and crockery, sizzle in pans, bubbling in pots, and Mad Davey whistling and singing and clucking and chortling to himself as he busied about their supper. Bard descended the ladder, enveloped in aromas that, not altogether familiar, nonetheless appealed to him to ingest and enjoy their sources. Under Davey's watchful guidance and direction, he joined in the preparations, washing and peeling and slicing or dicing whatever Davey handed his way. He was far from expert in his technique, but as Davey kept reminding him, with most things really important, will and passion will make up in large measure for an absence of practice and experience. Davey had enough will and passion, as well as practice and experience, for both of them, and by the time he told Bard to set out their plates and mugs on the table, Davey had convinced the child that he had the makings of an honest chef.

"Sit ye down there, Pilgrim," Davey glowed like the fire in his stove. "Tonight is a grand and special occasion. Tonight we feast." And feast, they did, on baked yams, golden and sweet, anointed with honey and cinnamon, "I swapped with a Trader for it," Davey confided. The wild leeks they gathered that morning emerged from the oven, now roasted and served with a sprinkling of walnuts. A big loaf of the acorn bread, such as they ate earlier, reappeared. They ate squashes, baked and stuffed with nuts and figs; large slices of eggplant, curried and battered, cooked with mushrooms, as delicious and filling as beef or venison; green beans, barely cooked, tender and sweet, a comb of honey, red and rich, from the poplars in the woods around. Davey did not say how he had persuaded the bees to share it with him. Along with all the rest, they indulged in beets, and tiny ears of corn, pickled and tart. They washed it all down with mugs of ginger beer which Davey had made and stored in one of the log buildings across the yard.

Later, Bard could scarcely believe how the two of them managed to prepare so much food. Davey had woven an elaborate dance of making and led him through it. They did what they did, and at the end of their doing, they feasted on their labors. The Keeper and his Pilgrim spent half the evening preparing the meal, and the other half indulging in it. They ate slowly and savored every morsel that passed their lips, not at all like eating with the cousins in the Gap, when the boy and the girls raced to see who would be first to finish. Mad Davey imparted to his young apprentice a revelation, that food is more than fuel, that a cook works for more purpose than to fill a belly, that the preparing and sharing of a common meal enriches the soul as it nourishes the body.

As they ate, they talked of dreams and ways, of comings and goings, of mysteries and puzzles. They conversed as might two old sailors upon meeting one another after long and arduous voyages. Late in the evening, Bard asked Davey again what he knew about the Weaver.

"What be all this interest in the Weaver, Pilgrim? What do you know of her?"

Bard confessed he knew nothing at all about the Weaver, but had been told in a dream that he needed to find her.

Davey set much store by dreams. "Dreams be more reliable direction than the doctrine of any priest, whatever the color of their robes. I reckon you need to find her then. Where she is exactly, I can't tell you, Pilgrim. She's up the North Road yonder somewhere, away atop the Alone, where none but her ever goes. If you are serious about finding her, you need to go and talk to the Herb Woman; she's about two days' walk from here. She's also a spinner. She grows flax and keeps sheep, and in the woods gathers fibers of whatever kinds serve, and spins them into yarn. Some of it, according to the Trader passing through, she passes to the Weaver. If anybody on the road knows where the Weaver lives, the Herb Woman could tell you. But if you go up there to see her, make sure she's had her breakfast before you knock on her door." This seemed to remind Davey of some private hilarity, for he stamped his feet on the floor as he sat in his chair, and unleashed a sound as much a howl as a laugh, then affecting a severe countenance, intoned, "I would think on it before I went to see her, if I were you," which set off another spasm of hilarity.

Suddenly, Davey leapt from the table and skipped over to the stove. The flue above it ran through a wide box-like affair with a door, which served as a warmer. Davey pulled out a huge apple cobbler, crusty gold and brown atop, dished it out with gusto into two large bowls, set down one before him at the table and pushed the other toward Bard. "I made this special for my birthday today. It was fully friendly of you to climb all the way up this old mountain just to share it with me."

"But I didn't know it was your birthday."

Davey's eyes actually glistened with tears, "And you didn't even know then. That is doubly sweet."

Bard thought Mad Davey deserved a present for his birthday. He had nothing of his own to give, though. Even the clothes he wore belonged to Davey. He pulled his medicine bag from beneath his shirt, and took out the little ball of tar soap. It wasn't enough to wash with, but at least it smelled good.

He dropped the soap into the old man's palm. "Happy Birthday, Davey."

Davey lifted it to his stubby little persimmon nose and inhaled. His eyes fixed on something far away and long ago. "Dear Callie, I haven't seen her since I was a boy no older than you, Pilgrim. You've given me a good memory tonight to take with me as I go."

As they cleared the table, Bard asked Davey if he had seen the green men riding past during the morning.

"No, Pilgrim, but I heard them. They were Couriers from Owl on their way down to Beaverdam. We've been having them right regular up this way of late"

"Owl?" the boy questioned, thinking of Ethan and of his own dreams of the old man and the bear.

"The Seer," Davey explained, "An old monk who lives cloistered with the Sisters at the Abbey away up the road almost to the Alone. They say he's very old. Some think he's immortal, maybe was in the Laurel in the Beforetime. The Sisters hardly let anybody see him, claiming he's renounced the world and become a hermit. But the

Traders are afraid to make a move without consulting him first. A Courier stopped here once when his horse went lame. He talked about Owl keeping a bear for a pet. And people talk then about me being crazy."

Bard asked no more questions about Owl, but hoped that since he was likely heading in that direction soon, the Abbey might be on his way.

Although they had consumed some number of dishes at supper, Davey had cooked enough of each for two, and so they had eaten most of the food. What was left, Davey packed in jars which he put in a bag and hung from the windless so they would stay cool in the night air. It would keep nicely for a day. "We're in luck, Pilgrim," he said with a wink; "We get to eat all this good stuff again tomorrow."

When they had washed and dried the dishes, Davey brewed them mugs of the spicy milked tea, and they took their drink out onto the deck and stood for a while looking out into the dark over the spring. Tiny fireflies swirled in a spiral from around the pool down below up along the rising air currents to above the house. They made Bard think of the sparkling gyre he had dreamt at the Circle. For by now he had convinced himself that the events at Council were just a sick child's dream, after all.

He told Davey he had seen the drawings in the upper room, and asked permission to look at them all.

"Mercy, yes, Pilgrim," exclaimed Davey with a hoot. "See in them what you can. An old man has to fill his time somehow with nothing to do all day." After another moment he said abruptly, "Right now, the old man is tired. "Goodnight, Pilgrim,"

Davey climbed down the stair and headed for the privy. Bard went in, washed the cups and set them on the table to dry, then climbed his ladder into sleep.

Bard had been in the Laurel for a week.

#

Sometime during the early hours of the morning, well before dawn, Bard awoke to see a light coming up through the opening at the ladder and sifting up through the cracks in his floor. He heard no sound, but quietly got up and went to look down past the ladder. Davey had pulled a chair from the table up close by the cookstove in which some coals still smouldered. A trail of steam drifted up lazily from the spout of a kettle on the stove. Davey perched with his feet on the rungs of his chair, tilted with its back resting against the wall. Across his lap lay Bard's washed trousers. He held a tattered shirt in one hand and plied a needle and thread with the other. His glasses drifted far down on his nose as his weary eyes strained to follow the needle. Davey was tending and mending. That was what he did. That was who he was. Davey looked very old. Bard wondered that he had never noticed. Then he crept back to his bed, and before he slept again, breathed to the sacred dark a prayer and a thanksgiving for his friend.

#

In the pale light of morning just before sunrise, Bard woke from another dream about Owl and his bear. In the dream, the Seer peered out from beneath a straw hat, with a wide brim past his shoulders. The edge of the brim turned down slightly to shed the rain that fell. Leaning on a staff very like Bard's own, Owl stood beside Bear in the middle of a narrow road, not much more than a path. He turned slightly and pointed up the road behind him. "Go," was all he said.

When Bard came down the ladder, he found Davey

setting at their places eggs scrambled with chives and mushrooms and bits of tomato and green peppers. Davey served the eggs like a sandwich between halves of large brown biscuits that reminded Bard when he tasted them of the biscuits the Trader had brought him the morning after he spent the night in the truck. Then Davey set on each plate a couple of sweet slices of the same golden melon Bard had seen before, and last, poured steaming mugs of what seemed to be his favorite beverage, strong tea, blended with milk and spices, and sweetened with honey.

As they ate, Davey said, "Don't let's work today. This seems a day for dally and wander. Let us indulge and heal ourselves." Indulging and healing sounded good to Bard, who had not rested much at all between his late supper and his dreams, and he still suffered some residual effects of his flight up the mountain. After they finished their breakfast and cleaned their dishes, Davey excused himself, "Give me a bit to myself, Pilgrim, and the rest of the day is ours to pleasure in." Bard watched from the deck as Davey ambled across the yard toward his outbuildings. Then he went back in, climbed to the upper floor and spent the next hour pouring over Davey's drawings.

When Davey eventually popped his head through the opening, he found Bard still at it, walked over, sat nimbly with the boy cross-legged on the floor, and began to tell him the story behind each drawing, for each had a tale between its lines, and although Bard knew as he heard that he would forget most of them, he wanted to keep them all in his mind and hold them in his heart.

Finally, Davey stood and stretched, went over to open the bottom drawer of the chest. He brought out several large sheets of blank paper, heavy and creamy in the light, the same as the drawings were made on, and laid them on the floor beside Bard. From behind the drop leaf, Davey fetched several blocks and sticks of charcoal. "Do your worst, Pilgrim," he said, as if he were telling an enormous joke, "I'll be down at the spring if you need me," and popped away down the ladder again.

Bard sat stunned and thrilled. During his summer in the Gap, he sketched practically anything that would hold still long enough to draw it, as well as those things he had observed close enough to hold still in his head. He had accumulated a bundle of drawings that he knew his father would likely consign to the trash as soon as they returned to town, but he made them for the joy of doing them and for the love of what he had seen. Their loss would only give him space to store new ones. Though untutored, Bard had a gift and a knack, and a rudimentary appreciation of what was required to render an honest image. He had never had real artist's tools or materials to work with. The trust and faith Davey had shown in sharing his own humbled and gratified.

Bard carried a sheet of paper over to the window and held it under the light. He weighed the heft of it, laid his hand flat against the surface and swept his palm lightly over the sheet, feeling its texture. When he held up the paper to see the sun shine through, it glowed warm and rich as fresh butter. He laid the sheet flat on the floor and sat on his knees before it. He found a stick of charcoal that seemed best to fit his hand, then for a long while sat looking at the paper, thinking about all the strange and mysterious souls he had encountered during his days in the Laurel. Finally, he leaned forward, laid the end of his charcoal upon the creamy void, and pulled a strong black mark across it.

For another hour and longer, Bard labored over his drawing. He arranged on the floor around him some of Davey's more accomplished efforts, and as he drew, he paused and looked from one to another of those, not to copy, but noticing the gesture and technique employed in them. By observation and practice, he found that with a finger or the side of his hand he could blend and blur the individual marks of his charcoal into fields almost like a wash of ink, achieve tones from a luminous black to the palest of gray. He discovered he could scrape the surface of the drawing with a hard edge, and the rough face of the paper would reward him with a multitude of textures. He learned that once he fixed the underlying shapes and forms in order, details and highlights would find their places readily. He knew his drawing was not close to being as finely wrought as any from Davey's hand, but he was happy to realize it went far beyond anything he ever thought he could do on his own. When at last he was certain he had put down faithfully as much as he could recall and render, he wrote some words across the bottom of his drawing, and being careful not to smear it with his smudged hands, left the drawing on the bed. Then he went down the ladder, poured some water in a basin and washed his hands, before bounding happily down the stone steps to the spring to find his Mad Davey.

When he reached the ledge before the spring, he saw no sign of Davey, although the rake stood leaning by the steps and the spring had been cleared. The split oak basket waited with some acorns inside, but more than that lay scattered about the stone underfoot, so Bard took off his hat and began to gather them. As he worked, more fell to replace some of those he had added to his basket.

From behind him then, "Pilgrim, you are ever the toiler; I thought we were going to play today." Bard turned. Davey stood in the pool, looking as if he had pulled a fine prank on his friend. The boy had no clue as to how the Keeper came to be there, and Davey never told him. It was as if he had stepped out of the cliff behind the spring.

Bard was mystified, "Were you invisible?"

"No Pilgrim, just dim."

Davey had left his sandals beside the pool, and as he passed he picked them up in one hand, leaving the wet tracks of his knobby feet on the stone, padded over to the basket, and with a giggle and a snort, hoisted one side, and nodded invitation. The basket was not so full today, and Bard could haul his part with one hand. With the other, he reached out and shouldered Davey's rake as they started up the steps.

When they reached the house, Davey gestured Bard to put down the basket by the steps, then pointed under the house where several hoes and rakes and shovels, a single-point push plow and several other garden implements rested against the cloven face of the split boulder. Bard deposited the rake there, and Davey started across the yard again, waving the boy after him. "Pilgrim, see my plunder room," and he skipped away toward the largest of the two log buildings as if he couldn't wait another minute to show off his loot. Bard ran after, hard put to catch up with the old man. Davey's plunder room, as he called it, was entranced by a double door without latch or lock, secured with a heavy oaken bar. Apparently, the doors didn't open often; there were no traces on the ground before them to mark their swing. Davey brushed off his feet with his hand, replaced his sandals, then heaved at the bar.

He seemed to have some difficulty lifting it, wheezed, "Pilgrim, help me out here." Bard put his shoulder under it and pushed, momentarily recalling the door on the gray man's corn crib. The bar gave before their combined force, and Davey lifted it and propped it vertically against the log wall. Then he threw open both sides of the door, pushed them back and around until their bottoms ground in the dirt, and vanished inside.

Bard looked after him. It was pitch black past the opening. Davey called, "Don't lag about, Pilgrim. Come on in." Somewhat hesitantly, Bard followed his direction, heard Davey speak a word that would have tangled his tongue had he tried to repeat it, and suddenly the interior was flooded with light from a row of clerestory windows in the roof. A loop of rope hung down from an opening contrivance mounted among the rafters, and swung like a pendulum in front of Davey's face. "Instant Light, Pilgrim," he exclaimed gleefully, "Now be that not magic?"

On at least one occasion, someone whose opinion he respected had told Bard there was no future to believing in magic. "You pulled on that rope,"

"It was a magic rope then," answered Davey, issuing gales of laughter to express his delight at his own jest.

Having never seen the inside of a Trader's kura, Bard was unnervingly disoriented for a moment; the interior of the building appeared to him several times larger than the outside. Down the center end to end, ran a narrow aisle barely wide enough for two to walk abreast. Davey's plunder packed the rest of the room. Innumerable boxes and crates and stacks and bins piled on either side one upon another. Bags and baskets and instruments and implements for purposes known and unguessable hung from the rafters as numerous as stalactites in a limestone cavern.

Bard stared in wonderment, "Are you a Trader?"

"Not a Trader, Pilgrim; I'm just a Keeper." Davey winked, "Whatever The Trader doesn't carry off, I keep. There is a need for every good thing by and by, whether or not it is valued by minds that claim to know all worth knowing."

To Bard the room seemed a maze and a mess, but Davey went straight along it until midway in the building he dove without hesitation into a pile of what appeared to be castoff military uniforms, and after a moment of intense rummaging among them, emerged with a cackle, holding triumphantly over his head a canvas rucksack. He held it up in front of Bard. "Be not this just the thing, Pilgrim, for taking on the road with you? You'll need it if you are bent on going to see the Herb Woman."

Bard realized he was indeed bent on going to see the Herb Woman. What had begun as a vague notion when Davey told him she would know how to find the Weaver, had, since his dream of the morning, acquired an increasing sense of urgency, and now crouched in his mind, as hungry and insistent as a wolf.

"Slip into this, Pilgrim and let us see how she fits you." Bard shrugged his shoulders beneath the straps of the rucksack, and Davey adjusted them. "These need a bit of padding but I can fix that in a cat's nap."

Davey helped Bard loose himself from the straps, then thrust the rucksack into his arms, and a little farther on, turned to a tall tier of shelves on which scores of large unlabeled cardboard boxes stacked to twice his height. Davey ran his hand up the face of one of the stacks, paused, about mid-way up the stack, and jerked a box loose quickly enough that those on top settled to the ones below with scarcely a totter or a teeter. From the box, Davey shook out a short coat of some dark, tightly woven oiled fabric. It had a double closure of large close spaced buttons and a wide collar that could be turned up in back. Davey held the rucksack while Bard tried on the coat. The bottom hung just below his hips.

"That might be easier to run in than your poncho if you ever find yourself in a place when you'd rather be somewhere else," Davey advised. The coat did not rest heavy on him, but was lined with a fleece that felt and smelt like wool, and Bard was warm in it as they stood in the closed space. Davey pointed toward the door and they started to leave. The old man paused once more and fetched a smaller box from what appeared to be a random pile, and said to Bard with another of his spontaneous giggles, "Ganny these will keep your feet, but we'll try them to be sure when we get to the house. Sandals won't do for sojourning over the countryside."

Davey grabbed hold of the rope as they passed by, swung himself off his feet from it, and the room went black with a clatter and a thump. Bard scurried for the light ahead and Davey popped out the door right behind him, swung the doors together and dropped the bar in place with a howl and a jig. "Be not the prospect of travel stimulating, Pilgrim?" He posed the question in an anticipatory tone as if he himself intended immediately to vacate to far and exotic lands.

Sitting on the deck, they found the shoes fit as if they had been sized and measured, and Davey fetched his sewing kit and a large scrap of heavy canvas he had on hand, cut and folded it over itself until he judged it thick enough, and began making padding for the straps of Bard's rucksack.

"Don't you think you might need these things sometime, Davey?" Bard felt guilty to be the recipient of so much of the Keeper's fine plunder.

"Pilgrim, the next time I wander from these woods, I'll travel light. All this gear would just weigh on me and tire me out."

They sat on the deck and talked about bears and squirrels until Davey finished his sewing project, then they went in. Bard put down his rucksack and sandals inside the door. He hung his new coat on a peg in the wall beside Davey's. He still had his new shoes on his feet.

Davey said over his shoulder, as he retrieved last night's leftovers from the windless, "Pilgrim, go up and look in the top drawer of the chest, and find yourself a pair of socks." Bard scrambled up the ladder, found the drawer full of wool socks, fine and soft. He pulled on a pair which almost reached his knees, but seemed to him a perfect size, and when he replaced his boots and laced them, they fit snug without being tight, and felt as if he had worn them for a season. His drawing still lay on the bed where he left it. If Davey had seen it, he had offered no comment.

When Bard came back down the ladder, he found Davey setting out their late lunch, now almost midway into the afternoon. Davey had taken the last of the bread and made sandwiches of eggplant and some of the vegetables left from their birthday supper. He smeared on the bread something yellow and tart out of a small jar from his shelf, instructed Bard to fill their cups from one of the water buckets, then as an afterthought, took a tomato from the window sill, sliced it, and added a slice to each of their sandwiches.

They sat to table then. Davey gazed expectantly at Bard until he recalled Mary's preamble to eating, and said, as if they were his own words, "We receive unworthily." The simple confession, he discovered, did become his own the moment he opened his heart and mouth to speak it.

They were hungry, and the sandwiches disappeared without much distraction or conversation. As they finished, Davey grinned at Bard from across the table, "Now twar that not tasty, Pilgrim?"

Bard washed their plates and cups while Davey sorted through their supper leavings to see what might be salvaged for yet another meal, and added what couldn't be saved to a covered bucket he kept to compost his garden. All at once, Davey giggled, and looking surprised, declared as if some angel had visited him a revelation, "Let us now perambulate." He seemed very pleased at making his pilgrim laugh out loud.

A few leaves fell around them as they walked through Davey's Wood. The gold and red among the maples and the oaks had broadened and deepened. All through the day, now and again Davey seemed preoccupied. The Keeper's laugh came as ready as ever, but the old man seemed watchful, as if listening for some summons that only his ears were tuned to hear. Bard thought perhaps it was because he was leaving. Davey obviously felt quite fond of him. Although Bard had never voiced a solid intention, they both spoke of his departure now as imminent and inevitable. Bard knew in his mind, and he was sure that Davey knew the time had come for him to go.

#

Their perambulations led them first out along the road to

143

a place where the ridge fell away steeply toward the south into smoke and shadows. Somewhere down there, Bard thought, lurked the gray man and his murderous little daughter. Beyond the dark valley rose a long steep of ridges higher than the one they stood on now. Davey pointed, "Those are the High Balsam, Pilgrim. I haven't been over there since I was a boy. Yonderside the Balsam runs the Long Broad, the heart's blood of Laurel. You must have crossed it on Charon's ferry, or you wouldn't have had Callie's soap to gift me with. Down below us there is the Dismal. The Grays, people brought over from Shadow, usually be sent to settle down there until they get adjusted to the Laurel. Some of them never quite do, and have to be taken back."

Davey pointed up the road. As they walked, it had been turning more east than north, "The Herb woman lives about two day's walk from here. She can tell you probably more than you ever wanted to know about the Weaver. When you get to Standing Stone, it will be best for you to overnight there. It is a fairy place and none but their sort will beset you while you rest there."

"Do fairies really live there?" Bard wasn't sure if he was quite ready yet to believe in fairies, but he had always been fond of the notion they might exist.

"Some say they once thronged the whole of Laurel," Davey answered, "but few alive now would claim to have seen one. For sure then, souls out of our time stood the Stone there. It was likely fairies as any. Who but fairies would go to so much trouble to make something that serves no purpose but to draw the eye? If you go there, you will see for yourself. You can read their lines in the rocks around the place."

As they left the road to return home through Davey's

woods, Bard saw black clouds banking up over the High Balsam, and heard far and away the faint rumblings of thunder as lightning flickered and played in the lowering sky.

Davey seemed to maintain an intimate personal friendship with every stone and flower and tree they passed on their circuitous meander back to the house. They loitered as much as they walked, while Davey named to Bard every flower they met, greeted each creature who crossed their path as politely and graciously as one would the parson out for a Sunday stroll, complimented the birds on their singing, and seemingly took perverse pleasure even in the assaults and predations of the hordes of tiny gnats and flies that swarmed them whenever they passed through a shadow.

Once, as they walked, Mad Davey burst into singing, at the limits of his cracked and quavering voice, a scrap of some old song of uncertain origin. It may have actually owned to a tune, which, during the course of his performance, Davey seemed once or twice on the verge of finding:

There is a place I've never been
Though I have lived there all my life,
There is a land I've never seen
More dear to me than kin or wife,
And I will go there now to stay
And I will travel night and day,
I will not stop along the way
Until I rest on home's sweet clay.

He seemed about to launch into another verse of it, and Bard wished he would, but Davey was distracted by the sight of a gnarled and twisted old holly tree ahead. Broad of bole and sparsely limbed, she appeared to have been broken by wind or perhaps struck by lightning sometime early in her long life. Davey rushed forward and threw himself upon her trunk and cried, "Dear Holly, I have loved you long, and last you will watch the woods alone!" Then he stood back and raised his hands wide above him and recited to the tree some words in a language Bard did not know, that had the music and flow of a poem.

At length, Davey could bear to part himself from his beloved Holly, and as they continued on, the boy asked the Keeper, "Do you talk to trees much?"

"Frequently," answered Davey with his normal good cheer. "Usually there's nobody else up here to talk to, and trees are the best listeners; they never interrupt."

"Do they talk back to you?" queried Bard with youthful skepticism.

"They talk constantly," Davey affirmed, "But the speech of trees is exceeding slow. It may take one of them a week to get out a single word, and a year to voice a sentence. A conversation with a tree can use up your whole life and never be finished."

As they went, Davey would stop and pull from his belt an old knife that had not held a cutting edge in half a forever, but which he used like a little spade to unearth various edibles along their path. By the time they reached Davey's clearing and followed the long shadows across the yard toward the house, the pockets of their jackets were bulging with roots and bulbs and tubors and shoots, of which each and every one as they came upon it, Davey informed Bard was the choicest, tastiest manifestation of vegitude in all of Laurel. Anyone who spent three days in Davey's company would suspect that Nature had determined to arrange herself primarily for Mad Davey's care and keeping, and as for his part, Davey did his best to return the blessing.

They took their turns at the privy and came in. Davey told Bard to leave the acorn basket by the steps, "Leave 'er there, Pilgrim," he said, without explanation. Davey asked him to stir up the coals and kindle a fire in the cookstove, and as it built, began washing and peeling and slicing their gleanings from the day. When the stove was hot, he set a pot with water upon it, stirred in a generous pinch of salt, and some spices, and dumped in the vegetables. He stirred it a bit, sniffed at the spoon, then diced a couple of small onions, which he added to the pot and threw in a handful of corn meal. When the broth began to steam, he fetched out a big spoonful, tasted it, smacked his lips with satisfaction, and put the lid on to simmer. While their stew cooked, he made up a cornbread batter, pouring it into a hot pan of melted butter, and set it into the oven to bake.

Then he turned to Bard and said, "Pilgrim, fetch your pack."

Davey patted the table with his hand and Bard brought his rucksack and set it before him. The pack divided vertically into two equal compartments which opened at the top and closed with a flap secured by two leather straps. Smaller pockets opened down the sides and on the front. Two straps at the bottom would serve to secure Bard's rolled blanket.

Davey dashed up the ladder and clothes began accumulating in a pile at the bottom. When he had followed them down the ladder, he sorted through them and pulled out two pair of canvas trousers, a set of suspenders, two sets of woolen drawers, several pair of the long wool socks, a couple of shirts, and Bards's own clothes, now washed and mended. Bard's old shoes, he held up appraisingly, before dropping them without comment into the compost bucket.

"Now, Pilgrim, watch and learn." Neatly, Davey folded each of the items he had selected, along with the coat from the kura and laid them snug together, inside the rucksack. He set atop the clothes a jar of his wondrous ointment, "Use this as often as you need, but not overmuch."

In the smaller pockets he stuffed packages of dried figs, a wrapper of hard biscuits, some nuts of various kinds, several apples, and a bag of raisins. Finally, Davey took his old knife from his belt and put it in, "Not much, unless you need to have it."

Bard brought his blanket roll and staff, Davey strapped the blanket roll on the bottom of the pack, and held it up. "Let's see how she rides on you, Pilgrim," and Bard slid his arms through the straps and let the load settle upon him.

His pack weighed heavier than he expected, but the padding Davey had added to the straps kept them from cutting into his thin shoulders. Davey slipped his fingers beneath the straps and approved, "It won't pain you, but you'll be glad to have your stick to lean on," and helped Bard ease out from under his burden. From one of the baskets overhead, Davey pulled out a large gourd stoppered with a wooden peg. The strap attached to it would reach across a shoulder. He filled the gourd with water from one of the buckets, replaced the stopper, and handed it over. "Don't wait until it's empty before you look for a place to fill it."

Then they settled to the table. Davey ladled out their stew, unpanned the cornbread and set it on a plate between their places. Bard filled two cups with water and brought spoons, and they ate heartily and gratefully. As they ate they talked about many things inconsequential, evading any reference to Bard's departure.

Finally Bard brought up the matter troubling him, "Davey, is it all right if I sleep out on the deck tonight? I want to rest close to the ground." He didn't want to say goodbye. He was afraid he might cry.

"Sure then you can, Pilgrim," Davey assented; "An old man needs his bed."

When they had eaten their fill, Bard dried the plates and cups as Davey washed. Davey covered the stew and left the pot on the table. Then he added some wood to the fire and brought the kettle to a boil, and made them each a cup of the spicy milked tea. They went out on the deck and sat with their feet over the edge watching the fireflies above the spring. Neither of them had inclination to speak. A long silence fell between them for the first time since Bard came to Mad Davey's house, an easy stillness in which their hearts spoke more clearly to one another than tongue is ever capable of.

At length, the dark deepened and the air began to chill. Davey reached up, grabbed the railing and hauled himself to his feet. His knees creaked audibly.

He rested his hand for a second on Bard's head, "Goodnight, Pilgrim," and went into the house. A moment later as the boy got up to follow, Davey's head popped out the door again, "One more thing, Son." Bard noticed Davey did not address him as *Pilgrim*. "Answer to no name they call you until you find your own."

"Where do I find it?" It was a sincere question.

Davey stepped back onto the deck, slapped the boy's chest with the flat of his hand perhaps a little harder than was friendly. In the distance, Bard heard the thunder of the gathering storm over High Balsam. "Right there, son. It is already in you."

Mad Davey placed a hand either side of Bard's face, bent and kissed him on the forehead, stood back and looked at him for a moment with that crooked smile, the old blue eyes krinkled all about and luminous with moisture. Without another word Davey went in and climbed the ladder to his bed.

Bard sat alone at the table, conflicted and confused. For the first time since he had come to the Laurel, he was about to leave a place where he wanted with all his heart to stay. He unstrapped his blanket roll, removed his bowl and stowed it in his rucksack, where he thought it would be safer kept. He rolled up the blanket again, but did not secure it. It would serve him for whatever sleep he had this night. He wondered if there were room in his pack for his sandals, but decided against it. He had taken overmuch from Davey without, he thought. When Davey's light above extinguished, Bard snuffed the candles on the table and windowsill, and as quietly as he could, carried his gear out onto the Deck. He rolled himself into his blanket and rested his head upon his pack. He held Mary's staff across his chest for comfort. He counted the stars until he slept, and woke again before dawn from another dream about Owl and his bear. All he could recall of it upon waking was that Owl had said again. "Go Now."

He went. He pulled on his hat, laced up his new shoes, rolled his blanket and buckled it to the rucksack, struggled into the unaccustomed burden, slipped the strap of his drinking gourd across his shoulder and over his head. He had to take off his hat momentarily to accomplish this maneuver. He went to the stair, dropped his staff to the ground below, and facing the deck with both hands on the rails, climbed down cautiously with his load, which tended to pull him away from the treads with each descending step. He picked up the staff and crossed the yard. Clouds were gathering, but the waxing moon gave enough light to find the path out to the road. To his right, far away, he could see just above the mountain the first paling of the dark that announced the new day. He began walking up the road, north by east. He slid his hand into his shirt to touch his medicine bag; he had forgotten it was empty now. Then, at last, he cried for lost love and home.

#

"Amos, I hear you have something for me."

The potter set out on his table an object a little larger than a man's fist, covered with a chamois. He unwrapped it to reveal a small bowl, glazed on the inside with a design of twined ivy. The Rider reached out and ran his fingers around the rim.

"You've mended well, Rider," observed Amos.

"It doesn't take long," the Rider answered. His hand still throbbed off and on, but thanks to Millicent's powers, the wound had healed. The Rider lifted the bowl, studied it closely for a few moments, then breathed into it and watched the ivy transmute into a silvered labyrinth, intricate past description, that traversed the inner face of the bowl, just below the edge.

"You did good, Amos," he testified, and took several dark coins from his vest pocket and laid them on the table.

"You can pay me when you get back." Amos offered.

"This trip may take me the long way round; best take your money now if you want to spend it." The Rider wrapped the bowl again in the chamois and dropped it

into the big pocket of his longcoat, and turned for the door
    "When are you leaving?" Amos called after him.
    Without breaking his stride, "I leave with the sun."
    "We'll miss you."

STANDING STONE

Morning came under a sunless, ashen sky, dim ahead and darker behind. Scraps of mist and cloud glided across the road, like ghosts lost in time. Bard felt the chill even through Davey's canvas jacket. He thought about getting out his coat, finally opted for the poncho, as mist began tending toward a fine rain. The poncho did not fit as easily over his rucksack, but once settled into it, he felt immediately warmer.

He walked; that was as much as he could say. He had no plan, no real goal, other than chasing after a name he heard in a dream. Tonight, if the road proved kind, he would sleep at Standing Stone. Tomorrow, he might or might not find the Herb Woman, who according to Davey, could tell him where to find the Weaver. What then? Why was he hiking alone in the damp when he could have stayed with Davey and been welcome? It made no sense. Everything in the Laurel, he thought, was strange and wondrous and powerful and made no sense at all.

Leaves skittered and scattered around his feet and away up the road as the wind rose at his back. Overcast and fogs muted the colors in the trees around. He could see the bare tops of poplars along the road. Bard had spent scarcely a week in the Laurel, and from the look of the land, a month might have passed. He walked high above the river and its valley now, to be sure, but it seemed to him that seasons in the Laurel birthed not in the slant and turn of the world, but that weather here manifest of some inner spiritual climate. The souls of Laurel, two-legged and four legged, lived out their summer lives, and whenever they finished, it was autumn.

Bard came round a bend to see a bear, darker and larger than the bear of his dreams, standing in the road ahead of him. She was fat with mast, no doubt headed soon for her winter den. Boy and Bear stood motionless for a time, watching one another warily. Finally, she raised her nose and swiveled her head, tasting his scent, then crossed the road and moved away among the trees.

Bard spoke aloud, to himself more than to the bear, "The difference between us, Bear, is that you know where you are going."

The road wound out along the crest of the ridge ahead, sometimes dipping to traverse a gap, sometimes dropping below the ridgeline to follow stable ground. Bard went with the road. He had food if he was hungry. He had water should he be thirsty. He had warm clothes and a means to stay relatively dry. He was getting used to the load and balance of his pack, leaning into his walk to keep his legs and hips under the weight he carried. He had begun to feel the music of walking with a burden. Most importantly, his shoes fit. He was as happy as any boy could be who believes he has just seen his best friend for the last time, and is afoot and alone in a place he does not know.

Unconsciously he measured his progress with the swing of his staff. Each time he planted the end of it upon the earth, he had traveled a distance approximate to his own height. Mile by mile the road tended gradually to his right, until the North Track, as Davey had called it, was closer to becoming the east track. It was not quite a road, though with care and caution a wagon could be brought along it. In places, however, it had eroded considerably, and small boulders the size of melons thrust up out of the ground, and would have rendered wheels a liability. In fact, Bard saw no trace of wheels along the track. Whatever humans trafficked this road went afoot, or rode or led their mounts and pack animals.

Sometime after mid-morning, his stomach reminded Bard he had missed his breakfast. The trees along the way provided ample shade and he had no difficulty finding beside the road a stone outcrop sizable for sitting. He shrugged out of his rucksack and from one of its numerous pockets, took out some of the dried figs Davey had packed and ate them slowly, magnifying their sweetness with occasional sips of water from his gourd. He bit into one of Davey's biscuits, and was fortunate to retain all his teeth. He thought he might try another for supper, if he had time to soak it a bit in some water.

Two crows sat in the broken stub of a pine just across the road. Bard broke off a small piece of his biscuit and tossed it into the middle of the road. He sat still as a stone upon a stone until one of the crows flew down, pecked tentatively at the crumb, and swallowed it down. Bard thought there might be some advantage in not having to chew one's food. The crow sat there, waiting with some expectation. Bard threw out another piece of his biscuit. The crow took it and flew back to the pine, where it perched beside the other crow and stuffed the biscuit down it's gullet as if it were a chick. The lower portion of the recipient's beak had been broken away. It was incapable of feeding itself. Watching, Bard recalled his encounter with Hawk as he was leaving the Gap. Without trying to put it to words, he acknowledged within himself that while death comes eventually and surely to all, without help and mercy, it comes much sooner.

He ate. He drank. Not what and all he might have chosen in fatter times, but enough to sustain him on his way. He doubted he was half the distance to Standing Stone yet. As the drizzle abated for a bit, and the sun finally burned through the fog ahead, he judged there was not much left of the morning. He shouldered his pack, looked to bid good day to the crows, but they had flown. He swung out his staff ahead of him and stepped off into the road again.

Bard had hardly fallen back into the rhythm of his going when he heard from somewhere up ahead the sound of horses, running hard. He stopped and looked along the road to where it veered sharply beyond a steep and stony bank, saw two horsemen, leaning low over their mounts, caps pulled down tight on their heads, their tunics as green as the pines they ran beneath. They raced one behind the other, as fast as their animals could be urged to carry them.

Bard raised his staff over his head, attempting to wave them down, thinking to ask directions, or if they were from Beaverdam as Davey had said, perhaps even send word to Robberlee that he was safe and well. The lead rider yelled at him as they bore down, but their pace never slackened. Bard thought that if he had not jumped out of their way, they would have ridden right over him and never looked back.

#

The Rider left Millicent at the edge of the Circle and came to stand before the Chestnut at the center. He removed the glove from his right hand and raised his fist above him. He spoke softly, "Callie, please talk to me."

Callie stepped from the tree, or more precisely, flowed from it until she was fully present. "We must be quick about this; I'm having a busy day."

"I need you to tell me about the boy, Callie."

"Rider, I know your heart is honest, as far as your mind will allow it to be. I knew you for a true soul the day you brought Liza to us, but you know I cannot tell you anything that might alter your way. You will find your boy in proper time as you must, but consider carefully that he may not be when you think."

"And that is as much as you will tell me?"

"I've told you more than is proper already. Now excuse me, I have souls to feed." Then there was only the Rider and the Tree together in the circle.

The Circle marked a Locus, a place that gathers power, so traces of passage lingered longer there, faded more slowly before time and weather than in ordinary landscapes. The Rider walked around the Circle deliberately, pausing often, confirming his observations from his previous visit. He identified and placed each of the Council members. The boy had entered from the south, left toward the east, down into the Dismal. He and Callie had sat either side of the North Track, the pack trail that wound northerly from the circle to merge with the Courier Road from Beaverdam, then gradually bore eastward through Davey's Wood until it ended away up at the Abbey on the side of the Alone. If the boy climbed the mountain straight up above Jude's place, he would have come to this same road eventually. Farther along that road, at the old abbey, dwelt the Seer. Of course, the Rider thought, Owl would have to be in this somewhere. The old monk had his finger in every pot that boiled in Laurel.

I am sometimes slow to lay hold of the obvious, the Rider told himself. Maybe the boy knew a lot more about Laurel than Robberlee had thought. The Rider raised his hand. Millicent came to him and they took the way north. Not long after they left the Circle, the Courier Road from Beaverdam joined the track on their left. There was no scent of the boy as they went, but the Rider was certain that somewhere not far ahead, there would be.

#

Except for the Couriers, Bard met not a single human presence as he traversed the afternoon. The road reached out before him, winding and turning with the flow of the ridge, dipping and twisting and rising again, tending generally higher and toward the east. Occasionally, as the track crested the ridgeline, he could catch a glimpse of the Dismal and the High Balsam to his right, or to left a range of dark mountains even higher, that tumbled up and away, one upon another, to the horizon, where all dimmed into Shadow.

As the sun lowered to west above Davey's Wood, Bard began to feel the weight of his full rucksack. His calves smarted at the unaccustomed stress, and he longed to walk unburdened as he had with Davey in his woods. He was glad he was not climbing up from the gray man's valley today. The sky ahead shone clear and blue, but behind and to south, grew ever darker, as the storm moved north and east over the Dismal, as if in pursuit. Thunder rumbled frequent and louder now. Bard figured the storm would overtake him by nightfall. He picked up his pace. He meant to reach Standing Stone, and hopefully, some sort of shelter for himself, before dark. He had no desire to spend a night in the open on a mountain in a storm. He chased his shadow along the road until the billowing cumulus occluded the sun. The air suddenly cooled, the wind picked up, and ahead, the eastern sky cast a golden light that purpled all the shades possessing the land around.

#

The Rider had just passed the fork with the Courier road when he met the Couriers making haste for Beaverdam, paired as they always rode, should one of them be somehow prevented. He stopped and raised his hand, and they reigned in their mounts before him. Yes, they said in answer to his question, they had seen a boy up on the Rising by Davey's Wood.

"Which way was he headed?

"We couldn't say, Rider. When we saw him, he was just standing in the road waving his stick at us. We don't stop for children."

"You should have stopped for this one," With that, the Rider moved past them up the track.

#

As Millicent and her Rider approached Davey's Wood, he sought some scent that would inform him where the boy came to the road. Although the Rider thought of it as scent, he did not track as animals do, by smell. The Rider was peculiarly attuned to all the souls around him and when he traversed a space, if any two or four legged had been there recently before him, he would have a sense of their passage. If they had left a clear and strong trace of presence, he could glean a fair idea of species, gender, emotional state, perhaps even a vague notion of physical appearance. He was not a psychic. He could not read thoughts and intention, but after years on the hunt, and his experiences of all manner of encounters with all nature and order of souls, he usually was able to venture a shrewd guess about these things as well.

They came all the way to Davey's Wood before the Rider felt any trace of the boy, then the trail was immediately hot. The boy had been all around here, for more than one day. The Rider thought probably he had come up by Davey's Wood, following the branch up from the Dismal by Jude's to Davey's house. Davey would certainly have known someone was in his woods, and likely taken him in. Davey, for all his claims to be a hermit, remained a lonely old man, always trolling for company. Possibly the boy was still with Davey. If not, the Rider determined he would by threat or promise find out where the boy was headed. Davey was inquisitive. Given a couple of days with the boy, he would know.

When they reached Mad Davey's clearing, the Rider left Millicent among the trees and stood in the yard before the house. "Davey, you have company."

After a moment, when Davey didn't materialize to hurl some mock invective at him, the Rider climbed the stair to the deck and went to the door, which was standing ajar, and looked inside. No one was in sight. He knocked on the jamb, "Old Man, are you to home?"

No response but thunder from the storm over the valley southward. The Rider looked up and saw black clouds boiling up over the trees. He went in. There was a pot sitting on the table. He removed a glove, lifted the lid from the pot and stuck his finger into the stew, then tasted. It was good, he thought, even though it had been cold since the night before. A bad feeling weighed upon his mind like a chill

"Davey, I'm coming up."

When he stepped off the ladder, he saw Davy lying on

his back on the bed, eyes closed, as if he were taking a nap. His right hand by his side was clutched into a fist and his left was across his chest, resting upon a sheet of his drawing paper. The Rider walked over to the bed and passed his hand over the old man's prostrate form twice, slowly, then a third time. He could sense no life at all. A soul had been there this very morning, he could tell, but resided no longer.

The Rider took off his other glove then, dropped the pair into the pocket of his duster, and gently pried open the fingers of Davey's right hand. He took the wee ball of tar soap, and held it to his nose. By the feel of it, he could tell the boy had held it, too, within a day or so. "Sooner or later, Callie touches everyone," He said to the walls. He tucked the soap into a pocket in his vest, and very gently laid Davey's hand back upon the bed. Then he lifted the left hand and drew the paper from beneath. Davey's shirt was slightly smudged with charcoal from the drawing the Rider saw when he turned the sheet over.

It was not one of Davey's drawings. The Rider judged it tentative, untaught, but not without aptitude. More than anything else, the drawing lacked experience. The strokes appeared often hesitant, false lines threading among the true. He would have seen the boy in the drawing even had he not felt in his own muscles the thrust and parry of the hand that made it. It was not a perfect likeness, but it was close enough that the Rider readily recognized Liza, with her fiddle tucked under her arm, her face lifted up, her mouth opened as if in a song, and her eyes closed as if in prayer. Across the bottom of the drawing, printed large and square as a boy would, *I LOVE YOU.* The Rider smiled in spite of himself. *Innocent youth,* he thought. Only later did it occur to him that the boy had addressed his inscription not to his subject but to his mentor.

With tenderness amounting to lovingness, The Rider replaced the drawing face down as he had found it, and laid Davey's hand across it. Before he turned to go, he bent over the bed and kissed the cold forehead. Riders do not cry, of course, but when he had gone down the ladder, there remained a drop of moisture on the Keeper's furrowed brow.

The Rider left the house, closing the door behind him. Millicent came to him, and he pulled the fairybowl from his bag, unwrapped it and took it to stand before the house and ponder his purpose. He had not intended to use the bowl for this, but he knew that if he had been found lying cold upon his bed, Davey would have done the same for him.

The Rider did not allow the urgency of his mission to hurry him. He took the bowl down to the spring, strode through the pool, and held it under the springhead until it was full. When he came back to the house, he stood beneath it, between the split faces of the boulder there, and held the bowl to his chest as he drew his rivener from its scabbard and raised it above him, pointing heavenward, it's tip almost touching the floor joists of the house above.

Without speaking an audible word, he breathed into his bowl, tuned his heart, his mind, his spirit, his whole body to one soul's plea, and called down heaven's fire upon Davey's house.

Had he not closed his eyes, the flash of searing light and heat that followed would have blinded him. He felt it even before the concussion of blue sound that made the Rider and the earth beneath him flinch and tremble. The whole roof of Davey's house blossomed into a great flaming flower. The rider saw sparks and brands falling all around him across the yard.

As the flames took the house, He went to Millicent and returned the dry bowl to its place. They would wait there until the rains came. Davey would not be pleased with him if he burned down the woods. And before they left, he would use the bowl for its intended purpose, and try to take a sighting on the boy.

They found a place among the trees to wait, and the Rider watched Mad Davey's house returning to earth. Flames wrote their eulogy against the dark, and smoke rose in billows and streams that seemed to take on forms as they ascended, hawks and bears and ravens and wolves and multitudes of fantastical nameless and unknown creatures, and a few human faces among them all.

#

The oncoming storm robbed Bard of the last sunlight of the day, and he began to wonder in the premature dusk if he had somehow missed Standing Stone. He felt certain he had put in a good day's walk, even by a man's measure. Then he saw right of the road ahead, a square wood post about twice his height, with a single wide groove cut around it about a foot from the top, obviously a way marker of some sort, and he breathed a prayer that it marked a way he wanted to go now. A foot path before the marker, led from the road in a descending curve through a wood, mostly hemlock, densely carpeted with ferns of several kinds. The trees there descended from regrowth of a primeval forest that flourished on the Rising before the Separation. Through the foliage, the sky still glowed a pale cerulean. A few fireflies ventured forth among the trees, and there seemed to issue from the whole place around a subtle luminescence, not so much a light to be seen, but a sightedness nonetheless, whereby every tree and fern and stone stood clear and revealed in the twilight.

As the path dropped away and below the road, the flank of the ridge manifest itself in a broad overhanging bluff of schist, riddled with fractures and seeps from which water dripped continually, echoing as in a cave. In several places, the face of the stone had fragmented, and fallen debris lay in heaps below, though none of the rockfalls appeared recent. Water from the various seeps pooled in depressions about the stone beneath, and coursed in rivulets down among the ferns to a little brook that skirted the base of the Standing Stone.

The Stone, as Bard stepped near, loomed as black as a raven's feather, and even in the dim light, sparkled with a multitude of tiny quartz crystals embedded in its matrix. He had seen such stone in the Gap. Mary referred to the gleaming specks of quartz as "fairy dust." No mark of artifice was visible upon the Stone. Moss and lichens encrusted its pitted and fissured surface. In a few places along its side, wee ferns had found purchase and sustenance. The stone was as broad at the base as Bard's outstretched arms, and tapered fairly evenly to about three times his height. He could have sat comfortably upon its blunt top, where several more ferns and a tiny hemlock seedling bore their mute witness to the continuance of Creation.

The stone's very stillness and solidity testified of its ancient origins. It was older than the mountain where it resided. Instinctively, Bard took off his hat as he stood before it, watching and listening for whatever revelation the Stone might bestow. A numinous awe settled upon him, as if he were facing a high and holy altar.

As he stood communing with the Standing Stone, his most immediate revelation was that it was getting dark around him. Then a flash of light above and a rattling rumble of thunder, loud and near, declared he was about to be wet upon. He stepped across the little brook and went up under the bluff where he found a dry spot and disengaged himself from his rucksack. Ice from some past winter had been kind to leave behind for him a number of broken limbs and branches from the trees overgrowing the bluff, that now littered about among the ferns around, and Bard was able quickly to accumulate enough of them that he thought he could fuel his fire for the night. Most of the branches were small enough to be broken in hand, and the larger limbs, he would lay to end in his fire once it established, and feed them to the flames as they were consumed. He still had seven matches in his canister to light his fire.

When he judged he had gathered enough fuel for the night, Bard cupped his hands beneath one of the more generous of the numerous dripping seeps and tasted. He detected no sign of stain or sediment in the water; it drank sweet and clear. He took his bowl from the rucksack and set it down on the stone beneath the flow. In less than an hour, he gauged, it would be full. He would have water tonight to drink and refill his gourd, which, sadly, did not seem to possess the same capacity for replenishment as his lost bottle. He unstrapped his blanket from the rucksack and rolled it out on the stone. He had found a space dry and clear, far enough back under the lip of the bluff to keep him sheltered in a steady rain, although if there came a blowing wind from the south, he might need to cover with his poncho to avoid being damped upon.

Bard found among his stash of deadwood, several

small cedar limbs. He stripped their bark, made a little heap of it, and above that a teepee of twigs and small sticks. He broke up some of the larger branches in his pile to add later. Then he took one of his matches from the canister, and as the first big drops of rain began to set the ferns out in the wood bobbing and waving, he lit the tinder. It caught immediately. He still had six matches. Vigilantly he watched and tended the life of his flame, and soon he had a moderate fire that offered him heat as well as light. Rain rattled louder in the trees, and began running steadily off the edge of the bluff above, weaving a liquid curtain between boy and night. Bard sat almost as snug as in Davey's upper room, unfolded his little square of oily paper, set it before him on the stone, and put upon it some of Davey's dried figs, supplemented them from a little bag of raisins Davey had packed for him, and began to crack the last of his chestnuts. The shells he used to encourage his fire. The nuts joined the figs and raisins to become his supper.

He ate with deliberate slowness, tasting and savoring not only the flavor of his food, but also the memories they evoked. In this potent place, the Council at Circle began to seem again a plausibility beyond a mere fantasy generated by illness and fatigue. He drank from his gourd, which, when he shook it now, felt light in his hand, sounded almost empty. He checked his bowl. It was about half full. Shortly he could refill his gourd. He broke up more of his firewood into handy lengths and added several sticks to his fire. He walked out to stand just shy of the runoff falling from the slope above and peered out into the rainy dark. For an instant, a flash of lightning limned the wood like day. He thought he glimpsed the Three, standing apart along the path past the brook, beyond the Stone. He waited for the next flash to verify his vision, but when it came, followed by a crash and extended echo of thunder, they were gone, if ever they had been there at all.

The storm generated more electricity than wind. Bard stayed dry behind his watery veil, and probably felt safer than his situation justified. He enjoyed the intense fireworks on high. He was a tired boy, though. Drowsy and fed, he lay back on his blanket and watched the play of firelight and shadow on the sparkled schist that sloped upward above him.

Then he saw it, and though he remembered what Mary had told him in that other world, whispered to the fire, "Magic."

The flames lighting the bluff from below revealed that not all the grooves and cracks that crazed the stone were natural. They had been augmented and elaborated by some ancient sculptor's hand and tools into a fantastic arabesque that covered the whole face of the arching rock above. Parts of the design had been erased where stone had flaked and fallen away, but most of the pattern was still discernible, and Bard saw illumined there the same swirls and twinings and overlappings that wound around the inside of his bowl.

He went and fetched it, by now nearly full, and put it down beside his blanket, then sat down again cross-legged, and reached behind him and seized his gourd, intending to fill it. He unstoppered it, held it before him, and was about to pick up the bowl when he saw reflected in the water the lines inscribed in the stone overhead. In the flickering light from the fire, the lines appeared to be moving. He set down the gourd, lifted the bowl in both hands close to his face and blew into it to see what effect the rippling of the water would have on the illusion. An intense blue light flared up around him, blinding him for a moment. When he could see again, the lines reflected in the water glowed and pulsed with what appeared to be blue flame. He looked up and saw the carvings overhead indeed ran with streams of living fire writhing and twisting along the incised maze in a continuous and accelerating flow.

As he watched, small streamers of flame began to dance and weave out of the stone into the air around. They drew broader and more numerous attenuations after them until the boy was enclosed by an undulating labyrinth of azure luminescence that rotated about him as it extended itself upward. As it grew, it gathered speed, tightened the strands of its weaving, drawing in until it held only Bard and his fire at the center, with the flaming torus rotating and expanding all around. Beyond the shining strands, he could see nothing but darkness. No trees, no Stone, no overreaching bluff, only the spinning labyrinth that rose higher and higher until all he could see through the open axis above him, far and away, were stars.

#

When rain did come, by which time Davey's house had been reduced to a bed of glowing coals, it came in torrents, punctuated by livid displays of lightning and mind-numbing percussions of thunder. During the storm, the Rider kept proximity with Millicent. As long as they were meld, her aura shielded him from the elements. The rain fell upon them, but did not touch them, passing through vertices of space where they had just been present or were about to be. When the worst of the storm had passed over them, and the rain still falling steadily, the Rider parted from her and walked with his fairybowl away toward the still smoldering ashes of the house. What he did now, he had to do alone, fully present and open to the moment in which he breathed.

He set the bowl upon the ground and watched in the rain until it gathered enough water for his purpose, then he knelt down in the wet grass with his bowl before him, and breathed into it, took from his vest pocket the talisman he had been given from Mad Davey's own hand, the wee black ball of soap which the boy had cherished and carried close to heart, and dropped it into the bowl. The water rippled and cleared. He could see the child clearly, but not his face, which was turned up away from the bowl, as the boy watched, entranced, the pulsing streams of light dancing and turning above him. It was a heartbeat before the Rider understood what he was seeing. At the same instant, he saw light and shadow playing on the ground around him. He thought the fire from the house had flared up again, and looked up just as the labyrinthine torus, ashine and wheeling, descended around him. He held up his hand to call Millicent, but by then the Labyrinth had closed around him into a sphere. It hovered, turning and shimmering for a moment until it had him all, then imploded upon itself to a single dimensionless point of light, and winked into darkness.

#

Bard did not know if he breathed or not, or if his heart hammered within him, or beat not at all. There was no time, no sound, no sight but the turning web of light, and the glowing threads following their endless and untraceable weavings, drawn by a music too deep and far for any ear to hear. If he had thought, he might have been reminded of the light that tented the Council at Circle, but encircled by the Labyrinth, Bard possessed no thought or questioning or understanding. His only knowing then was that he was fully and totally known.

Eventually the light weaving about him began to pale and slow and before he was aware of it, the shining threads around him imperceptibly began curling back into the carved relief on the face of the bluff as the gyre steadily drew itself back into the mountain from which it had manifest.

The patterns fired across the rock flared and dimmed until they became merely chiseled grooves on the face of hard stone again, and Bard heard the rain beyond and realized his fire had almost extinguished. He added some wood, and as light returned, looked at his bowl. It was dry and empty, except for a wee round ball, black and shiny, like a pebble. He knew it wasn't a pebble. He reached out and took it and held it to his nose, and inhaled the piney scent of Callie's soap. Then, with great care and deliberation, he dropped it into his medicine bag, pulled the drawstring tight, folded both his hands around it, and slept.

#

With a soft groan, the old man hauled himself up from sleep, rested on his knees to steady his breathing, then lurched to his feet. Some troubling dream he could not quite remember tried to follow him out of the dark as he wrapped his blanket about his naked and aching shoulders and crossed the room to the firecradle, where he knelt again, and blew the coals to life, then added fuel to brew tea. When the water boiled, he poured it into a bowl, stirred in twigs from his medicine bag, and allowed it to steep and settle for a few breaths. When he lifted the bowl to drink, he was startled to see reflected in the greenish liquid, the shining tracery of the Labyrinth, endlessly turning. Within it he saw the flailing form of the Rider, falling down and around like a drowning man.

A hesitant tap softly rattled his door, which slid ever so slightly ajar. Without looking in, the woman whispered, "And how is it then with my brother?"

The spell dissipated. He sighed and answered, "It is no worse or better than it should be with this old Owl."

In the morning, he thought, he would send word to Beaverdam that their Rider was having difficulties.

#

Bard woke to cold. When he opened his eyes, the girl stood among the ferns beside the Standing Stone in the misty morning rain, peering up at his shelter as if she had been patiently waiting for him to awaken. He thought she must be soaked, and motioned for her to come into the dry. He added some twigs to the fire, which had almost burned out, and when they flared, he added some larger bits from his pile, then looked up to find her just opposite the fire from him, standing barefoot, wearing a simple shift the color of Davey's drawing paper, with a green band of ivy embroidered about the neck. Her hair flamed in a luxuriant aurora about her face. She watched silent and still, seemingly listening for him to speak.

At first glance, he thought her about his age. She stood near his height, but as he looked he could not decide if she were waif or woman, youth or ageless. A movement of the air about her head and shoulders made him feel that she must have wings that remained somehow not quite visible. She was the strangest girl he had ever seen, and maybe the prettiest, he thought. But the strangest thing about her was that she had left no damp tracks behind her on the stone. In fact, she seemed as dry and kempt as if she had been strolling through a sunny afternoon. He decided then that he did not know what sort of soul had come to company him, but he was sure that she must be chilled in her thin garment, for he was trembling himself. He picked up his jacket and held it out to her, "I have another in my pack."

"Clothes are ever burdensome," She said pleasantly, "If you were not a shy and tender boy, I would not have bothered even with this," and she looked down and took the hem of her shift and spread it wide as she turned about as if to invite his approval of her attire.

"Well, I'm cold," Bard confessed, as he added more wood to the fire and pulled his blanket up around his shoulders and tried to still his shivering. "I'm not about to go running around the woods naked in any weather," he added in testament to his good reason and sense of decency.

The girl seemed to think they had talked enough about nudity, and held out her hands, "The Mother said you would need these."

Her hands had been empty, Bard thought, although it was hard to follow them as she kept waving them around in front of her as she talked. But now she held them cupped together to lift toward him three eggs, each a different color. They looked just like the eggs he had eaten at Davey's. Bard held out his hands to her and she placed the eggs there, holding her fingers upon their tops until she was certain he had them in his grasp, then she stood back and smiled a child's broad and open smile, waiting for his response as the rain ceased and the woods brightened under thinning clouds.

"Thank you very much, but I don't have anything to cook them in."

"Why not eat them as they are?" Pulling a crooked

172

little stick from above her right ear where it had been hidden by her fiery locks, she tapped each of the eggs with the end of it, and said, "It would be a waste now to boil them twice, Don't you think?" So Drum put them in his bowl and cracked the shell of one and found it boiled just hard enough and when he had shelled it clean, he bit into it as he held the bowl out to the girl, who spread her hands up before her in a gesture of refusal, "I never eat eggs, don't you know."

"How did your mother know I was here?" Drum thought as he spoke that he had posed this question somewhere before, and wondered what sort of mother would send her girl out into the rain to breakfast some stranger boy.

"How would she not?" answered the girl, waving her stick wide in a sweeping gesture. She looked like she was directing an orchestra.

Drum wanted to laugh. "Do you always answer a question with another question?"

"If you can ask the proper question, you must already know the answer, don't you think?"

"I think you are a riddle, that's what I think."

"I'm just Mathilda," she said, "And I've brought these to bless you with." She knelt and held out her hand toward him in a fist, and opened her fingers to reveal ten tiny pebbles, the size of peas, the same colors as the eggs. She laid them one by one on the stone between them, then tapped each in turn with her crooked stick, as she sang in a voice just like the fiddler girl's:

One to call and one to keep,
One for waking, one for sleep,
One for light and one for dark,
One to wield and strike the spark,

One for joy and one to dare,
One to carry all your care,
Time to gather up each stone,
Bind them close and then, be gone.

She sat back on her heels and smiled at Bard her wise and innocent smile, and he reached out his right hand to touch the stones.

"Not yet," Mathilda cried sharply, and swatted the back of his hand with her stick. It was barely more than a twig and had she hit him hard with it, her stick would have broken, but it felt to Bard as if her little wand had passed through his flesh like a knife. He howled and cradled his stricken paw to his chest, and looked down at it to verify that Mathilda had left him a whole hand. A deep and painful burn seared across the back of it, dark as the Stone.

Bard looked up with tears streaming down his face to ask, *Why?* but she was gone. He found Davey's ointment in his rucksack, and applied it liberally. Within an hour his hand ceased hurting as if it had never been injured. But the mark was still there, dark as ever.

#

It wasn't pleasant within the Labyrinth, but neither was it dangerous. Getting in and getting out was the tricky part, the Rider thought. While inside the gyre, one did not age or hunger or thirst. Perhaps a soul did not exist there in any sense that embodied mortals could conceive. For the Labyrinth itself had no measure. It did not fill a space. It had no duration in time. It simply was, here and there, any time, any place and every place and no place at all. What the Rider perceived as strands of pulsing light manifest from attenuated vibrations that coursed unceasingly in and among and through each of the others, intersecting at one or another time and place within the Laurel, and perhaps within Shadow as well.

The Rider had not been snared by a manifestation of these strands, so much as he simply hadn't been able to get out of their way. If he thought of the passage of time as a book, and himself as the reader, he reasoned that one normally progressed through the story by reading word by word and page by page from start to end. The Labyrinth pierced the book like a knife, and depending on its thrust, might instantly touch any point within the narrative. It was more complicated than that, the Rider knew, but he had gleaned that image from Millicent's mind. Millicent, as much of the Labyrinth as of the Laurel, had often taken him through the gyre to whatever time or place in Laurel their hunt might lead.

Now the Labyrinth had drawn him in without her, not that he found himself helpless on his own. Each of the strands resonated with its connection to Laurel. Unless he had been greatly displaced, he could sort them in his mind and find one to follow back to the Rising. Failing that, Millicent would locate him soon and bring him back to his own place. He would not be here long, in any case. Not long to him, but chronology became irrelevant here. What seemed an hour to him in the Labyrinth, might be weeks or seasons in Laurel. He could not afford the delay. He had been careless, and this was his reward.

#

When the throbbing in his hand eased, Bard realized he was still hungry. He ate another of Mathilda's eggs and put the last in his rucksack to save for lunch. While doing that, he saw the apples Davey had packed for him and ate one of those. He thought Davey would have fed him apples for breakfast, but would have fried them and

175

sprinkled them with cinnamon and honey.

The seeps were more effusive after the long rain the night before, and he sat out his bowl and soon had filled it twice and refilled his gourd. He looked long at the stones Mathilda had left behind. Finally, he reached out a tentative fingertip to touch one of them. When it didn't bite, he took them one by one and dropped them into his medicine bag. Then he wrapped his bowl in his burlap sack, and folded up his little square of oiled paper one more time, and put them in his pack. He rolled his blanket, strapped it on, tightened the laces on his shoes, and thought he was about as ready for the road as he could be. The sun was already well up and the morning, breezy and cool, promised a good day for walking. Bard wanted to reach the Herb Woman's house before the sun went down again, or some mad fairy assaulted him with a twig. He hoisted the rucksack and pulled the straps around, laid his staff across his shoulder, and walked down through the ferns, stepped over the brook, and past the Stone. He turned to look back at it one last time, and with the sun behind it, the stone seemed as black before him as a midnight sky. The little quartz crystals embedded in its surface winked at him like stars. Gazing fixedly at the Stone, he felt as if he were about to fall through a door that opened somewhere out in the unmeasured space beyond the world. A feisty squirrel barked from a hemlock branch just above his head and broke the spell.

RISING

As quickly as he could climb with his pack, Bard followed the path back up to the way marker. He made to step out into the road when he recognized a sound by now familiar. He moved back under the trees, as two Couriers swept by, riding hard for Beaverdam. He wondered if they changed their mounts somewhere along their journey. At the pace they were running, any horse he knew about would have been dead along the road before the day was out. The Couriers, intent on their way, did not see him.

Bard walked, and the sun rose higher, though the wind at his back carried away the warmth. He had gone close to two miles when the sun in his eyes reminded him that he had forgotten his hat. He supposed Mathilda didn't wear hats, either.

The wind honed its edge on him. Not long after mid-morning, he stopped and swapped his canvas jacket for the heavier coat from Davey's plunder room. He took out the last of Mathilda's eggs and ate it as he walked on. Warmer now, he felt his muscles loosen and his stride lengthen and the next mile went by more quickly.

Bard wished he might meet someone he could ask for directions. Davey said two day's walk to the Herb Woman's place, but gave him no landmarks. He hoped he wouldn't miss it. Bard passed no houses by the road that morning, though he saw a few lesser tracks trailing off to one side or the other. None of them looked to have been much used of late. No more Couriers appeared. Bard was not sure what he should do if he met any. He guessed that if they rode down the Rising every morning, probably they came up from Beaverdown in the afternoon. So far, he had only observed them making their run down the ridge toward the Circle.

Bard was still pondering logistics when he saw atop the next rise ahead a figure leading a pack animal with a monumental load piled on its back and hanging down over its flanks. He thought that if the load were as heavy as its size might indicate, the poor beast underneath could scarcely have carried it. As Bard drew near the base of the rise, the figures ahead passed over the crest and disappeared down the other side. When he topped the hill, the man and his mule had started up the next one, but they were larger in his view, closer now. Apparently they felt no hurry, whatever their destination, for he gained on them with every step.

The track rose and fell with the ridge as they went along it, rising always the more. The trees grew smaller here, the wind sharper than at Davey's Wood. In the more open landscape, wildflowers rioted in abundance, although many of them had already begun to fade. The more tender plants along the way looked to have been touched by a light frost within the last night or so. Where the larger trees thinned, broad copses of corylus had sprung up along the road. Their remaining leaves shown gold in the sun, and the bearded pods of their nuts weighed down their branches. Bard finally caught up with his fellow travelers when the old man leading the mule stopped to forage. While the man was picking nuts from their husks as they hung, his mule was gobbling up as many of the fallen ones as could be got.

As Bard approached, man and mule quit their harvest and turned their heads to inspect the new arrival, who thought the old man, tall and thin, with his long coat down to his boot-tops and a flowing white beard that reached his belt buckle, looked like a wizard from a fairy tale. His wide-brimmed, high-crowned hat, he held inverted in his left arm. The hat was half filled with nuts.

He reached out as Bard came up by him and shook his hand with a grip that belied his apparent age. "Sure now you don't live up here. You must be Robberlee's Bard; He told us to keep an eye for you. He's been wondering if you had found or lost yourself by now."

"If you know Robberlee, could you tell him I'm all right and that I'm not lost yet?"

"Son, you can be sure I will do that very thing, as soon as I see Beaverdam again."

Bard looked at the mule under her mountain of boxes, bags, and hanging utensils. "Are you a Trader?"

"Officially I am a Trader emeritus; but not enough families live on the Rising any more to make it pay a living, so I wander off up here on my own now and again just for the aggravation. It beats sitting around Beaverdam all day, watching the grays and waiting for dark so I can go to bed. You look awfully young to be a bard."

"That's what people like to call me by. Mainly I'm just a boy."

"Well people who don't know better like to call me Aengus, and mainly I'm just old. I'm on my way up to the Abbey, with a stop or two along the way. Maybe we can side by for a spell; I would benefit from some human company. Molly Dear is a good listener, but she doesn't make for stimulating conversation." Aengus nodded at his mule as he said this last, paused before his question, "What are you doing up here in nowhere, Bard? I'd think a fine boy like you would find more to occupy his mind in town."

Aengus had been friendly and open, aside from talking overmuch, which Bard decided must be an occupational hazard for a Trader, but something inside made him reluctant to tell the old man any more about his quest than he could help. He didn't lie. "I'm going to see the Herb Woman. She's a friend of Mad Davey's and he said I should go by her place."

Aengus shed his jovial demeanor at that, looked deadly serious, even sorrowful. "You don't know, then?"

"Don't know what?"

"Davey's house got struck by lightning and burned down with him in it."

Bard turned away. Without his hat to hide his face, there was nothing to do but put his hand up over his eyes and cry. His time in Laurel had been a parade of discoveries and losses. This loss was permanent and irreversible. Davey's death left something of his own heart gone forever. He wept for that loss. He wept for love. He wept out of his grief. He wept out of guilt, for there was a part of him, deeper than his sadness, that was glad he was not in the flames with Davey.

Aengus reached out as if to touch the boy's shoulder, seemed to think better of it and dropped his hand. Finally, when Bard's shoulders no longer shook with his stifled sobs, Aengus asked, "Was he family?"

"Better than family. He was my friend."

They walked on in silence for a time, listening to the wind and the sound of their own breathing and their feet upon the road, the clunk and thud of Molly Dear's hooves and the creak and jingle of her load. Aengus could not allow silence to go unmolested for long however, "How long has it been since you saw Davey, Bard?"

"Two days ago, at his place. I spent last night at Standing Stone."

"Me and Molly Dear walked all night. Not everybody wants to be at the Stone come dark. Ganny that proved an interesting experience for you."

"It got my attention." Bard decided not to tell about the dancing lights. "A bad storm came in the night, and I saw a girl. She said her name was Mathilda. Do you know her folks?"

"I met Mathilda a long time ago, when I was not too much older than you, Bard. I haven't seen her since, but I keep looking. She's got no kin that I know of."

"Must have been somebody else; she's only a girl."

"She always was." Now it was the old man's turn to be silent, recalling what was gone, and could never be found again.

Morning became afternoon. Their shadows gained on them, then passed them. The wind blew. They walked. Finally, Bard spoke, as much to distract himself from his mourning as to satisfy a lingering curiosity. "I've seen the Couriers riding the road. The only times I've seen them pass, they were headed toward Beaverdam. When do they come this way?"

"They don't ride up the Rising every day, Bard. Once a week or so, ten or twelve of them will ride up to their station by the Abbey. That way, there's always somebody there to ride if the monk has something urgent to message."

"What about if there's an urgent message the other

way?"

"Ganny they would send somebody, I've never heard of it. Anything drastic happen in Laurel, old Owl would know about it already. He's a seer. Robberlee can't tell him much. He waits to be told."

"Robberlee?"

"Robberlee's the mayor in Beaverdam. He's president of the Traders Guild. He's into a little bit of everything. If Laurel had a governor, it would be Robberlee. But if we had a king, it would be Owl."

"I thought he was some kind of hermit, or something."

"That's what we tell the tourists, Bard."

The road switched about and dropped down into a small gap in the ridge. As they crossed the saddle, a wide path led off to the left among some scrubby oaks and birches. Aengus said, "There's a spring right down here. Molly Dear needs a good drink, and I'm in the way of a little rest and refreshment myself. Let's lighten our load for a wee spell."

The well-worn track brought them to the spring, obviously a regular stop for those hardy souls who traversed the Rising. The spring, sheltered in a clear space below the road and out of the wind, had been walled about with stone. A little brook meandered away through a small meadow, and off through the surrounding thicket of corylus and birch. The springhead fed a large stone basin just below for animals to drink from. Molly Dear had obviously been here before, and made straight for it when Aengus dropped her lead. The two humans cupped their hands into the spring and drank their thirst away, then filled their bottles and gourd and settled down in the grass with their backs to the low wall, to eat a late lunch, and soak up the heat the sun had stored in the stones.

Aengus brought a wrapper from one of Molly Dear's bulging bags and set it before them on the ground, unfolded it and laid the paper back to reveal some slices of dried apples and peaches, and a couple of ripe plums.

Bard contributed some of Davey's dried figs, and the last of his raisins. "Davey gave me these for the road," he informed Aengus, unable to suppress the tremor of emotion in his voice.

From among Molly Dear's burdens, Aengus fetched a couple of cups and a bottle and poured them each a drink of golden apple cider, cloudy with lies. "Didn't trade for this, Bard. Made it myself."

Bard ate more than Aengus. Aengus spent more time talking and sipping his cider than eating. The old Trader tactfully avoided any further mention of Mad Davey's demise. He noticed the boy rubbing his reddened forehead, which was more than a little burned now from sun and the wind, "Bard, you need a hat."

"I lost mine back at Standing Stone."

Aengus grinned wryly, "No young man meets up with Mathilda without leaving something of his behind."

In answer, Bard held up his right hand for Aengus to see the burn across its back. This provoked another rueful smile from Aengus. If he had any marks of his own to show, he chose to keep them to himself. "I have a couple of fine hats in my goods, Bard." One of them might fit to you. Would you maybe want to trade for one?"

Bard did a quick mental inventory of what he might spare, "I have some apples. They're right good."

"I'm always looking for apples; red or gold, green or silver, I like them all." Aengus opened the flap of one of the bags draped across Molly Dear's flank and pulled out two hats, rolled tight with a string tied round them. He shook out one of them, which had a broad floppy brim and a flat topped crown, and put it on the boy, stood back and folded his arms, with a thoughtful look of appraisal. "You were made for each other. If you'll wear that one, we have a deal."

Bard opened his rucksack again and took out his apples, he had four of them left, wondering if that would be sufficient pay for a hat. Aengus seemed to think so. He stowed three of them with the other hat and bit into the fourth, "Dessert," he said with a wink, "Bard, you would make a fine Trader, yourself."

By the time they had finished their lunch and found some personal privacy in the surrounding coppice, the mule had grazed her way to the far side of the meadow. Aengus called after her, "Let's be gone now, Molly Dear."

She came to him and he took up her lead and led her to the spring, where he packed his water bottles, while Bard shrugged into his load, a little lightened by the departure of his apples. They climbed up to the road again, and walked away from the sun. The wind had become more blustery since morning. Bard was grateful for the chin strap on his new hat, otherwise he would have been chasing his shadow after it before he took ten steps.

#

Late in the afternoon, the wind lay and the air cooled precipitously. "There will be frost on the whiskers tonight," remarked Aengus. "I'll be glad for some shelter."

"Will the Herb Woman take us in?" Even in his coat, Bard felt the cold. In spite of Davey's padding, the straps of his pack were chafing his shoulders. He would have preferred to sleep beside the road rather than walk another mile.

"She'll offer, but I'll stay in the barn with Molly Dear like usual. I'll be comfortable enough there without being a bother, but you having come from Davey and all, she'll want to keep you to herself for a spell and talk. Those two share some considerable history. You'll do her a mercy if you let her give you a bed."

Another marker post came into view. This one had two horizontal grooves spaced a hand's width apart near the top. Beyond the day marker the road began to wind down and around into a deep gap in the ridge. Descending into the gap they could see about a half mile ahead the road winding back up to an even higher peak than those behind. As they dropped into the magenta shadow of the rise behind, the height before them still gleamed bright in the setting sun.

Within the gap, sheltered from the wind somewhat by the terrain, the forest growth became more dense, the trees a bit taller. Where the road leveled before turning to begin climbing again, off to their left, perhaps a furlong distant, they saw a light in the near dark among the trees there. As they left the road along a path toward it, Bard could see the light came from a house.

If they had passed during the day and not known a dwelling stood there, they might not have seen it at all. The house, long and low, with a sod roof, had been built into a hill. Unshaped stone, laid up between heavy timbers, formed the front wall. A wide porch ran its whole length. Near the house, a free-standing barn leaned ever so slightly into an attached shed. When they were within a stone's throw of the house, the door opened, and the light inside outlined a woman's form in the doorway. With the light behind her, Bard could not discern her features. From what he had heard of the Herb Woman, he guessed she was old, but whatever her age, she stood tall and straight in the lamplight.

Aengus called, "Lizzie, it's Aengus. I have a boy here with me you might want to know." Then he spoke softly to Bard, "Would you stay and hold Molly Dear for me? I may be about to bear some bad news here." Aengus took off his hat and walked to the house and stepped up on the porch. The mule brayed and snickered as he distanced himself from her, but stood quietly as Bard held her lead. He couldn't hear the conversation on the porch, but once or twice Aengus pointed out in his direction, so he guessed he figured somehow in their discussion. After a few minutes, the woman put her arms around the old man's shoulders and hugged him briefly, then Aengus beckoned. Bard led Molly Dear along as he went to stand in front of the porch steps for the Herb Woman's inspection.

The old woman had hair as white as Aengus's beard. She was also straight and spare as a poplar in winter, with eyes bright and piercing as a hawk's. Her face was lined and weathered like the stone face of a mountain, but warmer by far. Without saying a word, her gaze, stern though it appeared, enveloped Bard with welcome.

Aengus laid a hand across his back, "This is the boy Robberlee was telling me about, Lizzie, He was down to Davey's right before it all happened."

Lizzie regarded the boy in silence for a moment before she spoke to him, "Davey told you to come here, then?"

"Yes'm," Bard was reluctant to discuss his intentions before the Trader, "He said I was to ask you some things."

"All who come to me bring questions," replied Lizzie. "Maybe you can also speak a little comfort my way before you go." Aengus was already leading Molly Dear away toward the barn, "Aengus can't bear to be away from his mule overnight, but you'll sleep under my roof, won't you?"

"I'm honored you would ask me, and I'll be grateful to do it, Miss Lizzie."

"My mother named me Elizabeth, but any friend to me now just calls me Lizzie. And what is your name, then?"

"Didn't Aengus tell you?"

"I want to hear it from you."

"Everybody calls me Bard."

"You say that name like you pulled it out of a hat. We'll have to do better than that for you while you are here. Go help Aengus situate his animal, then you boys come in and I'll feed you supper."

Bard shed his load on the porch by the steps, and went after Aengus and Molly Dear to the barn. Intuitively, he liked the Herb Woman. Though she was much older, there was something about her that made him think of his own Mary, who seemed to him now so far away and long ago.

A lantern hung lit just inside the door, and Bard found a stall there to his right. Molly Dear stood patiently in the aisle, waiting to be admitted to her quarters, while Aengus, in his shirt sleeves leaned over the rail across the front of the stall, pouring grain from a bucket into a wood trough attached there. In one corner, a large metal tub had already been filled with water. Twenty or so curious sheep watched the proceedings from a pen at the far end of the barn.

"Would you lend me a hand here, Bard, and we'll liberate Molly Dear from her burden." Aengus, turned to his mule and began loosening knots and unbuckling straps and handing bags and boxes to the boy, "Just set them yonder where I hung my coat."

It took them a quarter hour to get Molly Dear loosed from her load. Some of the larger bundles needed the two of them to carry handily. When they were done, Aengus pulled a couple of blankets out of the stash and spread them across a drift of hay that had been loosed from the bales around. "I'll be as snug here as an old sow bear in her den," he predicted. It felt warm inside the barn. Bard thought it wouldn't be at all a bad place to spend the night.

Aengus turned Molly Dear into her stall, handed Bard several large parcels from among his goods, "Would you mind lugging these for me?" Then he doused the lantern, took a lidded box and bag under either arm himself, and they started toward the house, closing the door behind them with their backs. As they walked across the yard, Aengus regarded Bard thoughtfully, "If you are not in a hurry to get someplace right now, it would favor me mightily if you would stay on a few days with Lizzie, should she ask. The news about Davey was hard for her to hear, and I'd feel better not to leave her alone for a while."

If Aengus threw this out to bait him into telling his itinerary, Bard didn't take it, not that he had much to tell. Since his arrival in the Laurel, the cryptic directives Owl had issued in his dreams amounted to the nearest he had come to a purpose. It occurred to him that Owl seemed to be running all the lives in Laurel, including his. "There's no place I have to be. If she wants company, I reckon I could stay with her a spell. She seems right likeable."

"If she likes you, Bard, she has a golden heart. If she doesn't, she might eat you for her breakfast."

They stepped up on the porch, deposited their load beside the door. Aromas of cooking wafted from inside.

Aengus led Bard right of the door, down the porch, to a little counter with a sink and a hand pump on its top. A pipe ran down through the floor to a well or cistern somewhere below. A bucket of water with a dipper hanging over the side sat on the counter beside the pump. An enameled basin and a towel hung on the door in the front of the counter, and a bar of green soap lay in a little wooden tray behind the sink. Aengus set the basin on the counter, poured a dipper-full of water into the top of the pump to prime it, and worked the handle until water began to flow and filled his basin. Then he stepped back, "Bard, you go first," and in turn they washed the road from their hands and arms and faces. The soap made Bard think of Mad Davey, and he had to blink back some tears as he washed.

The opposite end of the porch had been walled-in to make a little room. As they made to go into the house, Lizzie stepped out the door, drying her hands on her apron. She looked at Bard with her hawk's eyes and pointed, "That's where you'll sleep tonight," and before he could get to them, she picked up his rucksack with one hand as if not conscious of the weight, and his staff with the other, led him to his room, and pushed open the door with her foot as she entered. The room provided little space to spare. A bed big enough for one, covered with a quilt, clean but patched and mended. A tiny window. A low table without a chair. A chamber pot with a lid sat under the table. A couple of pegs on the inside of the door for hanging clothes. A small mirror on the wall over the table. The mirror had a crack running half across it.

Lizzie dropped Bard's gear on the bed. As he took off his coat and hat to hang them, he said, "Thank you, Miss Lizzie, I could've done that."

"Lizzie"

"Thank you, Lizzie."

Perhaps she noted his subdued manner. Perhaps she just read his heart. He lifted his coat to a peg. Lizzie, passing through the door behind, reached to lay a hand on his shoulder, and almost in a whisper. "I'll miss him, too." Then she called to Aengus who was still waiting on the porch, "Go get your coffee, Aengus, we're right behind you."

When Bard came in after them, Aengus already stood with his coffee in hand in front of a big stone fireplace. An iron pot hung on a crane over the coals. From an oven built into the stonework beside the hearth, Lizzie was hauling a big iron skillet which she deftly inverted, and dropped a thick round pone of cornbread onto a plate. Bard went to stand beside Aengus and twisted to peer at the pot hanging over the fire. He figured it sourced most of the smells that had been enticing him on the porch. Lizzie saw him, and threw him a thick towel, "Son, lift that lid."

He did as he was told, and saw beans within, some simmering in their long green hulls, and some shelled out into the broth, bits of onions and peppers among them. Lizzie was obviously an omnivore, for a couple of large chunks of fat pork or bear swam amid the vegetables.

"Do you think you could stand to eat a little of that?" Lizzie teased.

He caught himself this time, "Oh, yes, Lizzie; I do believe I could manage."

She handed him a bowl and a big ladle, "Well, spoon it out then, and we'll have at it." While Bard filled the bowl and brought it to the table, she cut the corn bread into wedges, with as much enthusiasm but somewhat more precision than Davey, as she spoke over her shoulder to Aengus "Old man, be useful now and set the table for me. Then we can all sit down and shed the day."

Lizzie set the cornbread on the table beside the beans and handed a platter to Bard, "Hold this." Going to the fireplace, she raked the coals aside with a poker and uncovered the lid of a shallow cast iron pot. She lifted the lid with a pothook, revealing sweet potatoes baked in their skins, fat white shogoin, and a large filleted trout. All these she transferred to the platter; Aengus poured some cider into three mugs, and they did indeed sit down then and shed the day, as Lizzie put it, and perhaps gained a pound each in the process.

They ate and they drank. As they ate, they talked about everything but Davey. Now and again, they laughed. Lizzie offered them no dessert, as she usually avoided sweets for herself in the evening, but with Bard's help, Aengus brought in from the porch the parcels he had for Lizzie, and among them, a few pieces of bitter chocolate, which they let melt on their tongues between sips of the hot cider. Lizzie seemed to enjoy it as much as did the males. After they cleared the table, and washed the pots and plates, Lizzie brought out a bottle of something somewhat more potent and aromatic than cider. She and Aengus sipped it sparingly from tiny, handleless cups.

Bard would have been quite content with more chocolate and cider, but by this time had fallen asleep in his chair before the fire. While he dozed, Lizzie and Aengus talked business, or as close to business as they ever came. He had brought her implements and supplies for her spinning, two bottles of the same rice wine as they were drinking, some salt, a bag of buckwheat flour and a wheel of cheese, packed in its own wooden box, also a few other sundries from the plunder he shared with Mad Davey. Lizzie brought from her workroom at the far end of the house skeins of yarns and spools of thread, which Aengus would take for trade with the Sisters at the Abbey, who would in turn carry them to the Weaver, and bring her finished yardage back to the Abbey. From them, in exchange for yarns and the other needfuls he carried, Aengus would gain their stock of the Weaver's fabrics, and resupply with the spirits the Sisters made and stored in their cellar. Nearly all commerce in the Laurel was by barter. The bronze coinage, mostly used by Traders and Riders, had little intrinsic value other than to signify the receipt of services and thus an incurring of obligation to repay in kind, and was seldom used as payment for goods or property.

Bard woke as Aengus was rising to leave, "Molly Dear will be worrying I've been lost," he said in mock apology.

Lizzie kissed him playfully on his forehead as he left. "Give my love to your mule," she laughed. She lit a lamp and gave it to Bard, as he stood rubbing his eyes with one hand, "Don't fall asleep before you put this out," then she gently pushed him out the door after Aengus.

Bard went along the porch to his tiny room, shut the door after him, put out his lamp, and sat on the bed, fumbling groggily with his shoes. He lay back in all his clothes, too tired to think about the images thronging his head. A faint light from somewhere came through his little window and he could see fireflies or stars reflected in the mirror opposite. As sleep carried away his mind, he thought for a second he saw Owl's face in the mirror. "She waits," spoke the monk. If he said more, it was in a dream Bard forgot upon waking the next morning.

#

About an hour after sunrise, Bard woke atop all the covers, still fully dressed except for his shoes. The sun hung yet low enough to shine through his window and across his bed. The sunlight in his face had wakened him. He went down toward the barn, hoping to find a privy, or at least a private space for himself to do as he needed. He had been too shy to use the chamber pot in his room. He found the sheep still in residence, but Aengus had gone, along with Molly Dear and all her burdens. Without knowing quite why he felt that way, Bard was glad he had been left behind. He did find a privy, however, around the opposite side of the barn, a discovery which gratified him considerably and set his morning off to a satisfactory start.

As he stepped out from the privy, his disposition much improved, he could see through the trees to the road where it intersected with Lizzie's path. Aengus stood there, with his mule almost hidden under her hulking load, as he talked with two of the Couriers, who sat their horses before him. In the course of their conversation, they looked toward the house several times, then the green men spurred on toward Beaverdam, and Aengus led Molly Dear away and up eastward on the track. Bard had no sense of how he might have figured into their talk, or if he did at all, but he was glad he didn't tell the Trader more about himself than he had.

He went back to the house, followed Aengus' ritual for priming the pump, and took a boy's pride at doing some new thing successfully on the first try. He washed more thoroughly than most boys might, and since he was a guest, knocked on the door. When he got no answer, he opened it, "Miss Lizzie – Lizzie, are you to home?" Silence. He went in then, and saw no sign of Lizzie. The door to her work room was ajar, but he heard no sounds from there. On the table, at the place where he sat the night before, he found two plates, one inverted over the other. He lifted it to see two large biscuits, brown atop and slit across the middle. One sandwiched a fried egg, and the other held a thick slice of salt-cured ham. Hunger warred with timidity, and appetite won out. He sat down and ate them both. As he ate, he saw Lizzie's apron folded over the back of the chair opposite him.

Then he went outside again to look for the Herb Woman. It made him nervous to be in someone's house he didn't really know without their expressed permission. Although she had not quite invited him to stay on awhile with her, as Aengus had suggested she might, Bard found himself hoping mightily that she would.

He heard Lizzie before he saw her. On the side of the house opposite the barn, the trees of the wood above parted to admit a short path leading up to a clearing, slightly higher on the slope than the house. The little meadow stretched less than thirty yards across at its widest. As he started up the path, Bard heard very distinctly two sounds, a sort of swish, somewhat like the sound of Hawk's wings as she had flown past him along the road from Charon's crossing, followed immediately by a soft thunk, as would result from striking a tree with a stick. Bard froze, listening. Half a minute later, he heard it again, and half a minute after that, almost to the second, he heard the sounds a third time. They definitely came from the clearing.

As he passed the trees and came into the meadow, he saw Lizzie, her back to him just ahead, her white hair tied up in a scarf atop her head, and her long green dress gathered up above her knees and tucked into the sash tied round her waist. Drawing back on a bow almost as long as her height, she stood straight as the arrow notched to the bowstring. When she released it, the arrow flew true and embedded in the end of a short section of cedar log about eight inches in diameter, suspended in a frame of cut saplings on the far side of the clearing. Two arrows lay on the ground at her feet. Bard stood rapt and still as she bent from the waist to pick up the other two arrows in turn and sent them on their way to join the first. All found their target; the arrows clustered less than a finger's width between them each. Without turning around, Lizzie called, "Would you fetch my arrows for me?"

The end of the log was hollowed from strikes by many arrows, and it required more strength than Bard anticipated to extract them. He took the arrows to Lizzie and handed them to her, "Are you going hunting?"

"Not if I value my soul," she answered softly, with a smile, "These arrows never draw blood; but when I release them properly, they draw eye and mind and heart together in common purpose as finely and surely as a spindle draws strands into yarn."

"Where did you learn to shoot a bow?"

"It isn't so much about learning to shoot," said Lizzie, "But about learning to see. Once you really see the target, if you have strength to draw the bow, it becomes very hard to miss. But that isn't your question, is it? The old monk up at the Abbey taught me the way of the bow when he and I were a lot younger than we are now."

Bard asked no more questions, but decided then he would tell the Herb Woman, while he was here, about his dreams of Owl.

#

The Rider was still sorting through the ways of the

195

Labyrinth when Millicent found him, and brought him back to Davey's Wood, he judged, within two or three days of his unpremeditated departure. Mad Davey's outbuildings stood intact and unmolested. Somebody had been about the place since he left. The energy of the storm had rendered the trace uncertain, but the Rider was sure it belonged to Aengus, the trader, who stored his plunder there, where Davey, as landlord, had privilege to partake of the stash if he needed, and from time to time, he had.

It pleased the Rider to find his fairybowl where he left it. Millicent had veiled it before she came looking for him, and any passerby would have had to stumble over it to see it. He dropped it into the big pocket of his duster, and went back to the road, where he found traces of Aengus, several riders, and the boy. The Riders had all headed down the Rising toward the Circle and Beaverdam. Aengus and the boy traveled toward the Abbey. The boy, he worried about.

More than ever, the Rider believed the child posed a major threat to the continuance of the Laurel. He had slipped away from Robberlee, escaped Jude and his off-spring, and confounded a Rider more skilled at his craft than most of his kind. Everywhere the boy went, things happened to people. In his wake, Jude's sons had disappeared and Davey was left dead in his bed. The Rider had been sent on a detour from which, without Millicent, he might have been a long time returning. With or without knowing it, the boy held power. Be his intention evil or good or nothing he was aware of, he presented a danger, and would have to be dealt with.

Most disturbing to the Rider's mind was that the boy had appeared at a Council, in which Owl, through his avatar, Bear, had participated. Since then, the monk had given no indication that he had knowledge of the boy's whereabouts, while the boy evidently had been making straight for the Abbey. Either the boy, unlike every other soul in Laurel, could mask himself from the Seer's mind, or Owl had summoned the child himself, for some purpose of his own he chose not to share with those charged with maintaining safety and order among the people. Most of those the Rider knew in the Guilds believed that Owl's sight extended beyond Laurel, deep into Shadow. If the boy was not of Laurel, where else could he be from? Likely he came among them as an assassin, a spy, or something far worse.

So the Rider reasoned. If he were ordered now to abort his hunt, he would pursue the boy on his own initiative. By his logic, the boy, by his very presence in the Laurel, imperiled all the Rider lived for. He determined to act as he knew he must, and pray that mercy would be the only virtue he had to cast aside along the way.

#

Lizzie slid her three arrows into a quiver that lay in the grass beside her sandals. She had been barefoot as she made ritual with her bow. To Bard's questioning glance, she answered, "It improves my direction when I can sink roots into my place." She slacked the bowstring, unbound her hair and draped the scarf loosely across her shoulders, then freed her hem from her sash, letting it fall almost to cover her feet as she slipped them into her sandals. As they started back down the path again toward the house, Lizzie reached out and touched Bard's arm with the tips of her fingers, "I have work about the woods today. If you're not going to run away from me for a while, I'll ask you to take out the sheep."

Bard had no personal experience herding stock of any

race, but he was willing. "Do you think I can manage them, Lizzie?"

"The sheep will manage you." Fetch your staff and come along to the barn with me."

Bard stopped by his room on the porch to pick up his staff and his jacket, for though the sun had risen well above the trees now, the morning air held a chill edge. When he got to the barn the sheep had already begun pouring out the door and milled about the yard.

He tried to get behind them to urge them with his staff, but Lizzie laid a hand on his shoulder, "Come afront of them. You are trying to herd them, don't you know? You are a shepherd. Herdsmen drive, Shepherds lead. When the sheep know what you are here for, they will follow you across the world if you want them to." She tied her saffron hued scarf around the boy's neck like a bandana. "Now you look like their shepherd. Keep an eye for them, but walk ahead and trust them to trust you."

Lizzie walked beside him back up the path to the little meadow where she had practiced her archery. Bard wasn't sure if she did this for his own reassurance, or just in case the sheep realized he held somewhat limited trust in his own trustworthiness. They walked to the center of the clearing and the sheep followed just as Lizzie promised. The flock spread out and fell to grazing.

Bard had visions of chasing one stray while the rest of the flock took off in the opposite direction. "What do I do if they start to wander off?"

"Just keep reminding them that you are here. They will see you as their protector, and will not want to be out of your sight. Walk among them and talk to them; they will keep your company."

"What do I say?"

"Aengus said you are Bard. Well, Bard, sing them a story."

"I don't know any stories."

"Hand me your staff." It sounded like a command. He gave it to her, and she held it up vertically before her, as if it were her bow, then closed her right hand around it near the top, and pulled her fingers down the length of it. Above her hand as it descended, the smooth sheen of the wood yielded to an intricate and complex maze of tiny grooves that made Bard think of the lights that had fired from the bluff above the Standing Stone.

Lizzie laughed softly, "You can read all your stories right here. Every place you've walked in Laurel, every face you've seen, every voice you've heard, every story you've lived is in your staff. If you've lived them, you can read them here." She held out the staff to him.

He remembered Mathilda's stones and hesitated to take hold of it, but before Lizzie's intense gaze, he feared more not to. It did not burn him and Lizzie did not smite him with a twig. The staff did feel different in his hand as he took it, not just because of the change in its texture, but it seemed less of a weight, as if become an extension of his own arm and not just a stick he carried to lean on. He turned the staff in his hands and looked at the labyrinth carved around and along it. He found no text to be read there, but as his eye tried to trace the turnings and loopings of the maze, he could recall with clarity and detail, almost as if reliving them, moments of passage in his sojourn across Laurel. He was hardly reassured to be holding such a powerful wonder in his boy's hands.

"And I can't sing," he said, for lack of any further excuse.

Lizzie laughed, "Then say them your story, Even the

wisest bards may have no voice for song. They speak their stories, and the music is in the flow of their words, although some might have a flute or a drum to dress their tale. Maybe we can make you a drum."

Perhaps Bard read it in his staff, or perhaps her reference to the drum provoked his memory, but suddenly he could see in his mind's eye the boy sleeping under the tree and the chestnut falling and turning to strike him above his heart and release the music of the world. In a fit of playfulness, then, before he could curb the impulse, he clapped his fist against his chest and said, "I am the drum." Immediately from somewhere along the valley below, there was a loud grumble of thunder, and a sudden breeze stirred the leaves and rustled the grass around them. They both thought this a great joke on themselves, and laughed so loudly that all the sheep lifted their heads to look at them.

Lizzie said, as if in delighted surprise and recognition, "Hello, Drum, I wasn't expecting you today." And they both laughed again, with more zest and freedom than either of them had manifest for a long time.

Lizzie left him then, going to harvest the herbs and roots about the woods that she used in preparing her various potions, tonics, salves, ointments, unguents, tinctures and elixirs which she offered her neighbors to guard and restore their strength, soothe their aches, and mend them when they were broken. When Aengus came back down from the Abbey, he would stop again, and trade her some of the Sisters' soap and spirits, and perhaps a few yards of the weaver's cloth for a stock of her medicinals to carry down to Beaverdam to trade to town folk who had neither knowledge nor inclination to make their own cures and remedies.

While Lizzie garnered the woods, Drum told the sheep the tale of his walk through the Laurel in glowing detail and with few exaggerations, for in this strange place, the simple fact usually carried wonder enough to hold an audience. He kept his post right through noon, even though he was hungry. He learned soon that Lizzie only took two meals a day, with sometimes a slight snack between. When she called across the clearing to him in the waning afternoon, all his charges lay around him in peaceful contemplation of their napping trustee.

Lizzie addressed the sheep, "Let's go home," and the whole flock rose as one and trooped after her down the path with an enthusiasm that made it difficult for Drum to maintain his leadership position as shepherd. He thought then that one shepherd probably sufficed for any flock.

When they passed the porch, Lizzie went up the steps and into the house to prepare their early supper, and the sheep faltered in their migration. A few of them seemed on the point of following after her up the steps onto the porch. Drum didn't know what commands shepherds generally employed, but since it had worked for Lizzie, he raised his staff and called, "Let's go home!"

At the sound of his voice, the sheep pursued him through the barn door and into their pen. As he closed the gate, it occurred to him that he might have said *Let's go to hell*, and they would have come along after him with the same mindless alacrity. It was not the word, but the voice that bid them follow.

He found two buckets by the pen, which he carried up to the porch and filled at the pump, and after three trips the stone watering trough was full. He threw several forks of loose hay to the sheep, which did not seem to interest them a great deal except to lie in. They drank prodigiously, however, and before he left and closed the barn door on them, he brought two more buckets of water to replenish their supply.

Then he went to the porch and took off his jacket and shirt and Lizzie's scarf, which still hung tied round his neck, and washed himself at the pump as much as he decently could. Before he went into the house, he went down the porch to his room and found one of Davey's fresh shirts in his rucksack. He thought he must ask Lizzie about where to wash his clothes. Then he set his staff against the corner, pulled on his jacket, folded Lizzie's scarf and dropped it in the pocket, meaning to return it, closed the door behind him to shut out the evening chill, and went back up the porch to find his supper.

He paused at the door of the house, thought about whether to knock, when Lizzie opened it and said, "Come on through, and tend the fire for me while I cook." Lizzie had put bread in the oven to bake. She instructed Drum to watch the little dial set in the center of the cast iron oven door, and try to maintain a constant temperature. "Keep the hand straight up the middle."

By feeding the fire judiciously and adjusting the air vent in the door of the firebox below the oven, Drum managed more-or-less to accomplish his assignment. While the bread baked, Lizzie made a rich soup full of vegetables red and green and gold, as well as shreds of some sweet-tasting fowl, and when she judged it had simmered sufficiently, she had Drum ladle it into two bowls as she sliced a melon, then turned to check her baking bread. He savored the smell of the soup as he poured it, and finally overcame his shyness to ask a question that had been puzzling him since the morning. "Lizzie, I've been wondering."

"What else is a boy supposed to do? What have you been wondering about?"

"If you don't hunt with your bow, where do you get your meat?"

"I don't kill with the bow because it isn't a weapon. It is a tool to aid worship and prayer, to calm my mind and center my spirit." I have meat because people bring it to me sometimes when they come for my medicinals. Besides," at this she leaned over the table and continued in a mock whisper, "If I run plumb out of meat, I have a rifle in my closet." When they had done laughing, Lizzie poured out some strong green tea from a teapot that had been sitting on the hearth before the fire. She handed a cup to the boy, "Aengus brought this." Drum told her that he had never seen a firearm in Laurel.

"There are still a few about. Since the Separation they have dwindled. Some of us still keep arms up here on the Rising and in other hard scrabble places where one must kill meat in the winter or go hungry. We don't talk much about our weapons, and don't you talk about mine. Whenever the Traders come across powder arms they try to buy them, but they never offer one for trade, although sometimes you will find a Trader who can get you ammunition, or at least powder, so you can load your own. . The Traders say they turn in all the weapons they get to the smith in Beaverdam to be melted down into saw blades and plow shares and such. But a few skeptics say the Traders have them all in a warehouse somewhere, just in case. In case of what, nobody knows. I think our bread is ready."

Lizzie deftly slipped her long-handled peel under two round loaves and drew them from the oven, "Just right, you did good." Without waiting for the bread to cool, she began to cut into a loaf, and offered a slice, "Who am I giving this to then? Are you Drum or Bard tonight?"

"I reckon I am still Drum."

"In that case, maybe I'll let you stay for supper."

There was a square of honeycomb in a plate on the table, and as they sat down, Lizzie took her spoon and broke off a wee piece and dropped it into her tea. Drum watched and did the same. He tried to taste the tea, still hot enough to burn his tongue. He waited until Lizzie sipped from her cup and tried again. The flavor recalled to him the evening on Mary's porch when Ronan sang to them. Then he remembered the fiddler girl at Callie's house. He wished they had music now. He wished he was a real bard, and that he could sing a story for Lizzie.

If they lacked for music, they did not lack for blessing. They had good food and good company, and for all the difference in their ages, they felt an ease between them that comes from having shared a loss. Bard found himself ready to speak of it when Lizzie stopped suddenly as she lifted a spoonful of soup to her mouth, and said, "Tell me all about Davey."

He told his story as well as any bard, starting when he had fallen prey to the gray family, how he had escaped and fled up the mountain to the spring where Davey took him in. He told about his dreams of Owl, about Davey's drawings, and the one he had made for Davey. He wanted to tell about his love for the old man, but couldn't find the right words, finally settling for, "He was the best friend I will ever have."

Then he told about his night at Standing Stone, leaving out the part about the lights, but he told all about Mathilda, and said he still had the stones she gave him, and showed Lizzie the mark on his hand.

Unlike most other adults he had ever tried to tell anything important to him, Lizzie didn't interrupt. She just watched him talk, sipping on her tea once in a while, not commenting or questioning, just nodding from time to time to signal her engagement. When he was done, and could think of nothing else to add, she spoke quietly, "Davey was the best sort of man there is." Then she added, "Hold on to those stones from Mathilda. You wouldn't have them if they would not serve your need."

She got up and brought the teapot back to the table and poured the last of the tea into their cups, then set the pot aside, and asked, "Drum, do you know why Owl wants you to find the Weaver?"

He shook his head. "Maybe they were just dreams."

"We are all dreams, Drum. That's what makes us real. Davey wanted me to tell you about the Weaver, so now I shall."

#

"The Weaver's name is Thomasene. We grew up as friends, though she was a few years younger. When I went among the Sisters of the Abbey as a novice, nothing suited Thomasene but to go with me. The Abbey is very old, built on the Alone before the Separation. Then, when the world was broken, priests and deacons and wardens all fled to be bought and sold like the rest in Shadow, but the Sisters stayed, and prayed for the souls of Laurel, and lifted their lights to the Light in praise of the Mother, and gave hospitality to those few pilgrims who had kept their faith beyond the rending of the world. Fukuroo, the monk we know as Owl, came among them as a refugee, and stayed as their confessor. He heard without judgment, and advised without commandment. He taught those of us who were open to learning, the ways of prayer and

205

contemplation that he had learned among his old order. Thomasene and I learned from Owl how to use the bow to open a window of awareness into the sacred becoming of all things. I learned from Owl how to gather plants and roots to heal and restore life. The sisters taught us to spin and weave, and to make music and calculate numbers and read the old stories.

In time, I left the abbey, not because I disbelieved, but because the Mother became more present to me in the earth and the trees and the air and in all her creatures, than in chants and rituals and lives lived out bounded by a wall. No one faulted my choice, and I would be welcome to return today. Thomasene stayed, and I visited her in season, until I was told by one of the Sisters that she had removed herself to the summit of the Alone and embraced the vocation of a hermit. She had never spoken to me of such leanings, and I am puzzled about it to this day, but there is rumoring along the Rising, which the Sisters try to discourage, that she became a recluse as a penance for her disobedience to the Rule that she would love no single soul more than she loved all the souls of Laurel As for me, I doubt that loving any one the more need result in loving all others less. To wreck your own life or another's in the name of love would be sinful, but I do not believe the Mother would have us love any soul less than we are capable of.

Some on the Rising, who have wandered up on the Alone, claim to have seen Thomasene, though none near enough to speak. They tell that she has not aged in her solitude, but is still the fair girl who set herself apart from all the world so long ago. Perhaps they saw her. Perhaps they saw some girl on the mountain they wanted to think was her. But I have not seen nor spoken to Thomasene now for years upon years, although I spin her thread, and sometimes I see what she has woven it to become."

Saying this, Lizzie pointed to Drum's jacket hanging behind him on his chair. Her saffron scarf, which he had forgotten, was visible above the wide pocket. Embarrassed now, he reached to hand it back to her.

"No, keep it as yours, Drum. If the Sisters will let you see Thomasene, and if she will receive you, which would be unlikely, it will be a sign to her that you have come from me. If Owl has dreamed you this far, he may well dream you the whole way, for he has discerned some purpose in your meeting that the Mother has not revealed to the rest of us."

"The Mother?" queried Drum.

"God, Spirit, Maker, Mother, whatever word you use, it names the One who is all."

"God is a woman?"

Lizzie smiled at his query, "Sometimes She is; sometime He isn't."

#

When they had eaten and cleared the dishes, Lizzie and Drum sat before the fire and talked of the day past and the morrow to come. They both seemed to assume that he would be here to share it with her, and there was no further mention of his quest to find the Weaver. "Tomorrow, while you shepherd, I will gather nettles, and then we will split some wood." Lizzie told him.

She made for Drum a mug of the hot tea with milk and spices as Davey had been fond of, and she sipped a wee cup of her rice wine. When she set her cup aside, as if she read his mind, she gave him the music he had wished for. Lizzie brought out from her workroom an instrument strange to Drum. He thought it looked a bit like a guitar, but it had a longer neck and more strings. Lizzie held it upon her lap and played one after another, tunes that Drum had never heard, but seemed ever so familiar to him. Some of them sounded similar to melodies he had heard in church. Lizzie smiled at some remembrance of hers, and told him, "This is a song to the Mother that the Sisters taught us," and as she played, she began to sing. Her voice was not young like the fiddler, nor ruined like Davey's. She sang strong and steady, deep like the earth, and soft like the wind, and clear as a brook on a mountain:

As a farmer lives for planting,
As a sailor seeks the sea,
As a river finds the valley,
So we set our souls on Thee;
As a tree stands on the mountain,
As a swallow rides the air,
As a trout held by the river,
So we rest upon thy care;
As the grapes grow on the branches,
As the branches on the Vine,
So we live within thy presence,
Drawing every breath from Thine;
As the road leads ever onward,
As the journey has no end,
We will ever serve and praise Thee,
Loving Mother, Faithful Friend.

Later, alone in his room, Drum spread Lizzie's scarf upon his little table, opened his medicine bag, and counted his treasures. The scarf shone in the lamplight like fine silk. Lizzie had told him that the fabric was more durable than silk, that Thomasene wove it from nettles that Lizzie gathered and spun. He placed Hawk's ball of soap at the center and then arranged Mathilda's tiny stones in a circle around. It took him a second to realize the soap had vanished. He reached toward where it had been and the tips of his fingers disappeared, as if he had plunged them into water. But he felt the soap under them, and pulled it into view. When the marvel was no longer a surprise, something occurred to him. He took his hat, and tucked the stones into the band. He held then a hat he could not see. He put it on his head and stood before the cracked mirror. When he looked down at his hands and body, all was visible, but when he looked into the mirror, he only saw the wall and the window behind him.

Carefully, Bard removed the stones from his hatband, wrapped them with the soap into the scarf, and stuffed them into his medicine bag. The scarf folded tight upon itself, like silk, and there was just room enough.

#

When they reached the day marker above Standing Stone, the Rider found trace that the boy had taken the path down to the Stone. He also sensed the boy had continued later up the track along the Rising. Leaving Millicent by the road, The Rider walked down the path to the Stone. The boy had been here for a while, perhaps spent the night. He found the remains from a fire under the bluff, saw lying upon the stone there, where it had been dropped, the boy's hat. He turned it in his hand, noted the faded letters inked inside. Neither did he overlook the scrap of paper tucked behind the band. He pulled it loose, unfolded it, read Liza's message. He did not recognize her handwriting, and could not quite name the connection he felt, until he saw the *L* at the end. The Rider replaced the note, rolled the hat and dropped it into the wide pocket of his longcoat.

Mathilda, he called, without speaking. He waited. He

knew she was here, probably had been watching him since he came down the path. Then he said aloud, "Mathilda, tell me what has been going on here." And there she was, seated atop her Standing Stone. It was obvious from her appearance that she did not consider the Rider shy or tender.

"He came and he went, Rider, and now you have come round the circle again. Are we ever to keep meeting so? One day you shall meet yourself going." Mathilda laughed lightly, but there was little mirth in it.

"It would have been helpful, Mathilda if you could have kept him here for me. How did he get away from you so soon?"

"There is no staying a boy when he is following his dreams, Rider. You should know that, and look where it has gotten you."

"You are ever a riddle, Mathilda"

"And now I am gone, Rider, and so should you be." And she was gone, and soon, so would be the Rider. He walked through the ferns to stand before the Stone. The face of it was black, like the night sky. The quartz crystals in its matrix glittered like stars. The Rider summoned Millicent, held out his hand to her, and together, they walked into the Stone.

#

Drum did not take the sheep out next morning, nor did Lizzie gather nettles, for during the night a cold drizzle began to fall and by daylight a driving rain, riding on a howling nor'easter, swept across the ridge. The leaves fled the trees, and Drum was glad for Davey's coat. If Aengus had recognized that it was from among his stores at Davey's Wood, he never mentioned it.

During the morning, Lizzie and Drum split the

firewood already sawn to length and piled beneath the shed attached to the barn. Lizzie split while Drum stacked, thick pieces for the hearth, thinner splits for the oven and cookstove. They worked so for a couple of hours, Drum sorting and stacking, while Lizzie, with the same measured concentration with which she addressed her bow, wielded her long-handled maul and axe. Drum watched her work with a fascination akin to awe. He couldn't have described it in words, but somewhere deep he sensed that Lizzie had turned her labor into ritual. Time after time, she raised the axe straight above her head, until it almost touched the roof of the shed, then with her arms straight before her, let the blade fall in an arc to sunder the short flitch upended on her chopping block. She never missed, and almost always, the wood split cleanly with her first blow.

At length, she paused, and said, "I'm tired, Drum." Although she did not look tired at all, "Would you like to be the axeman awhile?" Drum had never been an axeman. He had played at it a few times when no adults were on hand to criticize his technique or forbid him altogether. Lizzie handed over the axe to him and stepped back, watching him, but pretending not to, as she stacked some of the splits onto a pile. Drum took off his coat and hefted the axe. It was heavier than he anticipated, but he raised it above his shoulders, trying to imitate Lizzie, then swung down with all his might. The blade struck his target a glancing blow and bounced off one side into the dirt. Inwardly, he cringed, knowing that his father would have berated him hotly for abusing a keen blade.

Lizzie, just kept gathering her wood, and said, "Try again, Drum. This time, leave a little room between you and your wood; try to keep the handle straight up like a tree as you lift it, and when your arms are almost straight, let it swing down. Keep your arms straight, and just let it fall, don't pull it down. If the axe does the work, you can split a whole pile of wood and not wear yourself down." Drum had another go at it, and did better, although his axe landed off-center and shaved a splinter off his flitch. "That will make fine kindling," Lizzie observed. "Next time, don't watch your blade. Look at the place you want to hit. If you keep your eye on it, your axe will swing to it." Lizzie set another stick before him and he lifted his axe one more time and let it fall of its own weight, keeping his arms straight so the arc would be true. He kept his gaze fixed on the end of his target and the blade halved it and he was astounded and elated.

Lizzie nodded her approval, "When you can swing the axe for an hour and not miss your block, you'll be ready to learn the bow. Now, I've things to do in the house. Mind your toes and fingers and when you've added another round to the stack, come on in." She left him, then. He still had misses and near misses, but whenever he remembered Lizzie's guidance, it went better. Before long the things he had tried mightily to do by will were becoming habit. Time passed him by, deep into the movement of his moment. He worked to the music of the rain dripping from the eaves of the shed, followed the cadence of his own breath and lift and swing, and added to the pile much more than Lizzie had asked of him before the rain slacked momentarily, and the sun broke through the clouds briefly to set the whole yard a dazzle.

ALONE

At the end of a road just before the Abbey cloister, Millicent and her Rider emerged from a Stone almost twin to the one beneath Mathilda's bluff. Behind and above the Abbey the bouldered bald of the Alone thrust against the sky. There Thomasene had been a solitary longer than most mortals are alive in the world. Down slope, across the road from the Abbey, stood the barracks for the Couriers, who, when they were not ferrying Owl's warnings and exhortations to Beaverdam, acted as rangers on the Abbey lands. It did not surprise the Rider to see three of the Sisters waiting for him. The Welcomers never left the Stone at Road's End unattended, although the rare arrivals there now were more often warned and rebuffed than offered refuge and shelter. Times had changed drastically in the Laurel since the Separation, and the Rider thought not all of the changes were for the good.

Sister Lucinda stepped toward him, eager as ever to do an unpleasant duty. She, at least, had not changed at all. "We thought not to see you here again, Rider." She seemed pleased to have one more opportunity to disappoint him. "Have you come to return to us Sister Tomasene's ring?"

"Sister, with all respect to you and to your Mother, when I give back the ring it will be to Tomasene herself."

"Then, Rider, I fear you will be forever burdened by

something that does not belong to you." She seemed to be enjoying herself a great deal.

The Rider judged such exchanges as this were probably the only pleasures she permitted herself, "Sister, I would see the Monk, if I may."

"You may see our Brother Owl when he summons you," She was definitely enjoying herself. "If he has not sent for you, then you have made your journey here in vain."

"He knows I am here, I'm sure, so I will not ask you to inform him. And I did not make my journey in vain, Sister, for I have come here to wait for one who will."

"Then wait with the Couriers, Rider. There is no place for you now in the Abbey."

For all of Lucinda's efforts on his behalf, she had not disappointed or offended him. He had expected no welcome, certainly not an audience with Owl. The Couriers, though they had no enthusiasm for a Rider's company, would be civil, and offer him bare hospitality. He did not need to pursue the boy any longer, for he was certain his quarry was sparing no effort to come to him. The Rider need do nothing now but wait.

He went into the Courier station to arrange his quarter, leaving Millicent by the Road near the Stone. Although the weather had taken a turn toward grim, Millicent was immune to it, and so the Rider to great degree when they meld. She could alter her nature to be at home in any conditions the world might bear upon her, and she could veil herself from the inhabitants of the normal flow of time, through her capacity to be in a place and absent from it in the same instant, thereby making herself dim, or totally invisible to ordinary sight. She could watch, and not be seen. If the boy came up the North Track while the

Rider was occupied, Millicent would call him.

Inside the station's day room, he found Aengus regaling the Couriers, or perhaps boring them, with another of his interminable tales of his wanderings, narratives that managed to skirt reality and flirt with truth without ever becoming in any but a broad sense factual.

As the Rider passed he clapped the Trader on the shoulder, "When you've finished lying to these men, Aengus, come let me buy you a drink." He went to the bar and ordered a bowl of a dark creamy brew, and Aengus, when he finished his story to great laughter and expressions of disbelief by his assorted listeners, wandered over to join him.

"Another," The Rider said to the bartender and lay a couple of coins on the counter, and when Aengus had his drink, motioned him to a table near the door, where there was less likelihood of being overheard, and from which the Rider could depart with dispatch, should need arise.

"How's your trip been, Aengus?"

"Tolerable, except for finding Mad Davey's house lightning struck. It looked like the whole top had been blown off it. Nothing left by the time I got there. Poor Old Davey; I'll miss him."

"I came by there before you. Davey didn't suffer. I found him dead in his bed before his house burned."

"Suffering's kind of moot when we're dead, Rider, don't you know? Still, I'm glad he didn't go roasted alive."

"Aengus, did you see anything of a boy along your way? He might have answered to the name, Bard."

"Yes, I did, the next day after I came by Davey's Wood. He was traveling fast for a young'un." Kept me company until we got to the Herb Woman's. I left him with her. He had come up from Davey's, must have been there right before it happened. He said he spent the night at Standing Stone. Claimed he talked to Mathilda while he was there, and had a mark to show for it. He said Davey had sent him to see Lizzie."

"How did the boy seem to you? He give you any cause to consider if he might have had something to do with Davey being dead?"

"When I told him, he didn't know. I'm sure of that much. Cried like a wee babe. He might have stole from Davey. He was wearing a coat from the plunder room, but I don't think he did harm to the old man."

"Did the boy tell you where he was going?"

"No, Rider, but there's more to him than he was telling. Lizzie was mothering him right considerable when I left. My guess is he'll be right there for a while."

Aengus had confirmed what the Rider already intuited. He did not believe the boy was a willful murderer, and he hoped he could do what had to be done for Laurel's sake without becoming one himself. At the moment, his chances seemed to him pretty slim.

#

Underneath the shed, beside the woodpile, a barrow leaned against the barn wall, and Drum filled it with split firewood and hauled it to the house. He brought the wood in and stacked it in a rectangular recess in the stonework between the fireplace and the oven, where wood was kept ready for hearth or cooking. Lizzie pursued her craft in her workroom. Drum could hear the rhythmic squeak of the treadle on her wheel as she spun. He made several trips to the shed until there was no room by the hearth for another stick. By the time he finished his chore, thick gray clouds, low and heavy, scudded across the ridge from the north. As he stepped up on the porch, the wind picked up, and rain began driving against the house again, cold and sharp, like needles pricking the skin. He went down the porch to his room, and hung up his hat and coat; he didn't want to take his wet gear into Lizzie's house. He wished he had a sweater. On his bed lay all his dirty clothes, washed and folded. He put on Davey's canvas jacket, and went into the house.

He wanted to thank Lizzie for washing his clothes, and apologize for leaving them for her to do. She had gone into his rucksack to get them, which would have irritated him had his mother done it, but he felt himself thoroughly known by Lizzie as if they were shaped from the same clay, or as Mary would have said, shared a soul. There was nothing he felt he must hide from her, for there was nothing she would judge him for. If it wasn't quite love between them, they shared an unqualified acceptance. He had been told by several that he was loved. Except for Mary and Ethan, nobody beyond Laurel had ever allowed him permission and approval to be himself.

On the table he found a plate with a couple of biscuits and some cheese. If Lizzie had not eaten herself, she had shown him the mercy of food for his midday, which he had worked right past. Seeing the biscuits, he realized he was hungry, indeed. It was hard to judge by the light, because of the heavy clouds, but he guessed it to be late afternoon. He couldn't recall seeing a clock or a watch in Laurel. Nobody seemed to keep time here, though there always seemed to be time enough.

He went out again to water and feed the sheep. The wind had turned colder now, still carried an icy rain. He went by his room, stuffing his biscuits and cheese as he walked, and pulled out his poncho before embracing the weather.

A rain barrel at the corner of the barn, already half filled, spared Drum repeated runs to the porch with his buckets in the rain. The sheep nibbled, without a great deal of enthusiasm, at the hay he gave them. He found several bags of grain among the bales and poured some into their feed trough, and they crowded after it. He sat and watched them for a while, listening to their shufflings and mutterings as they ate, and to the rattle and creak of boards and shingles as the wind clutched at the old barn. His days and nights in the road and on the mountain had taught him the blessedness of shelter, of being held dry and safe and warm in the midst of storm. He breathed a prayer to the God of all names, remembering the prayers he had heard from his grandfather, "Holy Father and Mother and Lover and Friend, Thank you. Thank you. Thank you."

He looked around him. It was getting dark. The day had fled. He blessed the gentle sheep and went to the house.

#

The Rider waited a day for the boy to appear. Sometimes he stood with Millicent by the Stone. Sometimes, to escape the disdainful glare of Sister Lucinda, he would walk away down the road. By late afternoon, he had detected no sign or scent of the boy. When a detachment of a half-dozen Couriers came up the track through the pounding rain that began now to be laced with sleet, the Rider left Millicent with the huddled Welcomers to keep watch at the Stone, and retreated to the day room to hear what gossip the new arrivals had brought with them.

He went to the bar and ordered another bowl of the dark ale brewed at the Abbey, and found an unoccupied table. As he sat, one of the fresh contingent of Couriers, not being informed of a Rider's acute hearing, bent his head close to his friends at the bar and said. "It makes me nervous having them underfoot. Riders go to Shadow and back all the time. Somebody has to do what they do, I reckon; but still, touched by gray, ever gray, my pappy always said. I don't trust one of them."

The Rider had heard such talk often before, a few times to his face. It did not alter his opinion of the man who said it. Idle talk seldom had much relation to reality. At another table, several Couriers engaged in animated discussion of current events in town, One of the new arrivals, proud to have something important to tell not already known here at the end of his world, informed his colleagues, "There were riots in Beaverdam three days ago. That's why some of us were kept back this trip,"

His audience included a skeptic, "I don't believe you. Souls don't riot in the Laurel,"

"It was the grays," the new man continued, "Some of them want to be let back into Shadow. They say there are no jobs for them here, and they are sick of our charity. They tried to set fire to the Guild House."

Another, who had listened silently until this point, interjected, "We ought to send them all back, then, every last one of them, and all their babes, too. There's barely room enough in the Laurel for us people of color to live decent lives."

The fresh face spoke again, "There's talk around the town about issuing rifleguns to the Riders."

"I've never even seen a powder weapon," from the youngest at the table. "I thought the Traders had them all melted down a long time ago."

Relishing his role as bringer of bad news, the one who

had initiated the conversation bent forward, trying to conjure an illusion of confidentiality, "A man who is in a position to know told me that the Traders have an arsenal, where they've been piling up weapons since the Separation. He said that if there was ever an uprising in Laurel, they would loose armed Riders on us as quick as they would on the grays."

At this point, the Rider chose not to hear more. He knew there were not enough guns left in the whole of Laurel to defend a town against a determined mob. A great part of a Rider's training involved techniques for influencing, directing and if necessary, intimidating souls without using overt force. Traders made an art of persuasion. For a Rider, it amounted to a religion.

He was about to down the remainder of his ale and go back to watch with Millicent at the road, when one of the Sisters from the Abbey came through the door, not the officious Sister Lucinda, but Wandalena, one of the novices. Her entrance attracted no undue notice from the Couriers, apparently used to seeing Abbey folk in their personal space. Their conversations and debates went on unabated. The Rider watched as she walked to the bar and said something to the tender. She seemed perfectly possessed and at ease among all these supposedly worldly men. He wouldn't have been much surprised if she had ordered a drink for herself. He thought Wandalena probably had a true vocation. He had often wondered how religious people prayed for a world they were afraid of.

The bartender pointed her in his direction, and she came over to his table, and stood waiting while he drank his last swallow of ale. "That stuff will rust your pipes, Rider." She seemed quite serious. "I know; I helped make it. If you are not pressed for other duties, would you allow me to see you to our Brother Owl? He would beg a few words with you."

#

Thomasene was freezing. The wind cut through her habit like a dagger. Sleet pelted her face and lay unmelted in her hair. But she would sit here beside the Gate Stone as long as she could endure the elements. She came here every day for her vespers. Once there had been hundreds of these stones all across the Laurel, and in Shadow as well. She supposed some had endured there after the Separation, although she imagined that most, as in Laurel, had been lost or broken or become anonymous. Before the rending of the world, not only Stones, but incredibly ancient trees had served as Gates. Thomasene thought they must all have been cut or burned generations ago. Few souls in Laurel could attune to the Gates now. To all others, the boulders were just big rocks that sometimes got in the way of human affairs. She had found the Stone on one of her walks up the Alone when she was a novice. It perched at the brink of a sheer stone cliff, in a cleft between two larger boulders. She thought it likely that no human souls knew of its nature other than her and Elizabeth. When they were still in the novitiate, they had walked through it to the place where Elizabeth would eventually go to build her house. It was their sworn secret. Thomasene chose this exposed and rocky height for her hermitage so she could dwell near the Stone. She kept close to it for the same reason a reforming drunkard keeps whiskey in his house. The only way she could bear to remain apart from the world that she loved, and from the woman she loved, was to know that they were never beyond her reach.

#

The Rider followed Wandalena out of the Courier station and through the biting wind and frozen rain toward the Abbey. As they approached the Stone, he sensed Millicent, who had veiled herself and discreetly extended her aura out to include the Welcomers, shielding them, without their being aware of it, against the worst of the elements. As they passed, the Rider caught a scrap of thought from her, tinged, it seemed to him, with sarcasm. He didn't get it all, but it had something to do with *dragonbait*. Two Sisters admitted them into the abbey, and they proceeded through the Gathering Room to a small door, which Wandalena opened for him, and closed after him as he passed through. It led into the colonnade around the cloister court. The sun was shining, though low in the sky, which domed blue and cloudless above. Flowers bloomed in profusion. Singing bees thronged the air. In a little apiary at the center of the court, Owl tended his hives.

The Rider did not like the Monk. He did not trust him, not because of the obvious powers he wielded, but because he bandied them with such extravagant obliviousness to the plight of those who were without. As the Rider saw it, people on the Rising were going to be cold tonight, some perhaps hungry, and down in the Dismal reigned dire poverty and want, while Owl dallied with his hobbies on an April afternoon.

Owl smiled at the Rider, "Thank you for coming. I know you must be busy. No doubt you are preparing to return with haste to Beaverdam to help resolve the troubles there."

The Rider saw no use in trying to play bluff with the Monk, who likely knew his thoughts as soon as he knew them himself. He answered with what was in his mind, "I think the games in Beaverdam are just a diversion. The real trouble, Monk, I believe is here with you. I do not understand why you are playing with your pets while a boy is loose on the Rising who may bring horrors upon Laurel that we cannot imagine."

"Is it the boy you fear, Rider, or just yourself? What will you think when I tell you now that I have brought him here?"

"In that case, I think you are either wicked or a fool. There is no safety for the souls of Laurel while he is on the land."

"Rider, you will put at risk the safety of Laurel and your own becoming if you interfere with what is unfolding here. I will not presume to command you, but I beg you to leave the boy alone to follow his purpose, and that you go back now to Beaverdam, where you can be of some real benefit to the people of the Laurel."

"I believe the boy's purpose, whether or not he is aware of it, is the end of Laurel. I was already certain that you brought him here, because I believe his purpose is your intention."

"Can you not trust me, Rider? Have I not proven my love for the Laurel a thousand times?"

"I carry a ring, Owl, which says I cannot trust you."

"Do you despise me now Rider, because Sister Thomasene chose her vocation, or do you despise yourself because she did not choose you? Neither of us had part or blame in her calling."

"Don't try to rewrite history for me, Brother. I was there."

"Don't let your history rewrite you, Rider."

Owl raised his right hand and clenched it into a fist. The flowers wilted in a second into dead stalks. The hives were still and coated atop with ice. The sky was black and starless and the wind stung the Rider's face with a swarm of frozen pellets. He lowered his head for an instant to shield his eyes, as Owl said, "This was for your comfort rather than mine, Rider. Would you embrace the storm that befalls you, and deride the bliss that is given?"

The Rider leveled his gaze to hurl a retort, but he was alone.

#

Drum came in from the storm to find Lizzie seated before the hearth, wrapped in a voluminous, richly embroidered robe the color of pomegranate blossoms, drying her long silver hair. It gleamed and flowed in the firelight like the waterfall he had seen on a mountain in a summer far away. As he entered, she gathered her silver into a large towel, and with a few deft movements, turbaned it atop her head, and slipping her feet into a pair of doe-skin moccasins, went to the cookstove, before which sat a large metal tub of steaming water. She added more from a kettle atop the stove, stirred with her finger to test the temperature, fixed on Drum her best eagle stare, "Drum, you need a bath."

"Right here?"

"It's freezing outside. Where else did you have in mind?"

"But you'll see me."

"I'm an old woman, Drum, and I have not forever lived alone. I doubt you could show me anything to further my education. I promise not to watch." And with that, she padded off to her workroom.

A towel lay folded on a chair beside the tub, with a bar of green soap atop. Drum undressed himself as quickly as he could, keeping a wary eye on the workroom door, then settled himself into his bath. It proved hot aplenty, but not overly. It got his attention without parboiling all his parts, and as he accustomed to the heat, the water embraced him with a comfort and healing akin to love. He washed himself for a while, forgot about Lizzie in her workroom, drowsed, and drifted away into sleep.

#

As the Sisters closed the Abbey gates behind him. The Rider was angry at himself for being angry. A Rider could not afford to let emotion cloud his judgment, and he feared he may have already transgressed. The monk's maddening equanimity had always riled him. Owl managed somehow to burrow under his hide whenever they met, and it would take him a while after to settle his mind, and arrange his thoughts comfortably again.

He went to the station, ordered another ale. He sat nursing it at his table until he could push Owl's inscrutable smirk out of his mind. Even a boy with powers would not likely travel afoot in the teeth of a winter gale, he reasoned. Most likely, the boy was waiting with Lizzie for the weather to clear. And knowing Lizzie, she would keep him close longer if she could. The Rider had experience to know that Lizzie had a soft spot in her heart for wandering boys. It was time to pay her a visit.

He went out to Millicent. Although he could have reached her with his mind from where he sat, he needed the touch of her aura to free him for rest. He went to the Stone. There were different Welcomers there this time, the night shift, he presumed. He noted Sister Lucinda was not among them. He supposed she was warm in her bed, dreaming up unkind things to say to unwary pilgrims. Millicent reached out to his mind, *So we are going*.

At first light, the Rider responded soundlessly. Then he

went to his room at the station, pulled off his boots and lay on the bed. He would rest tonight, but he wouldn't sleep.

#

"Wake there Drum. Dry yourself and try these on." Drum roused with a start, sloshing his now tepid bathwater onto the floor. He tried to disentangle himself from the dream that he had been having. A set of clothes lay on the chair beside. Lizzie was sitting before the fire with her back to him, tuning her lute. He took the towel and dried himself as he stood in the water, last his legs and feet as he stepped onto the floor. He tried then to wipe up the water he had splashed from the tub. As he dressed, Lizzie began to sing to the tune she was playing, in a voice as rich as the earth and as free as the wind

East along the ridge tops
Where dawn is growing bright,
Pines and oaks and poplars
Pay homage to the Light,
Throwing down their shadows
Upon the valley floor,
Lifting up their arms to greet
Day coming through the door;
Calling down Sun's blessing
To warm us through our day,
Calling up our dreams from sleep
To guide us on the way,
So praise to all our Sisters
Who whisper to the wind,
And praise our golden Brother
Who lights us to the end.

The clothes Bard put on were none he knew. But they fit him as well as his own. Drawers cut from soft, undyed cloth, long socks knitted from lambswool, and trousers, shirt and vest, all made of the same heavy fabric, stiff and rough to the fingers, but soft and pliable when settled upon his frame. Over the back of the chair hung a long coat, woven of black wool, with large pockets on the side. These were traveling clothes, made for life upon the road, which brought Drum's thoughts back to the dream that had overtaken him while he was asleep in his bath. He dreaded telling Lizzie about it.

"Thank you mightily Lizzie for these grand clothes. Whose are they?"

"They belonged to a boy very like you, Drum, who stopped by here a long time ago. He left them behind, and I saved them should he return. They wouldn't fit him now."

"Oh, Lizzie, I don't want to, but I have to go."

"Let me feed you then, and while we eat, you can tell me why."

#

Owl had come to Drum in his dream, morphing back and forth between bear and monk, finally settling into his human form, and smiled on Drum as he told him, "You are closer to her than you know. Let nothing stay you longer. Go unburdened and by no road. The door is in the Stone."

When Lizzie heard the dream, she didn't appear surprised, "Rest and try to get some sleep, Drum. Gather what you need to travel. Sleep by the fire tonight, I'll lay a pallet for you. It will be cold in that room off the porch. In the morning, before you go, I need to show you something."

Lizzie prepared them some soup and biscuits, and after this exchange, they ate in silence. When they had finished, Lizzie looked up at him with glistening eyes, "I'll clean up here and lay your bed. Go get yourself ready for tomorrow."

Drum went back to his room, grateful for the warmth of some strange boy's coat, and sat for a while on his bed, taking inventory of his worldly goods. Owl had told him to go unburdened. He would take the clothes he wore, his staff and his medicine bag which held the treasures closest to his heart. He would take Aengus' hat. The rest, he would leave behind. He set his bowl with its intricate cloisonné on the table. There was a drawer in the apron of the table, and he found a stub of pencil in it. He took his bit of paper that had come with him the length of the Laurel, and wrote on it, "I'll come back if I can. Thank you." He put the paper under the bowl, then pulled it back, and wrote below the rest, "I love you."

He went back into the house then, saw his quilts and pillow arranged for him before the fire. The house was quiet and Lizzie was nowhere in sight. He would ask her in the morning then if she knew a way to the Alone that did not follow the road. He hung his coat over a chair, and carefully folded his clothes upon the seat. He laid his hat atop the clothes, put his shoes underneath on the floor, propped his staff against the back of the chair. Keeping on his warm socks and drawers, he crawled between the quilts and lay watching the flare and flicker among the glowing coals in the fireplace. He would rest tonight, but he wouldn't sleep.

When the first light of morning shone through the windows, there was still no sign of Lizzie. Drum dressed and went out to the barn to say goodbye to the sheep.

When he entered their pen, they crowded around him, nuzzling at his hands. He shed among them the tears he was ashamed to loose before Lizzie. The clouds had thinned. The rain had stopped. The wind had stilled. The morning was cold, not freezing, although in the moist air, it felt as if it were.

When he came back into the house, his pallet was rolled beside the fireplace. The fire on the hearth burned bright and lively. Lizzie was at the cookstove scrambling sweet red peppers and chives into a clutch of eggs. Their plates waited on the table, and a dish of honeycomb, with several thick slices of bread, and a teapot under a cozy.

Lizzie pointed out some mugs on a shelf by the stove, "Would you pour us some tea, Drum?"

He did, and sat down as she ladled the eggs out onto their plates. Lizzie smiled toward him as she sat, but looked tired, older than he had thought of her. He guessed she had slept no more than he had. They ate, not hastily, but with purpose.

Lizzie said to him as they finished. "I guess it is time. We've had a good visit, Drum; I pray we will have more. Come along with me and see."

They went through her workroom. There were several spinning wheels, one with a treadle. Drum saw spindles and a niddy noddy, bobbins and spools, boxes and bins, a rainbow of skeined yarns, bundles of rushes and grasses and nettles and flax, bags of wool and cotton, vats for washing and soaking and dyeing.

Along one whole wall were shelves with little boxes and jars, and bunches of herbs and roots hanging from the ceiling to dry. Through an open door at the far end of the workroom, Drum could see Lizzie's unmade bed. Not like Lizzie to leave disarray in her wake. It confirmed to him that she'd had a bad night. Lizzie crossed the room to the far door; without a word, beckoned for Drum to follow.

In Lizzie's bedroom, there were two doors Drum thought might be to closets. She opened one of them to reveal not clothes but a space like a room between the stone wall of the house and the rocky face of the slope against which it had been built. Within this cavity stood what might have been a facsimile of Mathilda's Standing Stone. The face of it was black as midnight. The quartz crystals in its matrix twinkled at him like stars. Looking at it, Drum felt the same vertiginous urge he had felt facing the Stone below the bluff.

Lizzie was speaking to him. "This is a Gate Stone. There used to be many of them, all over the Laurel. Owl believes they may all be occasions of the One Stone that resides forever beyond all times and places. This Stone will take you to the Weaver."

"Can you really travel through this?"

"Not me, but I believe you can. For a very long time now, it seems to me, I have been unable to follow the Stone's music. It is closed to me now. Besides, I am at home right here. Where would I need go? I might meet myself someplace yonder and that would be confusing to us both. One life at a time is quite enough."

Drum thought she might want to go visit her friend, but he asked instead, "How does it work?"

"It doesn't work, Drum; it just is." Fix in your mind where you want to go, or who you want to see. Step into it, and it will take you there. Don't let your mind wander, or you may wind up someplace you didn't intend. If that happens, think of where you started, and you can return immediately."

"You need to go soon, Drum. I had dreams of my own

last night, and I don't think it is safe for you to stay with me longer." Drum went back through the house and fetched his coat and hat and staff. When he came back, he threw his arms around Lizzie's waist and hugged her close. She sounded to him like she was whispering, "Go, Drum. Now."

Drum had always been a daring boy, even when he was Bard or Little Bear or Ben. He had also been not without a precocious prudence. He took the scarf from his medicine bag and removed Mathilda's stones, and tucked them into the band of his hat. As he did so, the hat faded into the air, though his fingers assured him that he still held it by the brim. He returned the scarf to his bag, and on impulse, handed the ball of soap to Lizzie. She lifted it, smelled of it and smiled at him, and he put on his hat. Lizzie, in spite of herself, immediately burst out laughing, "Drum you always were a trickster."

"Can you see me?" he asked.

"Only in my mind's eye. Now go!"

Drum reached out and touched the Stone, "How do I open it?"

"Don't think of the Stone," she said, "Just think of Thomasene. Imagine a rocky cleft, away up on top of the Alone. He closed his eyes and tried to forget about the Stone. He could see in his mind vaguely, but convincingly, a woman sitting among boulders on some rocky height, her head bent as if in prayer. Something about her reminded him of Mary. For a second, he wondered if she missed him now. He stepped forward, hoping he wouldn't bump his nose on the Stone. He felt only a cold wind, and opened his eyes to darkness.

#

Lizzie could not see Drum enter the stone, but she heard

the sigh and felt the rush of air that informed her the Stone had received him. "Holy Mother, keep him," she whispered, wiped her tears, and turned to see the Rider standing at the door to her room.

"Elizabeth," he spoke quietly, though fury was in his face, "You have no idea what you have done to us all." In his left hand, he held his bow.

Lizzie could not keep her voice from trembling, "Remember who taught you. Misuse that and you damn us both." The Rider raised his right fist and summoned Millicent, who entered the house as a whirlwind. Furniture toppled and slid across the floor. The air filled with tufts of wool and streamers of yarn and covers from the bed and bits and pieces and shards and fragments of all that was in the house. Lizzie knelt on the floor and covered her face with her arms as the maelstrom swirled and raged about her. Before she could recover and voice a plea to stop them, Rider and Flyer were meld and through the Stone.

#

Time did not flow within the Gate. No light. No place or form manifest there. One sensed destinations, not physical doorways from place to place, although a traveler often perceived them so, but visions of arrival. A mind attuned to the Stones could reach through one to touch an object of thought in proximity to another stone. Drum sensed two arrivals before him. As the first drew near, he looked out over the tumble of Pinnacle, above Ethan's cabin. He heard people calling him. It took him a moment to recognize his name. He saw his father, and Ronan, and some other men working their way up among the boulders. Ethan was standing in his yard before his cabin looking up at them. Drum did not recognize any of the men at first, then he understood. Mary had missed him indeed. It was a search party.

But he was here to find the Weaver, not to be found himself and wrapped back into a world he never felt was his. Since his arrival in the Laurel, Drum's memories of his former life had been fading steadily. They were no more than vague dreams now. Soon, if he stayed, he would not remember his time in Shadow at all. Drum pushed the vision away and turned to the other. It moved toward him. He no longer saw the woman he assumed was Thomasene, but he saw the rocky cleft before him, and he saw the brink of a precipice high and away above all the distant peaks around, and he nearly slipped and tumbled over it as he stumbled out of the Gate onto the Alone.

The air was cold. Even the light was cold. Ice skinned the stone underfoot. Carefully he moved away from the brink before him, and with his back to the rocks rising behind the Stone, using his staff to steady and anchor him, he worked his way up and out among the sundered boulders until he had an expanse of stable soil underfoot. The sun was breaking above the ridges to east. The world below seemed to be resolving itself out of night, taking form before him as he watched. Above him slightly, he saw the rocky bald at the summit of the Alone, worn and rounded by time and weather. In the shallow soil gathered between the bones of the mountain, patches of grass proclaimed their intention to live. Within two or three days past, there had been flowers blooming on the height; their frosted corpses brown and withered now. Below him on the slope that fell back gradually from the cliff, Drum made out the outline of a stone cottage, not much more than a hut.

A narrow path twisted over the stony ground toward

the cottage. He commenced walking along it when he saw the Three a little distance ahead, still as death. He might have passed by them without knowing, had he been less aware. He did not know if they had followed him through some way only they could discern and traverse, or if they had foreseen his destination and waited here for him. Beyond them, there were no lights visible in the windows of Thomasene's little dwelling. If the Weaver was there, she must be asleep, he thought, or else she preferred to pray in the dark.

Drum could not know that for the Weaver darkness was not a matter of preference. It was the element in which she moved through her life, where she followed hour by hour and day by day the endless tracery of the Labyrinth manifest within her own consciousness. Over her years on the Alone, her heart and spirit had attuned more and more to all that is too deep and vast and beyond visible creation or conscious thought to be defined by any human mind.

She was kept fast in her place not by some secret knowledge she had attained of things beyond ordinary human understanding, but by a ceaseless and expanding awareness of being totally known. Her soul flowered now in the deep time before Creation and in the boundless dark beyond all dissolution. She no longer looked upon the world but held it within herself by the same Power in which she was held.

Owl ordered the affairs of Laurel by the force of his purpose. Thomasene upheld the Laurel solely by being in it as she resided at the Stillpoint from which all order and being are spun. Her simple presence in her world was a sustaining Grace.

#

234

The Rider had no trouble tracking the boy beyond the Stone. Within the Gate, nothing passed except what was real. In the outer world of Laurel, physical senses sometimes diverted a hunter down a false trail, or faded before they revealed their end. Here, the boy's track lay as bright and clear as a strand of the Labyrinth. There would be no losing him. The Rider sensed ahead of him two portals. As he came upon the first, he realized the boy had passed it without entering. The Rider stilled his mind before it and looked out upon a steep piled and strewn with weathered boulders, a few straggly pines clinging to whatever soil gathered between. A hoard of motley grays were toiling up among the rocks, calling out plaintively in some Shadow tongue that sounded familiar to him, but he could not translate. He knew now the boy's purpose. The grays were calling for him to open the Gate that they might descend upon Laurel. But the boy had passed them by here. What was his plan then?

Millicent's thought touched him, *Yonder*.

He fixed on the other portal as it moved toward them. He saw through it the rocky aerie where he had sat with Thomasene the day when she had handed him the ring their friend Elizabeth had given her for her birthday.

"Return this for me. Tomorrow, I'll wear the Mother's band," Thomasene told him. His heart had broken then. Thomasene never once said she loved him, but she seemed plainly fond of him; he had hoped he held enough love for them both. He wondered what magic Owl had unleashed to make her forsake her life and those who loved her. Many girls in those days went to the Abbey to be taught. Few girls ever stayed to become one among the Sisters. Most left skilled and learned to make their own place in Laurel as Elizabeth had done.

The Rider never delivered the ring. Whenever his grudge against the Monk began to ease, he would take out the ring and gaze upon it to feed his anger.

Elizabeth knew he had it, and guessed why he cherished it, and never demanded it back. "It is still among friends," was all she said.

By custom, anything of value belonging to Thomasene should have become property of the Abbey when she took on the habit, and when Sister Lucinda found that he had Thomasene's ring, she had branded him as a thief. In her mind, that it was intended to go back to Elizabeth made him a thief twice over. He had no doubt she prayed for his punishment daily.

Her prayers, he thought, were about to be answered. If the boy opened a gate here, the grays would sweep down the Rising like a pestilence, and there would be nothing between the Alone and Beaverdam to stop them. Poor Thomasene would never see them coming. The Rider and Millicent swept from the Stone to the edge of the precipice, then turned and flowed upward among the boulders behind, following the trace that hung hot and bright in the frigid air. The boy was the grays' door into Laurel. The Rider meant to close that door now, else within weeks, everything north of the Long Broad would be gray, and that would be just the beginning of the end.

#

Suddenly the Three leapt toward Drum. He had no time to react before they swept right past him and up the path. He turned to see the Rider and his black Flyer taking form as they emerged from the boulder field atop the cliff. The Rider raised his bow as they hurtled toward him and loosed an arrow. *How could he see me?* thought Drum, as the point sifted his hair without drawing blood and took his hat away, scattering Mathilda's stones across the mountainside. The Three went not for the Rider but for his Flyer. Millicent went down, tried to slip from the moment, but they were already inside her, tearing and rending. She screamed and splintered into a burst of darkness and went out of the world.

The Rider was already clear of the melee, running toward the boy, his rivener raised to cleave the child's skull. Drum hurled at the death closing on him now the only defense he could muster, his name. He shut his eyes and raised his staff in both hands above his head. "I am Drum!" he shouted. He felt but did not see the glowing torus of the Labyrinth blossom from both ends of his staff. He did not see the look of astonished bewilderment on the Rider's face, as, when he was poised to strike, the Labyrinth took him.

#

As Millicent carried him up onto the bald of the Alone, the Rider could taste the boy, close enough now to hit with a stone, he thought. Why couldn't he see him? He saw Charon's dogs watching him from down the path. Of course. The grays' plan would need the ferryman. The Three lunged toward the Rider as he unslung his bow and drew an arrow. He figured he might get one shot away, if he was lucky. Elizabeth had told him when he was learning, "Shoot with the eye but see with the mind. Don't aim for what you see, until you know within where your target is." As they ran to attack, one of the dogs veered inexplicably to the right as if avoiding some invisible obstacle. The Rider aimed above that spot and let his arrow fly. His intuited shot almost found its target. The hat flew, and the astonished boy stared gape-mouthed at him as Millicent went down among the Three and released him. He drew his rivener as he ran. The boy did not try to fight or flee. He raised his staff over his head, lifted his face and closed his eyes as if in prayer, and it sounded then to the Rider like the boy called him by name. He was raising his weapon to strike as the Labyrinth flared about him, and he realized he was looking into the upturned face of his own youth.

Idiot! his mind screamed at him, *You've run this wrong from the beginning.* He raised his left hand and the Labyrinth snared it and folded him into time.

#

When Drum dropped his staff and dared open his eyes, there was no Rider, no Flyer, no Three. There was just Drum standing in the sunlight on a cold morning upon a treeless mountaintop. Something glittered in the path at his feet. It was a woman's ring. He picked it up and watched it sparkle in the sunlight as he turned it over in his hand. He reckoned the Weaver must have lost it here, for who else would have come this way? He didn't know what about it made him think of Lizzie. He put it into his medicine bag so that he wouldn't lose it again before he spoke to the Weaver, and went off down the path to the cottage.

Once there, he stood at a little distance from it for a long while, as the sun rose higher and began to warm his back. He had come at last, and now he didn't know what to do. In frustration he clapped his fist to his chest. There was no drumming. No trembling in the earth nor signs in the sky, just the thump of a little boy's fist against his bony sternum. The occupant of the cottage must have heard something however, for she came out her door and onto her porch, holding a long stick like a pendulum before her in her hands. The stories about her were true,

Drum thought, for she looked not many years older than himself.

"Is anyone there?" she called, the tone of inquiry, free of fear or trepidation. She came down into the yard and stood for a while, listening. Thomasene looked several times straight in Drum's direction with no sign that she saw him standing before her, and he wondered if somehow he had become invisible again. Then she turned, swept her stick across the steps, went up onto the porch and into the house, closing the door behind her. Drum knew then that the Weaver was blind.

Had he come so far, at so much cost to be her eyes, her warder? He believed he might knock on the door and be welcomed into a fine and useful life where he would be well-loved for all that was in him to give. It would give reason to all the hardships he had suffered in Laurel and for all the trouble others had endured for his sake. Yet, it seemed almost too easy, too neat to be true. He hesitated.

Not yet, Drum. Her way is not yours. It was Millicent. Somehow, she had come back from whenever she had fled. As she spread her presence around him, Drum could feel her hurt and her pain, and he could feel the healing at work in her. He could feel her love for him and her yearning for embodiment, not to possess him and constrain him, but to be in him, to be present through him into the world. And he knew she was right. The Weaver's life was not his life. She had lived alone and blind for longer than he had lived at all, and she had not suffered for his absence. His need for needfulness would not answer her need, whatever that might be. She was called to be apart from the world. His calling was to be immersed in it, with all the struggle and hurt and laughter and weeping it might bring. With Millicent, he could explore worlds within worlds and worlds beyond. Thomasene wove the yarns and threads Lizzie spun. Millicent would weave him into the tapestry of times past and times to come.

Drum knew then what he had to do. He took the medicine bag with Thomasene's ring and Lizzie's scarf in it, and went quietly and hung it on the door. Then he came back to Millicent and held out his arms to her as she meld with him, lifting him within her form.

My darling, darling boy, she thought toward him, *Where shall we go now?* Drum knew not the place whereof he spoke then, but he trusted Millicent, who touched all beginnings and endings, would know, when he lay down his head upon her warmth and, clutching Mary's staff to his chest, whispered, "Take us home." At that word, Millicent unfolded her great wings into the morning, and they flew.

SECESSION

As they lifted into the light, Drum lost all sense of place and time. Millicent began to flow in the morning air, finding in the tendril of a cloud a strand of the Labyrinth, following it across worlds and years to the one place Drum could become himself again and be at home forever in the Mother's music. They soared through lights and darknesses as Drum fell into deep and deeper sleep, rose northward high over the Black Mountains, plummeted deep into Shadow, tracing Raven's flight to a dead pine away up on the side of Standing Stone Mountain. They passed over Lon's Anvil in the dark of a late-summer's night, swept around the pine and down into the Gap to the house Ronan had built for his wife Mary. Drum, now more deeply alive than sleep or wakefulness, but aware as only an everliving soul can be aware, saw rising up from below him a light that as it drew near took on the form of a sleeping child's face. The child opened his eyes and Drum looked out through them from his bed on Mary's porch at a world that, false and broken though it was, looked to him as real and in need of love as the one he had just departed. Still shedding sleep, he heard Millicent whisper in his head, *Beloved, when you are whole and ready, I will come for you again*.

As Drum came to wakefulness, he could not quite remember what Millicent had said to him, could not quite remember Millicent as the Laurel faded from his consciousness like a dream. Mary's staff lay across his chest. He could not remember Circle now, but in his moment of waking he felt the same as when Callie had taken his hand beneath the chestnut. He reached out to touch the welcoming dark. "I am Drum," he announced to the shadows as they fled.

#

When the first streaks of day brightened above Pinnacle, Drum got up and looked in his mirror to make sure it was really him. He couldn't see much in the faint light filtering in from outside, but it seemed to him his reflection wasn't entirely familiar. He opened his suitcase and took out the rock Mary had given him at the beginning of their summer. Afraid of losing it, he had put it away except for once when he took it to show to Ethan. It was a binding stone, the old man had told him, would always bring him home when he needed to be there. Now he looped the cord over his head and let the dark weight fall against his chest. He could feel the edges.

Drum dressed quickly and quietly and slipped out into the yard. He paused at the door to leave Mary's staff, puzzling as to when in his restless dreaming he had fetched it to his bed. He wished it was his to take with him. He loved the smooth feel of it, polished by hands he loved more than any in his world. Obeying a sudden impulse, residue perhaps from some forgotten dream, he held the staff upright before him and drew his right hand down the length of it. Then he grinned at it in pure wonderment and joy and left it by the jamb as he passed through.

Standing in the yard under the gathering dawn, he knew he must be away now, for Mary rose early. Without much ponder, he walked away toward Standing Stone Mountain. He had not often wandered there. It would not be the first place they came looking for him. Beyond that height was another state, and taller mountains, and people who did not know him, but who would recognize his soul. Somewhere up among the laurel beyond the Anvil, Drum would find friends. He stepped among the trees, a shadow within a shadow. From an old pine among the rocks high above, Raven watched him go.

ABOUT THE AUTHOR

Henry Mitchell grew up in the upcountry of South Carolina where his family has resided for eight generations before him. He presently lives and works in Greenville South Carolina with his wife, Jane Ella Matthews, a Feldenkrais practitioner, and their spiritual guide and German Shepherd, Simon.

Mitchell worked as a painter and sculptor for fifty years before beginning to write fiction in his seventies.

His short stories have been published in the UK by Alfie Dog Fiction. *The Summer Boy* is his first novel.

7959360R00137

Made in the USA
San Bernardino, CA
25 January 2014